the
VOYAGE
to MAGICAL
NORTH

CLAIRE FAYERS

SQUARE
FISH

HENRY HOLT AND COMPANY
NEW YORK

T 91916

SQUARE
FISH

An imprint of Macmillan Publishing Group, LLC
175 Fifth Avenue
New York, NY 10010
mackids.com

Our books may be purchased in bulk for promotional, educational, or business use. Please
contact your local bookseller or the Macmillan Corporate and Premium Sales Department at
(800) 221-7945 ext. 5442 or by e-mail at MacmillanSpecialMarkets@macmillan.com.

Library of Congress Cataloging-in-Publication Data
Names: Fayers, Claire.
Title: The voyage to Magical North / Claire Fayers.
Description: New York : Henry Holt and Company, 2016. |
Summary: "Twelve-year-old Brine Seaborne and her friend Peter find themselves
in an adventure with pirates, invisible bears, and a seriously evil magician"—
Provided by publisher.
Identifiers: LCCN 2015022325 | ISBN 978-1-250-11538-6 (paperback) |
ISBN 978-1-62779-658-3 (e-book)
Subjects: | CYAC: Magic—Fiction. | Voyages and travels—Fiction. | Adventure
and adventurers—Fiction. | BISAC: JUVENILE FICTION / Fantasy & Magic. |
JUVENILE FICTION / Action & Adventure / Pirates.
Classification: LCC PZ7.1.F39 Vo 2016 | DDC [Fic]—dc23
LC record available at http://lccn.loc.gov/2015022325

Originally published in the United States by Henry Holt and Company
First Square Fish Edition: 2017
Book designed by Anna Booth
Square Fish logo designed by Filomena Tuosto

5   7   9   10   8   6   4

LEXILE: 710L

For Phillip, in memory of Musashi

CHAPTER 1

Brine sat at the driftwood table in Tallis Magus's library, her chin propped on one hand as she read. Aldebran Boswell could have been describing her life, she thought. A long, straight line of cleaning the magician's house, cooking the magician's food, washing the magician's disgusting socks. Nothing ever changing.

Brine Seaborne's life will continue in a straight line . . .

There was one big difference, of course. A moving object might have some idea of where it came from, but Brine had no idea at all. She had one clear memory of waking up in a rowing boat three years ago, surrounded by people, and that was all. They'd asked her her name, and she couldn't remember—she couldn't remember anything. So they named her Brine because she was crusted head to foot in sea salt, and Seaborne because that's what she was. Sea borne: carried by the sea.

She'd been so ill that no one had expected her to survive, Magus told her often. Lucky for him that she had recovered, or the magician would have had to do his own cleaning all these years.

Brine crumpled up the cloth she should have been using to dust and threw it at the door. As Boswell predicted, it flew in a straight line.

Unless something happens to knock it off its course.

The duster bounced aside as the door opened.

Brine slammed Boswell's book shut and jumped up as Tallis Magus swept in. He looked cleaner than usual, and he was wearing his best robe—the one he kept to impress rich visitors. Right behind him came a man who was a bit shorter than he was, a lot fatter, and had a face like a fish on a bad day.

Brine gaped at him. Penn Turbill? Why was *he* here?

"What are you doing, Seaborne?" Magus barked.

"Dusting," said Brine. She rescued the cloth. "Sorry. It slipped."

Magus gave her a disbelieving glare and shook back his robe, sending off a flurry of stale magic that made Brine cough. "Get out!"

Brine dropped him a curtsy and fled.

Outside, she shut the door firmly and leaned against it. Something was definitely off course. People came to Magus's house for two reasons—either he owed them money or they wanted him to cast a spell. But Penn Turbill was the richest man on the whole of the Minutes island cluster, and the biggest miser. No way would he have lent Magus anything, and what could Turbill want that he could get only by magic? He already owned almost everything.

Very carefully, Brine turned her head and pressed her ear to the door.

". . . Smaller than I expected," Penn Turbill was saying.

"She's only twelve," replied Magus, "as far as we can make out. She'll grow. And she works very hard—as long as you can stop her daydreaming."

Brine twisted her duster into a tight knot. They were talking about her, but why? She was just the magician's servant. Why should Penn Turbill care how big she was? She waited, listening as a floorboard creaked inside the library, followed by a rattle of keys and the louder creak of the door into Magus's private study. Then silence.

Maybe they'd just been making conversation. Maybe Turbill had asked about her simply because he'd seen her on the way in. Yes, and maybe a flock of flying sheep would swoop down on Magus's house and take her home. Not that she knew where home was.

A hand grabbed her shoulder. Brine yelped and lashed out backward with the only weapon she had: the duster. It connected limply.

"Watch what you're doing, can't you?" said Peter Magus irritably. He picked off a lump of fluff exactly the same beige as his hair, then paused and looked at Brine as if waiting for something.

Brine glared back at him, not moving.

Peter flicked the dust at her. "Didn't we decide that servants were supposed to curtsy to family members?"

"You might have," said Brine. "I didn't. Anyway, you're no more family than I am." Peter's real family were fishermen on one of the smallest of Minutes Islands. He hated it when Brine brought this up, which Brine thought was quite ridiculous. He seemed so determined to forget where he came from; Brine would have given anything to remember.

She sneezed into her duster. "Have you been practicing magic again?"

That was the other thing she hated about living with Tallis Magus (one of the many other things): She was allergic to magic. No one could explain why, not that anyone had really tried to. Magus didn't care how often she sneezed as long as she also kept the house clean.

"Not that it's any of your business," said Peter, "but I had a lesson this morning." He drew a squiggle in the air in front of her and grinned. "Don't worry. I won't turn you into a frog—yet."

"I'd like to see you try."

"I might one day." Peter jerked his head at the library door. "What's Bladder-Face doing here?"

Brine almost smiled, but turned it into a scowl. "Penn Turbill? How should I know? I'm only the servant." She tucked the duster into the waistband of her skirt and stalked away. At the top of the stairs, she turned back. Peter was leaning against the door, his ear to the wood. "But if you ask me," Brine added loudly enough to make him jump, "it's going to mean trouble."

▶┅┼┼┼●

Penn Turbill didn't leave the house until the sun was setting. Brine watched from an upstairs window as he hurried down the steep little path to the beach. Magus was plotting something with him—something that involved her. She didn't like the cold feeling that swam in her stomach. This was her own fault. She'd wanted something to change; she'd practically wished for it in the library. For all she knew, it might even be a good change, but she couldn't quite convince herself of the fact. There were many, many things worse than a boring straight line of a life.

She heard footsteps behind her and spun round. Peter stepped back quickly. "Don't throw anything. Magus wants to see us both downstairs."

Tallis Magus was waiting for them in the sitting room, smiling. Brine felt a prickle of worry. In the three years she'd lived in the magician's house, she'd seen him smile maybe four times. Mainly he alternated between a vaguely irritated frown and a full-blown thunderous scowl, the latter usually happening when he found Brine somewhere she shouldn't be. The grin that stretched his face now was so alien that Brine pinched herself to make sure she wasn't in the middle of a nightmare.

"Peter, Seaborne, come in," said Magus. "Have a drink."

Brine stopped in the doorway. This was definitely all wrong. Magus stood up, still beaming, so that his smile seemed to lift him out of the chair by his teeth. He poured wine into three goblets and held two of them out. Peter tasted his cautiously. Brine stared into hers, wondering how much Magus had already drunk.

Magus took a long gulp and wiped his chin on his sleeve. His gaze bumped around the room. Brine started forward, thinking he was going to fall over, but he waved her away. "I am perfectly well, Seaborne." He fell back into his chair. "In fact," he said, "I have good news for you both. I spoke to Penn Turbill today, and we reached an agreement. Peter, you are very young, but you're a good boy, and you're going to be a magician one day."

Peter shot Brine a sideways glance. She shrugged. She didn't have any idea what this was about, either.

Magus didn't seem to notice that neither of them had spoken. "Money and magic are a good mix," he said. "And Penn Turbill has more money than anyone. His daughter's not the prettiest girl on the islands, but looks don't really matter. You'll like her."

"I will?" asked Peter.

Magus's smile slipped. "Of course you will—you'll have to. You're going to marry her."

Peter turned red, then white. "Marry? But . . . but I can't get married. I'm too young."

"Stop gawking at me like a fish," snapped Magus. "You won't stay too young, will you? You and Turbill's daughter will get betrothed next week, then she'll move in here and you can get married as soon as you're fifteen. That'll give you nearly three years to get to know her. That should be enough, even for you."

Peter shook his head. "I don't want to get to know her. I don't want to marry her."

Magus slammed his goblet down. Wine slopped over the sides. "You will do as you're told. Who else is going to marry you—the fisherman's runt, the magician's useless apprentice? Drink your wine and be happy."

Peter's goblet fell from his hand. He didn't appear to notice.

Brine looked down at the spreading wine stain and tried not to smirk. "I'll get a cloth," she said.

Magus stopped her. "That's not the only thing we agreed. Obviously, Seaborne, I'll have no need of a servant once Turbill's daughter moves in. Penn Turbill has considered your youth and your—ah—questionable origins, and despite them both, he has agreed to take you on. You will be going to live with him as his housekeeper."

A dull clatter sounded, a thousand miles away.

"Make that two cloths," said Peter.

»→+++‡‡●

Brine wasn't sure how she got to sleep that night, but she woke to the sound of shouting. She groaned and rolled over, burying her face in the pillow.

Peter's voice came through the ceiling. "I'm not going through with this. You can't make me."

"Don't talk back to me, you ungrateful child."

Brine would have stayed in bed if she could, but staying in bed wasn't going to solve anything. Magus and Peter continued to argue as she dressed. From the sound of it, Magus was winning. She could still hear him calling Peter names as she got the fire going in the kitchen and laid three fish on a rack over it. She might have felt sorry for Peter if he wasn't such a pain. It would serve him right to be stuck with someone he couldn't stand but still had to be polite to—see how he liked it. Anyway, Brine had enough problems of her own to worry about.

"I'm not marrying Bladder-Face's daughter," announced Peter, marching in on her some time later. His left cheek was scarlet, as if he'd been slapped.

Brine turned a fish over and stabbed it hard with a fork. "What are you going to do, then? Run away and join the pirates?"

Peter's other cheek reddened to match the slapped one. Brine didn't care. As far as she was concerned, he'd gotten the better part of the deal. She'd spent three years working for Tallis Magus. She had cleaned his house, cooked his food, washed his clothes until her hands were raw, and in return, he was swapping her as if she was an old robe he'd grown tired of.

"At least I won't have to live with you anymore," she said. "And Penn Turbill is rich. Have you seen his house? It's huge."

"Ten times the house, ten times the cleaning," Peter said.

"Yes, well, I don't have to get married. Your children are going to be *so* ugly."

Peter scowled at her and sat on the table. Brine watched the fish smolder. The nearest one looked a bit like Penn Turbill—it certainly had the same glazed expression.

Ten times the house, ten times the cleaning.

"I've heard," said Peter, breaking into her thoughts, "that Bladder-Face can't read. There's not a single book in his house."

Brine turned cold inside. Peter flashed her a triumphant grin. "Magus might not have noticed you sneaking into the library all the time, but I have. I was planning to blackmail you one day." He tapped the side of his nose. "You know what they say—knowledge is money."

"No it's not, it's power."

Actually, it was neither. It was freedom, the chance to escape, even if only for an hour or two. In Penn Turbill's house, there would be no escape. Brine turned the fish again, watching the juices spit as they hit the fire. A dull weight settled over her.

"Why don't you try talking to Magus again?" she said. "Tell him it would be bad for your studies to have a wife."

Peter pointed to his reddened cheek. "Why don't you talk to him if you're so clever?"

Because Magus definitely wouldn't listen to her, Brine thought, and Peter knew it. She sighed.

The smell of burning fish wafted between them. Brine

sneaked a glance at Peter and caught him looking back at her. They both jerked their gazes away.

"Well," said Brine at last, "if Magus won't change his mind, we'll have to make Turbill change his."

"Yes, brilliant idea. How?"

One of the fish ignited. Brine snatched it off the rack by the tail. "You're a magician, aren't you? I'm no expert, but how about you cast a spell on him?"

CHAPTER 2

Magic is the art of making shapes. The magician takes a quantity of magic, forms it into the correct spellshape, and releases it. The process appears mysterious because most people cannot see magic. All they see is the magician's hand moving and the flash of light as the spell is released.

(From ALDEBRAN BOSWELL'S BIG BOOK OF MAGIC)

The library was a different world at night. Shadows crawled together, piling up against the door that led to Tallis Magus's private study. Brine could feel the door behind her, a heap of dark at her back, even while she tried to read by candlelight.

In the daylight, her plan had seemed easy: get what they needed here and row to Turbill's island, where Peter would cast the mind-change spell—then back and into bed while Magus was still snoring. Now, with shadows yawning around her, she could think of a hundred things that would almost certainly go wrong.

She opened another one of Boswell's books at random.

The island cluster of Minutes lies in the northwest of the Atlas

Ocean. It consists of more than twenty islands, many of which are so close together that you may sail between them in a matter of minutes. Beware, however . . .

The library door opened. Brine bit back a scream.

"Scared you," said Peter. He held up a key.

Brine stood up, trying not to show that her heart was hammering and her hands had begun to shake. "Where's Magus?"

"Snoring like a blunt-nosed whale."

They both paused, watching each other in the candlelight. Peter looked back over his shoulder. The night was getting to him, too, it seemed.

"What if we cast the spell on Magus instead?" Brine asked. At least that way, they wouldn't have to row across the sea at night.

"Don't be stupid. The spell would wake him, and he'd know exactly what we were doing."

Whereas Turbill was as blind as a sea slug when it came to magic. Whether the spell worked or not, he'd never know Peter had cast it.

"I could try talking to Tallis again," said Peter. "Maybe he'll—"

Brine snatched the key from his hand. If they thought any more about this, they wouldn't go through with it, and then she'd be stuck with Penn Turbill for the rest of her life.

She opened the door to Magus's study and coughed as the stink of sweat and old magic wafted out. The dryness in her mouth spread straight down her throat, and her nose began to prickle. She'd never set foot in this room before, not even to clean it: Tallis had never allowed it. Shelves covered every wall, and books, boxes, and bottles covered every shelf. A table leaned against the only clear space, below the window.

"Magus is going to kill us," muttered Peter. The candle shook in his hand.

"Only if he catches us. Hurry up."

He nodded, his lips tight. He passed Brine the candle, wiped his hands on his trousers, and went to the shelves.

Brine walked to the table. It was full of sheets of paper with the same few spellshapes drawn on them, over and over again in neat rows. Some of them bore notes in Magus's handwriting— mainly comments such as "rubbish" and "must try harder." So this was what Peter did in his evenings, hunched over the table in his bedroom. Somehow, Brine had thought that practicing magic would be more exciting.

"Watch out," said Peter. He dumped a leather-bound book on the table, scattering papers everywhere.

"Now you decide you want to read," said Brine.

"I'm looking up the spellshape, stupid." He started turning pages. Brine looked over his shoulder. Boswell said there were thousands of different spellshapes, and the best magicians might have memorized five or six hundred, while the worst ones would know twenty or thirty at most. Some of them were so simple a child could draw them. Others twisted on the page and made Brine's eyes hurt to look at them. But every single one could be drawn in a single line without taking your pen off the page.

Casting them was different, of course—you drew the shape in the air with your fingers, and instead of ink, you used magic.

"There," said Peter, stopping at a shape that looked like a lopsided spiral. Brine pinched her nose hard, willing herself not to sneeze while he copied the shape onto a scrap of clean paper and slid the book back into its slot on the shelf.

Brine hopped impatiently from foot to foot. "Can't you hurry?"

"Can't you shut up? We're nearly done." He reached up again, moving books out of the way to get to a set of wooden boxes. He hesitated over them, then took down the biggest one. Brine held her breath as he lifted the lid. She'd expected it to be locked.

Carefully, Peter slid his fingers into the box and lifted out . . . Another box.

In that box was another box. Inside that one, a tiny casket made of gold-plated wood.

And inside that, nestled between twenty layers of wool that were already fraying under the corrosive onslaught of pure magic, lay a narrow sliver of amber shell. It was no longer than Brine's little finger, and it was the most precious thing in the whole world.

>++++++●

According to Aldebran Boswell, starshell fell to earth in the wake of a shooting star, hence its name. According to everyone else, this was nonsense. Starshell was the fossilized remains of the silver jellyfish tree that grew everywhere before the Great Flood and the reason it was called starshell was because people like Boswell didn't know any better. Either that or it was the claw of the tentacled lurk-weed that once crowded the ocean bed. Or oysters made it when they wanted a change from pearls. In some parts of the world, people still risked their lives for it, diving hundreds of feet through the coldest parts of the ocean and sometimes, only sometimes, emerging half-drowned with a glistening shard in their hands. Even they couldn't agree on what it was.

But whatever it was made of, one thing was known for sure: Starshell was the only thing in the whole world that held magic. Somehow—how and why was a mystery—it drew magical energy out of the air and stored it ready to be used. Without starshell, there would be no spells, no magicians, no Tallis Magus.

For half a minute, Brine forgot the urge to hurry and gazed down at the glowing piece of shell. All starshell was precious, but this one was special to her. It had been found on a gold chain around her neck when she herself had been found adrift in a rowing boat. A shivering, sneezing child with skin as dark as hazel-wood, half-dead from sickness and thirst, and wearing the price of the island as jewelry.

Magus had been quick to lay claim to the starshell to add to his stock. The islanders had insisted he couldn't have the shell without the child, so he'd taken Brine in and kept her as a servant. If it weren't for that piece of starshell, she might have been a fisherman's daughter by now. And yet, the one time Tallis

Iagus had let her hold it, she'd sneezed so hard she'd almost dropped it.

Peter didn't look at her as he lifted the starshell out of the box and folded the layers of wool over it. "I thought you wanted to hurry," he said.

Brine shook herself out of her daze and nodded. It wasn't her starshell anymore; it belonged to Magus—and they were about to steal it. Gripping the candle like a weapon, she led the way back through the library and down the stairs.

The front door stood before them, a faint crack of moonlight showing along the top where the wood had warped. Brine's heart quickened fearfully. They were really doing this. They were going to steal Magus's starshell, steal his boat, and cast a spell on the richest man in the whole island cluster. She paused a moment to steady herself. It was fine. Magus was asleep, the rowing boat was waiting for them down on the beach, and nothing bad was going to happen.

She opened the door and blinked in the flood of moonlight. The grass looked silver, crisscrossed with the long shadows of the trees, and the path to the beach curved away between them. Brine glanced at Peter. His face was set in a grin of mad terror.

"Are you sure you can cast the spell once we get there?" asked Brine.

He jerked his head in a nod. "Of course I'm sure. I'm a magician, aren't I?"

An apprentice magician, which wasn't exactly the same thing. Brine didn't say it. She started along the path as quickly as her trembling legs would allow. They could do this. Get to the boat, row to Turbill's island, Peter would cast the spell, and then—

The sound of the door banging back stopped her dead. Peter turned and let out a low cry of dismay.

Tallis Magus burst through the doorway. He was wearing his dressing gown and slippers, and his hair swung loose about his face. Brine might have laughed, except for his eyes. They glittered with a light that went beyond mere rage. They were twin shards of ice, full of vengeance and the promise of long and painful punishment. Brine felt a whimper rise in her throat and clamped her lips together to stop it from escaping.

Magus advanced upon them with steps that made the grass tremble. "Thieves!" He pointed at them with a long, shaking finger. "I take you into my house. I treat you as my own children. Ingrates! *Give me back my starshell.*"

Brine tensed. Peter put his hands behind his back. "What starshell?"

Magus's eyes flashed. "Did you really think I'd leave it unprotected in an ordinary box? The moment you put your thieving hand on it, I knew. Give it to me."

Brine felt the air thicken. Peter tossed the starshell back at her. She sneezed. The wool-wrapped packet missed her hands and hit the grass.

Magus curled his fist and drew his arm back.

"It was Brine's idea!" shouted Peter. "She took it, not me."

Brine's cheeks flooded with heat. "Liar!"

"Thief!" Magus roared and took a step forward.

Peter stumbled away from him.

Crunch.

The sound froze them all where they stood.

Slowly, reluctantly, Brine looked down. Down at the imprint of Peter's shoe on the grass, and the flattened square of wool, and the starshell that lay in the middle of it. Her mouth turned dry with pure, cold horror and the certain knowledge that now Magus really was going to kill them.

Magus let out a wordless bellow. Peter yelped, scooped up the broken starshell, and bolted down the hill. Brine hesitated a moment, then ran after him. Magus, cursing loudly, was just behind, but she was a lot younger and much faster. And, at this moment, a lot more desperate.

She sprinted past Peter and felt the path give way to loose sand beneath her feet. Dark against the shoreline, the rowing boat bobbed as if it were waving to her. With a final burst of speed, Brine flung herself inside. Peter landed beside her with a crash.

"Come back here!" shouted Magus.

Brine threw off the mooring rope and heaved on the oars. The boat shot away from shore. Magus ran onto the beach, shouting threats and waving his fists, but he was too late. A wave caught them and swept them out of his reach.

B rine kept rowing until the shore was swallowed up in the night and Magus's angry shouts were faraway squawks that could have been the sound of a gull. Finally, she paused and leaned on the oars, trembling. Peter's face was white, his hair standing up in sweaty clumps. He gave Brine a wobbly smile. "Well, at least we got away." He unwrapped the starshell, and his face fell.

Brine leaned over to look. The front half of the shell had snapped in two. The back, where Peter's heel had hit, was crushed almost to powder, and the bits were already turning dull gray, too small to hold any magic. Peter shook the useless fragments over the side of the boat and wrapped up the two larger pieces. He looked like he was trying not to cry.

Brine shut her eyes tight. There was no point going to Penn Turbill's island now. Even if they cast a spell on him, it wouldn't make any difference. They couldn't go back to Magus's house, not yet. Maybe not ever.

A sudden, irrational longing for home came over her—a home she couldn't even remember. Ever since she'd arrived at Tallis Magus's house, she'd dreamed of leaving. Then she'd discovered the magician's library and Boswell's books, and she'd known straightaway that she was going to be an explorer, too, and see the whole world. Now, however, with the ocean before her, she felt like she was a small child again. Huddled in a boat with no food, no water, nobody to hear her crying or to care whether she lived or died.

"At least we've got the boat," said Peter. "And we've got two pieces of starshell now, where we only had one before."

Brine opened her eyes. "We've got two much smaller pieces of starshell, thanks to you. And thanks for blaming me, by the way."

"Well, it *was* your idea to steal the starshell."

"I didn't notice you objecting."

"That's because you never listen to a word I say."

The boat swung in a lazy circle. Peter didn't offer to help as Brine took up the oars again. The constellation of Orion hung above them, the three bright stars that made up the mast pointing the way north. She turned the boat in that direction, feeling it pick up speed as the waves swept them farther from Minutes. She lost track of time, letting the sea carry them, resting for long minutes between each oar stroke.

A long while later, she noticed a rosy pink creeping across the sky from the east. She sat up straight and looked around.

"Uh, Peter," she said, "I think we might be lost."

CHAPTER 3

The island cluster of Minutes lies in the northwest of the Atlas Ocean. It consists of more than twenty islands, many of which are so close together that you may sail between them in a matter of minutes. Beware, however, the sudden currents around the Minutes Islands—they can sweep an unwary boat onto the rocks or straight out to sea.

(From ALDEBRAN BOSWELL'S BOOK OF THE WORLD)

Peter followed Brine's gaze full-circle around the empty gray waves. A speckle of dots to the east might have been Minutes or just a result of staring at the rising sun. He sat back rubbing his eyes. Great—now he was stuck in a boat with Brine for company and they had no idea where they were.

"This is your fault," he said. "You've rowed us in the wrong direction."

"Really? Feel free to take a turn if you're so good at it."

Peter gave her his magician's sneer, though he didn't know why he bothered—Brine never took any notice. He had put the starshell pieces in his pocket for want of anywhere better. He slid them out and folded back the layers of wool. His palms prickled with sweat.

The first time Peter had ever touched starshell, he'd been six years old. The youngest in a family of eight children, his main memory of that time was of his parents yelling at him for getting in the way. Then Tallis Magus had come around to the villages, looking for an apprentice, and Peter was shoved into line to meet him. He'd been scared stiff of the big magician, but when Magus had grabbed his hand and forced it onto the starshell, Peter had felt the magic swarming inside. He hadn't known how rare a talent it was. All he knew was that after less than a minute's discussion, his mother handed him over to Magus, his father slapped him round the head and told him to behave, and that was the last time Peter had seen either of them.

"What are you doing?" asked Brine.

"Finding out where we are. Be quiet, can't you?" He tried to ignore her—easier said than done when she was watching him from right across the boat—and started to draw magic out of the starshell. He'd never cast a spell without Tallis Magus standing over him before, but he wasn't about to let Brine see how nervous he was. The magic came out in an uneven strand, but it came.

The finding spell was one of the first spellshapes Magus had ever taught him, because Magus kept losing things, Peter guessed. Many people thought it was one of the easiest spellshapes to form—a simple circle—but anyone who thought that should try drawing a perfect circle in the air with nothing to guide them and see how they got on.

"Did you know," said Brine, watching Peter try, "that the world was once made entirely of ocean, before the mariner Orion stole fire from the stars and drove back the waves to make the islands?"

Peter grunted. "Pity he didn't get rid of the oceans altogether, then we wouldn't be in this mess." The circle spellshape was slightly flat on one side. He tried again.

"Why don't you hold your wrist still and just turn your hand?" suggested Brine.

"Because . . ." Peter tried it and found to his annoyance that it worked. The magic formed a little ring in front of him and, gazing through it, he pictured Minutes. All the islands, the houses with stones on the roofs. Magus's house, cold all year except for the kitchen, where Brine always kept a fire burning. He released the spell and watched as a blob of light the size of his hand leaped high in the air and shot off southeast. Several seconds passed before he felt it connect.

"Well?" asked Brine.

"Minutes is that way. A long way that way." His stomach twisted as he said it.

Brine shrugged. "It's not like we can go back there, anyway. Can you find us another island?"

Peter shook his head. To find something, he needed a mental image of it, and he couldn't form an image of something he wasn't already familiar with. He knew he didn't have the imagination for it. He wrapped the starshell pieces back up. "We have to save magic. If we use it all now, it'll take days for these pieces to recharge, and then we'll really be stuck. If we row for long enough, we're bound to find another island, or a ship. Or something."

"If who rows for long enough?" asked Brine pointedly.

Peter sighed and took the oars.

Rowing was harder than it looked. The oars kept slipping, and every time he missed the sea with one of them, Brine rolled her eyes and groaned.

"Is this why your parents gave you away to Magus?" she asked. "Because you couldn't row to save your life?"

Peter accidentally cracked himself across the knuckles. "At least my parents knew where I was going. Your parents stuck you in a boat and pushed you out to sea. You must have been a horrible child."

A flash of hurt on Brine's face told him he'd gone too far. He bit his lip. Brine looked away from him. Peter bent his head and kept rowing.

Brine heaved a sigh. "You'd think I'd remember being lost at sea, wouldn't you? It's not the kind of thing most people would forget."

"I'm certainly not going to forget this in a hurry," Peter agreed. He shifted his grip on the oars again, and one of them flew out of his hand altogether.

Brine retrieved it and grabbed the other one from him. "You just keep watch. Shout if you see land."

Peter tried to hide his relief. He sat, rubbing the blisters on his palms, and watched the sea for any sign they were not alone.

It couldn't have been more than ten minutes later when he spotted a dark smudge on the horizon. It might have been an island, except that Peter was sure there hadn't been an island there a few minutes ago. Also, islands didn't usually appear to be heading straight toward you. A rhythmic thudding reached his ears, something like the beating of a giant heart. Peter wondered what it was, then he knew: the sound of sails.

"Brine." It came out as a croak.

A ship. They were saved. Peter scrambled to his knees and waved both arms. "Ahoy!" A ship! He could even forgive Brine for getting them into this mess. A ship could take them back to Minutes—or anywhere else, for that matter. They could work for passage. Brine was good at cleaning, and he . . . he'd think of something.

He lowered his arms. "You won't tell them I'm a magician, will you?"

Ships and magicians didn't mix, Tallis Magus always said. On the one hand, magicians were so useful to have around that some ships, especially pirate ships, had been known to kidnap them and force them to work on board forever. On the other hand, sailors were notoriously superstitious and hated anything they couldn't understand—which was most things, but especially magic. So magicians found themselves both wanted and not wanted, sought after and hated.

Brine pulled a face at him. "Maybe I'll blackmail you. Knowledge is money, hmm?"

"Don't be stupid."

"You started it." She went back to rowing the boat. "Don't worry. I won't tell them you're a magician, because you're not a magician. You're an apprentice, and you're not a very good one."

Peter sighed and turned his back on her to watch the ship approach. It was close enough now to make out the four masts and the sails that bowed in the wind. And also close enough to see the black-and-white flag that streamed out from the tallest mast.

A black skull and bones on a white background. Pirates.

A moment of pure terror froze Peter's voice. All he could do was point.

Brine's eyes widened as she looked. She dug both oars into the sea, hauled the boat round, and began to row in the opposite direction. She was far too slow. The thrum of sails pursued them, growing louder with every second. Peter gripped the sides of the boat. Brine rowed hard, but the pirate ship sliced through the water behind them like a knife through . . . well, like a knife through water.

Brine's face shone with sweat. The boat creaked with every smack of the oars. Bells clanged on the pirate ship, the sound echoing across the smash of waves and the sudden howling in Peter's ears.

"Do something!" shouted Brine. "Use magic."

"I can't!" Peter's chest felt tight. Almost every spellshape he'd ever learned had fled from his mind. "All I can do is find things and pull them."

"Then pull Minutes!"

She'd gone mad. "Brine, Minutes is all islands."

"I know." She plunged the oars back into the water. "Boswell's third law of motion. Every action has an opposite reaction."

Which meant if he tried to pull Minutes, it would pull them closer instead. Peter's heart leaped. But Minutes was too far away; he couldn't do it. Could he?

It was either try or be captured by pirates. Forced to cast spells for them forever. Or they'd discover that he was only an apprentice magician, and not very good, and they'd throw him overboard. Peter took the starshell pieces out of his pocket and drew out enough magic to make the spellshape. It was only a simple downward arrow, but he let it go too soon and the pieces flared, jerking him forward.

Brine hauled him back up by the collar. "They're gaining on us. Try again."

Peter rubbed his forehead where he'd banged it. A wave broke right over him, and he gasped and spat out salt water, his ears ringing with the thunderous roar of waves and sails. This wasn't working. He needed quiet to work magic: quiet and calm and plenty of time. He had none of those.

Brine kicked him.

In a burst of painful clarity, Peter saw Minutes—not only

saw the islands but felt them. They settled into his thoughts, heavier than a thousand anchors. He braced his feet on either side of the boat, drew a new arrow in the air, and heaved.

The boat picked up speed. Peter kept pulling. He had no idea how much magic the starshells had left or how long it would last at this rate. He didn't dare think about it.

The pirate ship thundered down on them as they fled. The ringing of bells grew louder, mingled with voices yelling at them to stop. The boat skimmed faster across the waves with every second, until it felt like they were flying. Peter felt like laughing. He was doing this—he was actually doing it!

Brine screamed. Peter's eyes flew open.

The pirate ship had changed direction. Now, instead of following them, it cut across the sea behind them. A surge of water lifted the rowing boat high and slapped it back down with a jolt that snapped Peter's teeth together. Brine dropped one of the oars, and the boat swung wildly as the starshell pieces let out a final blaze of light and turned gray, their magic exhausted.

Brine leaned out and grabbed the floating oar, her face red with effort and fury. "This is not fair!" she shouted. Whether this was at Peter, the pirates, or the universe in general, he didn't know.

Together they stared up at the approaching ship. Dark planks gave way to a lighter patchwork, scoured to the color of old bones by the sea winds. High on the prow, in faded paint, Peter could just make out letters. Half an *O,* an *I,* the bottom strokes of an *N.*

The bells on board the ship slowed, then stopped. The silence was worse than anything—it meant they'd lost. Lost their chance to escape, lost their lives, probably. Peter found the paper he'd drawn the mind-control spellshape on. He looked at it one last time, trying to memorize it, then he crumpled the paper and dropped it overboard. If the pirates found it, they'd know what it was, then they'd know what *he* was, and after that, it would be kidnapping or death. He ought to throw the starshell into the sea as well, but he couldn't bring himself to do it. He tucked the pieces into his pocket with numb fingers. Whatever happened, he wouldn't let the pirates have them.

That was all he had time for. A rope rattled down and slapped into the boat right at his feet. Peter gazed in silence at the man who climbed down. He was short, and so broad across the shoulders that he was almost rectangular. His arms were blue with tattoos and thick enough to double up as oars. He grinned at them both, revealing uneven off-white teeth. "Ahoy, my hearties," he said. "Cheer up—you've just been rescued by the *Onion*."

CHAPTER 4

Is your life dull and friendless, your misery endless,
Do you just need a shoulder to cry on?
Then shout 'hip hooray' for she's coming your way
On a ship that is almost Orion.

Oh, she's strong and she's swift and if you get my drift
She is all that your heart could desire.
For one chance to see her, fair Cassie O'Pia,
A man would walk naked through fire.

(From THE BALLAD OF CASSIE O'PIA,
Verses 1–2, Author Unknown)

The *Onion*. Even on Minutes, Brine had heard the stories. The
oldest and most glorious pirate ship on the eight oceans,
named after the first stars that burst upon the midnight sky—and
but for an unfortunate misunderstanding at the sign writer's, the
ship would bear the name of *Orion* still. Her crew were the fear-
somest warriors ever to have left land, and her captain, Cassie
O'Pia, was a woman so beautiful that her face had not only

launched a thousand ships but caused several others to capsize with excitement. The *Onion* saved the Columba Islands from the bilious plague. The *Onion* slew the Dreaded Great Sea Beast of the South. The *Onion* defeated the evil pirate magician Marfak West and his amphibious desperados.

After all the stories, Brine had expected something more exciting. The woman who faced her was only a little taller than Peter, and the only way her plain, square face could have launched any ships was if she'd head-butted them into the sea. Her eyes, it was true, were a pair of dancing sapphires, and her hair fell to her waist in a tumble of curls that might have had a hint of red if she'd bothered to wash, but right now they were more dirt colored than anything else. Apart from a crescent of emerald around her neck, she was dressed like a common fisherwoman, sea-stained and scruffy.

"You don't look like a pirate," said Brine, and she could have bitten off her tongue as several of the crew grinned.

The woman's eyes crinkled. "What did you expect—wooden legs and parrots?"

"I don't know. What's a parrot?"

"A type of vegetable, I think. Which reminds me—welcome to the *Onion*." She put out her hand. "I'm Cassie O'Pia, but you can call me Cassie."

Brine continued to stare.

"She wants to know your names," one of the pirates growled.

Brine knew what Cassie wanted. She just wasn't sure she

wanted to answer. "My name's Brine," she said reluctantly. "And this is Peter. Thanks for rescuing us. We were—uh—fishing, and we got blown off course."

Cassie followed Brine's gaze to the little boat, with its noticeable lack of nets and fishing equipment. "Fishing," she agreed. She smiled. It was a brilliant smile, one that might be able to launch a ship or two, after all. "The first rule of the *Onion* is we don't ask questions. Once you're aboard, it doesn't matter where you came from." She paused. "Where are you two from, by the way?"

Brine scowled. "I thought the first rule of the *Onion* was you didn't ask questions."

"And the second rule is we don't follow rules," said Cassie. "So?"

"Minutes," said Peter. "We're from Minutes."

Cassie raised an eyebrow. "You look like you could be." She turned to Brine. "But you're definitely not. You look more western to me."

Brine's heart missed a beat. She'd read about the Western Ocean in Magus's books. Not a lot, because hardly anything was known about that part of the eight oceans, and nothing she'd read had felt even the slightest bit familiar.

"Not entirely western, though," said Cassie, dashing Brine's hopes straight back down again. "And I thought I'd seen almost everywhere. Where *are* you from?"

Brine shrugged.

"She doesn't know," said Peter. "No one does. She was found at sea."

Trust Peter to open his big mouth. Brine tried to kick him but he sidestepped. Everyone turned to look at her, and she felt herself grow hot under the pirates' scrutiny. She pushed a hand through her hair. "What happens now?" she asked, trying to look as if she didn't care. "Are you going to make us walk the plank?"

"Do we have a plank?" one of the pirates asked.

"I'm sure we can find one," said Cassie, still looking at Brine, "but it seems a lot of effort for two children. The thing is, we can't take you back to Minutes, either. There are currents around the islands that would drive us straight onto the rocks, and I don't risk my ship—not for anyone. However . . ." She stretched the word out as if she was about to do them a big favor. "However, we're on our way to Morning. It's the biggest trading island in the Columba Ocean, and you can buy pretty much anything there—including passage back home if you want it. Or information about the western islands." Her smile broke out like lightning through a cloud. "Or, I suppose, if you want to go back into the sea right here, you can do that instead. What do you say?"

Brine looked at the rolling waves. Her stomach rolled in harmony, making her feel queasy. She reached three conclusions in quick succession. One: If they went home now, Magus would kill her. Two: Even if he didn't, she'd still have to go and live in Penn Turbill's giant, bookless house. Which led to three: What was so bad about being a pirate, anyway?

"We'll stay," she said.

"An excellent decision." Cassie clapped her on the shoulder. "Mr. Hughes, take them to the galley."

The short rectangular man stepped forward with a grin. "Call me Ewan," he said.

►┼┼╫┼╫╉╺

Don't take this personally," said the cook. "It happens to everyone." Her name, improbably, was Trudi Storme. Short and sunburned, with a frizz of yellow hair and a figure that started going out at her neck and didn't return until her knees, she looked like a mushroom that had been struck by lightning.

Brine prised another sucker off a tentacle. "What, everyone you know has been kidnapped by pirates and forced to chop octopus in a kitchen that smells like a whale's stomach?"

"Quite a lot of them, yes," said Trudi, who appeared to be one of those people who'd heard of sarcasm but thought it was some sort of exotic fruit like a pineapple. "Except that it's a galley, not a kitchen. You can tell because it's on a ship."

A fat, cream-colored cat wandered through the door. Trudi tossed it a tentacle. "This is Zen, short for Denizen of the Deep. Cassie bought him to catch rats and mice, but he really only likes fish." She turned sharply. "Peter, don't touch that!"

Peter had been poking at a pot over the fire. He jumped back.

"What's in there?" asked Brine, peering into the dark red liquid. It looked like something had died in there—unpleasantly.

Trudi swelled with pride. "I call it a Cataclysm of Pot-Roasted Cephalopod with a Concasse of Alginate in a Black Spice Sauce." She saw their puzzled looks, and her shoulders drooped. "Tentacle and rum stew," she said with a sigh.

➤┉╫╫🐟

Some careers, Brine thought, were simply not meant to go together. On Minutes, it was quite normal for a fisherman to also make furniture, and the island doctor spent his evenings painting seascapes. Pirate and gourmet chef, on the other hand, combined about as well as oil and honey—which is to say, you can do it, but it won't do either of them any good.

"When I was a girl," said Trudi, "I dreamed of keeping house for a rich man. I was going to spend all day in his kitchen, prodding at pans and saying things looked interesting. But the only prodding we do here is with a cutlass, and if something looks interesting, it usually means trouble."

Trudi didn't often have people to talk to, Brine guessed. She nodded, pretending to listen while she worked, pausing now and then to slip Zen pieces of tentacle under the table and glare at Peter, who was peeling the skin from a fish so slowly the oceans would freeze before he finished.

Trudi chattered on. "The real problem is ingredients. Nothing keeps on a ship, and there's only so many times you can mix fish with more fish before people get bored. I'm hoping we can restock on Morning. Cassie did say everything would be all right this time."

Peter put his knife down. Brine stopped, her own knife midair. "What happened last time?"

"Nothing. Nothing happened." Trudi looked away. "Would you like to hear the story of how Cassie O'Pia fought Marfak West on the Island of Rats? It's really good."

"No, thank you," said Brine. "I'd like to hear the story of what happened last time you visited Morning."

Cassie put her head round the door. "Didn't I tell you we don't ask questions on the *Onion*? Is that stew ready? Grab some plates, you two, and follow me."

She smiled, but her voice carried an edge that warned them not to argue.

Brine picked up a stack of wooden plates and followed her up on deck. The day was bright, but it felt like a cloud hung over the ship. Brine didn't dare meet Peter's gaze. She knew he'd be feeling the same as she was, and he'd be blaming her for all this. She was the one who'd agreed to stay on board, after all.

What exactly had they gotten themselves into?

CHAPTER 5

Magic in its natural form is too weak to be manipulated, but
when naturally concentrated in starshell, some people are able
to draw it out and use it. This talent is rare, and many believe it
is unnatural.

Because starshell pieces are constantly absorbing magic
from the air, even if a magician empties one completely, it will fill
up again in time. Oddly enough, the bigger the piece, the faster
it replenishes.

(From ALDEBRAN BOSWELL'S BIG BOOK OF MAGIC)

Peter had already decided he was going to murder Brine.
Maybe not completely, just enough to teach her a lesson. He
should never have let her talk him into this fish-brained plan.
He tried to catch her eye so he could glare at her, but she was
very carefully not looking at him. Of course, this was all one
big adventure for her. She probably didn't even understand that
they were in real danger.

He could feel the outline of the starshell pieces in his pocket
as he climbed the ladder to the deck, and he had to concentrate

on walking normally so Cassie wouldn't guess he was hiding something. Right now the starshell pieces were useless to him, and they were dangerous. It would take days for them to get their magic back, and if any of the pirates found them and realized what he was, they'd make him stay on board, casting spells for them forever.

Cassie reached across Peter and handed a plate to a man who was as tall as a mast and the color of burnt toast. "This is Tim Burre from Auriga. That's in the west," she added, with a sharp glance in Brine's direction. "All right, everyone gets a helping of stew, unless they're on punishment rations, in which case they get two helpings." She tripped over the cat. "And watch out for Zen. Octopus is his favorite."

For the next half an hour or so, Peter put plates into hands and ladled out stew. By the time he'd finished, he was hungry enough to eat some of it himself. It tasted of the sea: too salty and with an unpleasant undercurrent of seaweed. He found a corner to sit down in, away from the rest of the crew, and hoped they'd forget about him for a while. He couldn't avoid Brine, though.

"Thanks for blabbing about me to everyone," she said, sitting down next to him.

Peter lifted his head. "I was trying to stop them from asking questions about me. If they find out I can do magic, they'll never let me leave. Magicians are too useful."

"You?" She laughed. "You're as useful as a paper boat."

"And you're so much better than me, I suppose?"

She flicked stew at him. "Don't be childish. We're stuck here together for now. We need a plan."

"I seem to remember it was one of your plans that got us stuck here in the first place," said Peter.

Brine stared at him unapologetically. Peter sighed. Unfortunately, Brine was right: They had to do *something*, and like it or not, she was the only person on board he could trust at all. He lifted Zen away from his plate. "This doesn't mean we're friends."

"No, of course not."

They shook hands.

"What's the plan, then?" asked Peter.

Brine shifted closer so she could whisper. "Did you notice how Trudi went a bit odd when she mentioned Morning? I think we should find out why."

Hello," said Peter, approaching one of the crew. "I just wanted to say thanks. If you hadn't spotted us, I don't know what would have happened."

The pirate shoved his hands into his pockets and grinned. Half his teeth were black and the rest were either yellow or missing. "You're welcome. The name's Rob Grosse. Third in charge of boats and rigging. What do you think of the *Onion*?"

Peter tried not to recoil from the blast of Rob's fishy breath. "She's nice."

"No she's not. She's glorious. Greatest ship on the oceans, never defeated in battle."

"Not even at Morning?" asked Peter.

Rob's smile snapped off. "You don't want to hear about Morning. Have you heard how we defeated an army of swamp beasts on the Isle of Bats?"

"No," said Peter, "and I—"

"It's called the Isle of Bats because it's full of bats." Rob sat down on a bucket. "What they don't tell you, though, is that the island is basically one great swamp. The insects get eaten by birds, the birds get eaten by the bats, and the bats are massive. Big enough to lift a man off the ground." He spat on the deck. "But Cassie had heard there was treasure in the swamp, and so there we were, digging about in the sludge."

"I'm sure it was very interesting," said Peter, "but what about—"

"Night fell, and so did the bats. It was as dark as the inside of a whale, and we were covered head to foot in swamp until you couldn't tell us one from another. The bats screamed round our heads like demons. We kept killing them, and more kept coming. Then, just as Cassie was saying not to worry, because it could be worse, monsters came rising out of the swamp."

"Nothing like Morning, then," said Peter.

"No, not a bit like Morning. Haven't you been listening? Swamp monsters, as big as horses and with teeth like sharks. You don't get them on Morning."

He stopped as Ewan Hughes appeared.

"Bored already?" asked Ewan. He handed Peter a mop and

bucket. "If you've got time to talk, you've got time to work. You can clean the deck."

"Hello," said Brine. "You're Tim Burre, aren't you? Do you need any help?"

Tim looked up from the pile of ropes he was mending. He seemed a little surprised to find her talking to him. He handed her a rope. "I can teach you to tie knots, if you like."

"Great," said Brine, sitting down next to him with fake enthusiasm. "Cassie said you were from the west. How far west have you traveled?"

"I haven't," he said. "If you go west of Auriga, you'll fall off the edge of the world. Everyone knows that."

Brine laughed, then realized he was serious. "The world's round. You can't fall off."

"That's what they want you to think," he whispered. "Do you want to learn knots or not?"

It was a silly hope that Tim would be able to tell her anything about her home. Brine made a deliberate mess of a knot and tried to appear young, incompetent, and eager to learn. "You'll have visited Morning a lot, then, I guess."

Tim's fingers fumbled on the rope. "You don't want to hear about Morning. It's the world's most boring island. Do you know the story of how the *Onion* fought the Dreaded Great Sea Beast of the South?"

"Yes," said Brine.

Tim sat back. "It started like this. . . ."

▶⊶╫╫☙

Can I help with anything?" asked Peter.

The blond man on the rigging leaned down to shake hands. "Come on up if you like. My name's Bill Lightning."

Peter grinned. "What, because you never strike the same place twice?"

Bill gave him an odd look. "No, because it's short for William."

The whole crew was mad. Peter shook his head. "You're making these names up."

"Someone has to," said Bill. "Why not us? Some people want a new start when they come on board, and a new name helps. Like you're becoming a different person."

Peter had never considered being anyone but himself. He hadn't exactly enjoyed being Tallis Magus's apprentice, but magic was all he knew—and it was important. He'd been doing something that most people found impossible. The idea that he could just forget all that and do something different was strange and a bit scary. He climbed up to join Bill on the rigging. "How long until we reach Morning?"

Bill shrugged. "We'll be there soon enough. Do you want to hear how I fought ten wild bears armed with nothing but a lobster claw and a dishcloth?"

Peter didn't, but he had a feeling Bill was going to tell him anyway.

He was right.

▶⋯⊦⊦⊦⊱

"Hello," said Brine, approaching a group of pirates who were playing a game involving dice and a set of colored sticks.

"It's no use asking us about Morning," one of them said. "We're not allowed to tell you anything."

Brine tried to look as if she didn't know what they were talking about, and kept walking.

▶⋯⊦⊦⊦⊱

Days passed. Peter couldn't remember the last time he'd felt so tired. Anytime he paused, someone would give him a job to do, generally involving scrubbing some part of the ship. The *Onion* had three levels—or layers, as the crew called them—all connected with a single ladder that ran top to bottom. First, the main deck; then the mid-deck, which held the galley, a work room, Cassie's cabin, and the sleeping quarters; and finally the bottom deck, which was used for storage and was mostly empty save for the ominous shape of the brig. Trudi assured Peter it had been ages since anyone had occupied the iron cage, but he still kept well away from it.

Between jobs, he talked to the crew. There were around fifty people on board, and they were all very quick to launch into stories of past adventures, and even quicker to change the subject when he asked about Morning.

After four days, he and Brine between them had learned:

1. *Cassie O'Pia was the greatest hero who'd ever lived.*
2. *Cassie O'Pia had run away from home at age fourteen, after her father had lost her in a game of cards. She'd swum for forty days until she found the* Onion *and emerged dripping with seawater and diamonds.*
3. *Cassie O'Pia was the daughter of the dreaded pirate captain Rasalhague the Second. She'd run away from him at age sixteen and swum for sixty days until she found the* Onion *and emerged dripping with seawater and gold coins.*
4. *Cassie O'Pia grew up in the magical south where people have fishes' tails and live underwater. She'd seen the* Onion *sailing by and followed it. She'd swum for a hundred days until she emerged from the water dripping with seaweed and emeralds.*

What they hadn't learned was:

1. *Anything about Morning.*

That evening, they sat on deck beneath the stars and ate something that Trudi said was barbecued crab claws stuffed with peas and semolina.

"What's Morning like?" asked Peter.

Most of the pirates avoided his gaze. Trudi tried to hide behind a plate. Rob sucked noisily on a crab claw.

"It's fine," Ewan Hughes mumbled. "Big. You'll like it."

"If they let us land," Trudi added.

A shadow fell across her. "Whatever this lot are telling you," Cassie said, "it's not true." She eased herself down into the middle of them. "We are going to Morning because they buy and sell anything. Which means we can restock and you two can get home. Is everybody all right with that?" She looked around the crew. Trudi reddened and stared at the deck, and Ewan Hughes scowled, but nobody said a word.

"Good," said Cassie. "Now, why don't we tell our guests how the *Onion* defeated the evilest magician the world has ever known? Marfak West."

Peter shivered despite himself. Marfak West: the name of nightmares. According to the stories, he stood as tall as a mast and was as thin as a shovel, and his soul was as twisted and sour as an eel in vinegar. While everyone knew he had died at the hands of Cassie O'Pia, everyone secretly believed he had survived, and even thinking his name too loudly would bring his ghost rising from the sea, seeking vengeance.

The pirates all sighed happily. "There has never been another fight like it," said Ewan. "The *Antares*—that's Marfak West's ship—and the *Onion* were evenly matched. Marfak West had his magic, but we had Cassie. We fought all day, and then as day gave way to night . . ."

"The *Antares* fell apart," said Bill. "Just like that. It was as if the magic had been the only thing holding her together, and when the magic ran out, everything stopped working."

"It didn't hurt that we rammed her head-on, either," added Rob Grosse with a grin. "Good riddance. I hate magicians. They give me the creeps."

There was a general chorus of agreement and several suggestions as to what to do if you met a magician. Most of the suggestions involved cutlasses.

Peter shifted uncomfortably. "What happened to Marfak West? Was he really eaten by giant crabs like the stories say?"

Ewan Hughes shook his head. "If there'd been any giant crabs around, Trudi would have cooked them. No, we watched the *Antares* sink and picked up the survivors. Marfak West wasn't among them. Either the sharks got him, or . . ." He cast a glance at the sea. Shadows crept closer, long and jagged. "No, definitely the sharks," said Ewan after a while. "The sharks got him."

▶⤙╫╫●

Peter slept badly that night, his dreams alternating between lessons with Tallis Magus and visions of Marfak West chasing him with one of Trudi's kebab skewers.

"Always remember," said the dream Magus, "magic corrupts. Never hold starshell for long. Magic does not want to be held— it needs to be used."

"Then why is it held in starshell?"

"Insolent boy! How dare you question your master?" Magus turned into a giant squid and began slapping Peter with tentacles.

Peter woke with a yell. Ewan Hughes was shaking him. In the hammock below him, Brine sat up, groaning.

"Morning, both," said Ewan. "Which, coincidentally, is both the time and our location. We're here."

Scrambling up the wooden ladder and onto the deck, Peter forgot the aches in his back and the fact that he hadn't washed in over a week. He'd known Morning was big, but he hadn't realized quite how big. Golden sand swept in an impossibly long curve. Behind that, trees bristled, and beyond the trees, the yellow walls of tower after tower rose into the sky.

Peter put his hand down to his pocket without thinking and only just stopped himself from taking the starshell out. *Calm down*, he told himself. Not long now, and they'd be free on Morning. He could do whatever he wanted then. He slid his fingers into his pocket and bit back a gasp. Just for a second, he thought he'd felt the tingle of magic on his fingertips. He had to try again to be sure—yes, it was faint, but it was there. Carefully, he removed his hand from his pocket. The tightness in his chest eased a little.

"Impressed?" asked Cassie, coming up behind him.

Peter turned around and lost his voice completely.

The pirate captain was glowing, and not just because of the

wind on her cheeks. In place of her shapeless gray clothes, she wore tight black trousers, long boots, and a shirt that sagged under several pounds of red lace. A belt around her hips held a cutlass, two daggers, and a silver buckle in the shape of the *Onion*. The emerald crescent sparkled at her neck like a slice of frozen sea.

"Uhn . . . ," said Peter, fighting to dislodge his voice from his throat.

Cassie grinned at him. "Are you ready?"

Two rowing boats bobbed in the sea, waiting. Peter climbed down into one and squeezed onto the seat next to Brine. The starshell pieces dug into his leg, reminding him of their presence. Was knowledge money or was it power? Peter wondered. He'd forgotten. In any case, he was keeping this piece of knowledge to himself.

The boat rushed into land.

Straightaway, the shore rang with Cassie's name, and a surge of people almost knocked Peter back into the sea. A lone man sat on a rock, writing furiously. A seagull waited beside him.

"That's a news-scribe," Brine whispered excitedly. "See his messenger gull? What do you think he's writing?"

Peter turned to look. He'd never seen a real-life news-scribe before—the men and women who wrote down everything that happened on an island and sent their reports by seagull to the library island of Barnard's Reach. Peter didn't care what the scribe was writing. The important thing was that if he and Brine wanted to know anything about Morning, the scribe would be able to tell them. Peter started across the sand.

A hand came down on his shoulder, stopping him. "Where do you think you're going?" asked Ewan Hughes.

"Nowhere. I was just—" Peter stopped. Everyone did. The crowd shuffled back, leaving the pirates in an expanding semi-circle of empty sand.

Twenty men in identical black uniforms came marching across the beach. At their head strode a man who, for some reason, thought that leather armor and a heavy black cloak were appropriate clothing for the hot weather. As a result, his round face was pink and shiny with sweat, and he had a glassy-eyed look that made Peter think of Penn Turbill. Peter felt his mouth twitch and hurriedly looked down. Something told him that smiling would be a very bad thing to do.

"Baron Kaitos!" Cassie cried, dropping into a curtsy that threatened to split her trousers. "I never thought you'd still be here!"

A scowl darkened the baron's face. "So I see." He spoke the way you'd imagine a lizard might: dry lips and flicking tongue, and he matched it with a heavy-lidded gaze that seemed half-asleep, though he never quite blinked. "Didn't you promise never to set foot on Morning again?"

"And didn't you promise to slaughter me on sight if ever I came back? So we're both promise breakers."

"Not yet," said Kaitos. He dropped a hand to his sword.

Peter tensed, ready to run, but Cassie spread her arms wide. "We're here to trade, not to fight." She grabbed Brine's arm with one hand and Peter's with the other. "As a starting point, to make up for any damage caused on our last visit, I'm pleased to offer you this pair of fine young servants free of charge. What do you say?"

CHAPTER 6

The world, as everyone knows, is made up of eight oceans. The
Columba, the Agena, the Andromeda, the Dragon's Head, the
Gemini (which is actually a pair of identical seas), the Perilous,
the Atlas, and the Western Ocean, of which little is known. The
Columba is the most populated, with many large islands, including Morning. The twin Gemini Seas in the north are the
greatest source of starshell. Beyond the Gemini Seas, there is
nothing, only a barren plain of ice where monsters roam. Or so
everyone believes.

(From ALDEBRAN BOSWELL'S BOOK OF THE WORLD)

Brine felt like a sword had gone through her. Cassie couldn't
be serious—but one look at Cassie told Brine that she was.
This was exactly the reason people were afraid of pirates. From
the moment Brine and Peter had set eyes on the *Onion*, it was
inevitable that they'd end up at the bottom of the sea or as pris-
oners somewhere. They should have known.

"This isn't fair," said Brine. Her voice shook. "You said you'd
let us go."

Cassie kept her grip on Brine's arm tight. "I might have lied a little. Sorry." She didn't sound sorry at all. "Baron, do we have a deal?"

Kaitos wiped a trickle of sweat from the side of his face. "You have a stay of execution, that is all. Come with me." He swung round and strode away. Cassie eyed the waiting guards, then nodded to the rest of the crew, let go of Peter and Brine, and followed the baron across the sand.

No chance to run. Ewan Hughes nudged Brine and Peter along together. "Looks like none of us are going anywhere soon," Ewan murmured in Brine's ear. "Best do as he says."

Something in his voice suggested he wasn't entirely happy with the situation. Brine looked back and opened her mouth to speak, but Ewan shook his head and hurried her on, frowning.

After a few minutes, the sand leveled out into a path between trees. Brine shrugged her shoulders, trying to unstick her shirt from her back. Her mind tumbled with thoughts. She wondered if the baron had a library, because if he did, it might not be too bad living here. She wondered about running, but Ewan Hughes was right behind her and guards had moved in to march on either side. Most of all she wondered if she could get away with murdering Cassie.

The baron's tower came into view above the treetops.

"Is it just me," asked Peter, staring up at it, "or is that tower leaning?"

Kaitos stopped dead. The guards all put their hands on their swords.

"You've added another story since last time, haven't you?" Cassie called cheerfully.

A faint look of pride passed over the baron's features. "I might have made a modification or two. It's all very well having a thousand servants, but they have to live somewhere."

"Whatever you do, don't say the *L* word again," whispered Ewan as they walked on. "Yes, the tower leans—the baron built it too high—but you mustn't talk about it. He beheaded the last person who pointed it out."

Ewan could have told them that sooner, Brine thought, before Peter had opened his big mouth. She watched Baron Kaitos uneasily. Ewan was probably joking, but she couldn't be sure, and she didn't want to take the chance that he wasn't.

Finally, the trees opened onto a grassy slope that ran down to the tower. A set of high gates led into a shaded courtyard. A servant ran up with a tray of drinks as they entered. The baron took one and drained it in a single long gulp. Brine watched jealously, her own mouth full of grit.

"This way," ordered Kaitos, leading them into the tower. He ushered them into a room that was perfectly square and big enough for all of them to sit down and still be surrounded by guards. The only furniture was a table in the center.

The sudden relief from the sun made Brine dizzy. She sat on the floor.

Cassie walked to the table and leaned against it. "Well," she said, "we're here. What now?"

The baron's mouth twitched, as if he was trying to smile without letting the rest of his face know about it. "Wait and see."

He gave a mocking little bow, turned on his heel, and went out. The door swung shut behind him, trapping the edge of his cloak. The flap of black cloth wriggled, then disappeared with a force that Brine was sure must have torn it.

"Well," said Cassie, "that could have been worse."

Brine glared at her. She wanted a wash and a drink, and she wasn't sure she was going to get either ever again. "You tricked us," she said. "You said we could buy passage home from here."

"You probably can," agreed Cassie. She picked at the edge of the table. "Look, you're nice kids, but the *Onion* is not a place for children. This way, we all win. I get back on the baron's good side, and you two get to live here on a nice big island. The baron's not a bad man underneath all the bluster. Work hard and stay out of trouble, and you'll be fine."

"What definition of *fine* are you using, exactly?" snapped Brine.

Cassie looked straight at her. "The one that means you're still alive when you could be dead and drowned."

Brine started up. Peter grabbed her wrist. "Brine, leave it."

"Leave it?" She should have known Peter would give in without so much as a whimper. The pirates shuffled their feet and avoided her gaze. Trudi turned crimson.

Ewan Hughes cleared his throat. "Cassie's right, Brine. You're far better off here than with us. You've only seen what it's like on the *Onion* when the wind is good and there's plenty of food and little work to do. You wait until we sail into a storm or we're becalmed for a week with nothing to eat. You'd soon change your mind. Stay here, and you'll have a home."

"A home?" Brine shoved Peter away from her. "Some home, stuck here with Seaweed-Brain."

"You think I want to be stuck here with *you*?" Peter shot back.

"Kids—" murmured Cassie.

"Shut up," they both shouted.

They broke off as the door opened and Baron Kaitos strode back in. Everybody stood up. The baron had taken off his cloak, but his face still glistened with sweat, though it was far cooler in here than outside. A muscle in his cheek jumped as if he was nervous. Brine stared so hard at him that she almost missed seeing the man who followed him.

He wasn't hard to miss. He was not much taller and not much shorter than anyone else, his hair was the color of ordinary sand, his face was so utterly forgettable it was almost remarkable. Only his eyes held Brine's attention, and it took a moment for her to work out why. They were an entirely unexceptional shade of mid-brown and rimmed with nothing. The man had no eyelashes.

The baron cleared his throat, and Brine's gaze jumped back to him. "Allow me to introduce Bartimius Boswell," he said. "Great-grandson of the scientist and explorer Aldebran Boswell."

Boswell's great-grandson. Brine gulped and sat down slowly. No wonder the baron had been acting so strangely. The descendant of the most famous man in the world was here in the room with her.

"Never heard of him," said Bill Lightning cheerfully.

Something dark flickered in Bartimius Boswell's lashless eyes. Brine felt a moment's unease, which disappeared before she could wonder what had caused it.

This ordinary man was the descendant of the greatest scientist and explorer who'd ever lived, and he was here, standing right in front of her. She felt like her heart was about to explode. She wanted to say something—tell him she'd read all Boswell's books, that she wanted to be an explorer like him—but she knew that whatever she said would come out wrong.

She kicked Peter, who was grinning at her, and watched as Boswell patted several pockets and drew out a square of yellow cloth. He held it in both hands for a count of ten seconds, then bent over the table and smoothed it out. If it was a ploy to get everyone's attention, it worked. The pirates all shifted forward. Brine got up and joined them at the table.

She was looking at a map, and not a particularly impressive one. The eight oceans were sketched in blue ink and a scattering of different-shaped spots showed the positions of the islands. Morning was marked; the Minutes cluster, unsurprisingly, was not. On the western side, a curling sprawl of letters said *Here Be Dragons*, and at the top the letters *MN* stood above a mark that looked like someone had tried to draw a ship and gotten it wrong.

"What does 'Here Be Dragons' mean?" asked Brine. Her nose itched.

"It means we don't know what's there, of course." Boswell gave her a sharp look. "I thought all sailors knew that."

She met his gaze without blinking, then spoiled the effect by sneezing. "I'm new at it."

"And the rest of us are getting impatient," added Cassie, reaching for the map.

Boswell slid it away from her. "Then I won't keep you. You all know the stories of Orion, I assume?"

Everyone nodded. Who in the world hadn't heard of Orion? The first and greatest sailor. The hero who stole fire from the stars and drove back the oceans of the world to create the first islands. If the stories were to be believed—and Brine knew they weren't—Orion had sailed around the whole world, fought a thousand monsters, and married a thousand wives. Then, at the end of his life, he'd turned his ship north and sailed off the world altogether and up into the sky, where his ship became the first-ever constellation, a guide to all those who sailed the eight oceans.

"It's just a story," Cassie said, but her gaze was fixed on the map on the table.

Boswell's eyebrows rose. "Just a story? It is *the* story. The first tale ever to be told when people were looking out to sea and wondering what might be over the horizon. Aldebran

Boswell once said all stories have to start with a grain of truth, and the greatest story of all must surely carry the greatest truth." His gaze took in the whole room. "That is why, one hundred years ago, Aldebran Boswell set sail to re-create Orion's journey to the top of the world. He was never seen again."

The room was silent. Brine sat still, barely daring to breathe. So that was how Boswell had died. None of Magus's books had said anything about the end of his life. She'd always assumed he'd retired from science and died naturally of old age.

Trudi yawned loudly.

"It might have escaped your notice," said Cassie, "but we're pirates, not scientists. Do you want to get on to the bit where there's a big stash of stolen gold?"

Boswell's face creased in annoyance.

Brine wanted to hit Cassie. She'd spoiled things again, upsetting Boswell just when they were getting to the interesting part of the tale. "No one would sail to the top of the world just because of a story," she said quickly. "Your great-grandfather was looking for something." Cassie frowned at her and tried to push her out of the way, but Brine stood her ground. She'd been pushed around enough for one day. "I'm right, aren't I?"

Slowly, Boswell took his hands off the map and nodded. "You are quite correct: He was looking for something. Somewhere, to be exact. Even pirates should know that there are three north poles—geographical, magnetic, and magical." He pointed to the top of the map. "This is what Aldebran Boswell gave his life to find. Magical North—the single most concentrated point of magic anywhere. It lies in the ice plains at the top of the world, where the sun only sets once a year. It is guarded by a monster a thousand times more terrible than the Dreaded Great Sea Beast of the South, and it is surrounded by the Sea of Sighs, where the wind howls like the souls of the dead and men have drowned themselves rather than listen. Only a madman would attempt such a voyage—a madman or a hero."

Nobody spoke. The room seemed to have turned colder. Boswell rested his hands on the edge of the table, his long fingers splayed out. "But once a year," he said, "on the thirty-first day of the month of Balistes—Orion's Day—the sun sets over the ice plains. And if, during this annual twilight, you stand on the exact point of Magical North, you will be able to see the whole world. Imagine it—everything that exists spread out before you like your own personal map. You could look up the locations of all the treasure of the world, or all the starshell. You could see your own past if you wanted to—maybe even your own future. Great-grandfather was unclear on that."

Brine couldn't take her eyes off the map. The letters *MN* stood out at the top like bruises.

Boswell looked around at them all. "Imagine it," he repeated softly. "Imagine what you could do with that knowledge."

"Magical North is just another story," said Ewan. "It doesn't exist."

"Aldebran Boswell would disagree," said Boswell, "and he was a far cleverer man than you'll ever be. But if the thought of unlimited knowledge doesn't tempt you, think about this: Boswell's writings speak of a vast treasure trove in the northern plains. Gold, diamonds, rubies. More riches than you can possibly count, just sitting there waiting for you."

He paused to let them think about this. The pirates all stared at the map while trying to pretend they were looking somewhere else. Ewan Hughes crossed his arms and frowned. "What you're saying is, all we have to do is follow a man out of a legend to a place that doesn't exist, pile the ship with imaginary gold, and Bob's your oyster."

Baron Kaitos stepped forward. "I'm willing to make you an offer," he said, evidently deciding he'd been quiet long enough. "I will restock the *Onion*, taking in return the servants you brought with you today. Upon successful completion of the voyage, I will pay you a chest of silver plus one-fourth part of whatever treasure you find at Magical North."

Cassie stepped back from the table. Her swinging fingers casually brushed her cutlass hilt. "Only a fourth part?"

Kaitos glanced at Boswell—Brine noticed the movement. *Strange*, she thought. The baron owned the whole island and must have been used to ordering everyone around, yet the way he looked at Boswell was as if he was waiting to be told what to do. He looked almost afraid.

"This is no mere treasure hunt, Captain," snapped Boswell. "You need someone with scientific knowledge. Someone who can steer you safely through the howling oceans and the icy coils of the sea monster. Someone who knows how to survive when the temperature drops low enough to freeze wood. And most of all, someone who has a map." He picked it up and folded it.

"No," said Cassie.

Everyone started talking together. Cassie held up her hands for silence. "The answer is no. I'm not risking the *Onion* on a dubious treasure hunt. Baron, thank you for your hospitality, but we have other places to be."

She started toward the door. The baron pushed in front of her. "You're a fool, Cassie O'Pia." His face reddened, but then he caught Boswell's gaze and snapped his mouth shut.

"I suggest we all take time to consider the idea," said Boswell smoothly. "Until tomorrow, at least. The captain may change her mind by then."

Kaitos nodded. "Until tomorrow. Let my servants know if you need anything." His gaze found Peter and Brine. "Speaking of servants, you two come with me."

CHAPTER 7

Magicians are rare. Very few people can see magic, and even fewer can manipulate it into the correct spellshapes. This is a good thing, because magic corrupts. Only the purest metals and gemstones can survive its presence, and we have to wonder what this corrupting power does to the minds of those who control it.

(From ALDEBRAN BOSWELL'S BIG BOOK OF MAGIC)

Once again, Peter and Brine found themselves in a kitchen. A whole pig hung over a fire the size of a rowing boat, its juices running down like sweat into the flames.

Peter couldn't believe this was happening to him. His only consolation was that it was happening to Brine as well.

"This is your fault," he said.

"Oh, good, that means everything's back to normal, then." Brine turned her back on him. "I suppose it was my fault that Cassie double-crossed us."

"You're just mad because the *Onion*'s going on an adventure and you're not invited."

A hand caught him between the shoulder blades. "Work, not talk," shouted the cook. The man was huge and missing most of his teeth. He thrust a tray of drinks at each of them, slopping liquid over the sides of the goblets. "Take these."

"Take them where?" asked Peter, earning himself another slap. Brine took her tray and turned away without a word. Peter followed, shaking his head, his ears still ringing. "What are you doing?"

"Being a good servant."

A guard walked by, his gaze sliding over them as if they'd suddenly become invisible. Brine gave Peter an I-told-you-so grin and stopped the next guard. "Excuse me. We have to take these drinks to Mr. Boswell's room. Can you tell us the way?"

The guard's eyes flicked down at her and glanced away again indifferently. "Top floor," he said, and walked off.

They looked up at the stairs. The steps spiraled away from them, fading into shadow. Peter felt another of Brine's plans coming on, and his heart sank. "You can't just go up there. What are you going to do—ask Boswell for a job?"

"I don't see you coming up with any better ideas." Brine started to climb.

Sighing, Peter climbed after her. "Just because he's Aldebran Boswell's great-grandson, it doesn't mean he knows anything about him."

"He knows about Magical North."

"Yes, well, that might be the only thing he knows. And he could be making it all up. He looked shifty. The baron, too."

Brine hesitated.

She'd also seen it, then, Peter thought. He was glad he hadn't imagined it.

"They were probably nervous being around so many pirates," said Brine.

"I don't think so, and neither do you." He tried to overtake her, but she only climbed faster, giving Peter the choice of following her or giving up and going back to the kitchen. He followed.

The first ten stories had carpets on the floors and paintings on the walls. After that, the walls were bare and the plain stone floors looked like they could do with a wash. Everything smelled funny. Peter guessed the baron was one of those people who liked to put on a show where it mattered and let everything fall apart behind the scenes. Which made it odd that an important visitor like Boswell should be all the way up on the top floor.

Peter paused. "Brine, I really don't like this. Can we just stop and think for a minute?"

"Since when did you start thinking?"

A guard turned to look at them. "Boswell's room?" asked Brine.

"Top floor, end of the corridor. What do you want with Mr. Boswell?"

"Room service," said Brine.

Seventeen floors. Twenty. Twenty-five. Forty. Peter's legs burned with the effort. Finally, just when he thought his knees were going to give way altogether, the stairs ended in a narrow corridor. The uneven slant of the tower was obvious here. Gashes of light leaned at odd angles from the narrow windows, and even the floor felt wrong, as if it were trying to throw them down the corridor to the door at the end.

Peter's heart bumped. This was definitely not right. "Remember what happened last time we went somewhere we shouldn't?" he asked.

Brine set her tray down. "We're already servants. What else can they do to us?"

"Do you want a list?"

She threw him a scornful look and started down the corridor. Peter sighed, put his tray down next to hers, and followed. If this turned out like her usual bright ideas, they'd both end up in the dungeon, assuming Baron Kaitos had dungeons. Peter wondered if there would be rats.

Brine stopped outside the end door and raised her hand to knock.

"Wait," whispered Peter. Something didn't feel right, and he wasn't going to go barging straight in. He nudged Brine aside and peered through a crack in the door.

Boswell was sitting upright in a wooden chair facing him. His eyes were closed. That, in itself, wasn't unusual. As far as Peter knew, scientists often closed their eyes when they were thinking. From what Peter could see, the rest of the room wasn't unusual, either—books open on the floor, a giant map on the far wall.

No, what was unusual was the way that yellow light

trickled in a thin line out of Boswell's palms and curled in front of him, forming a shape that Peter recognized because he'd been studying it only days before. A mind control spell. And, judging by the amount of magic Boswell was pouring into the spell, it was going to be a big one.

Peter's skin prickled. The starshell pieces in his pocket buzzed softly. He straightened up from the door and met Brine's gaze.

She rubbed the end of her nose. "What is it?"

Peter put his finger to his lips. Carefully, terrified one of them would make a sound and Boswell would hear, he tiptoed away until his back hit the far wall of the corridor. "He's a magician," he whispered, motioning for Brine to stay quiet. "Boswell's great-grandson is a magician." If the man was Boswell's great-grandson at all. Peter spread his hands flat on the wall to keep them from shaking. He remembered the look on Baron Kaitos's face. *You're a fool.* And Boswell's words: *The captain may change her mind.* The baron knew. He knew, and he was afraid.

Brine looked like she was trying to suppress a sneeze. Peter gripped her arm. "We have to warn Cassie." Even though she was a pirate and a promise breaker and deserved to be mind-controlled.

Brine's face twitched. She pinched her nose and nodded. Together, they began to edge back toward the stairs, which suddenly seemed a thousand miles away.

And then Brine sneezed.

A chaotic starburst of amber light flared out around

Boswell's door—the light of a spell being released too early, Peter thought. He let go of Brine's arm. For once, her allergy had done something useful. Now Boswell would have to start his spell all over again, if he had enough magic for it at all.

But then Peter noticed the silence. It was not a good silence. It oozed out through the cracks in the door, filling the corridor with the dark sense that something bad was just about to happen.

"I think we should go," muttered Brine, but Peter couldn't move. He stood frozen, his gaze fixed on the end of the corridor, where, slowly, as if it were happening in a dream, Boswell's door swung open.

"Can I help you?" asked Boswell, and for a second, everything felt so normal that Peter's knees sagged in relief. But then he saw the gold chain swinging from Boswell's pocket. Gold— the most valuable metal in the world, because it was one of the few metals that survived in the presence of magic.

A lump gathered at the back of Peter's throat. "I don't think you're Boswell's great-grandson at all," he said.

Boswell's teeth gleamed as he laughed. "Of course I'm not." His voice slithered unpleasantly in Peter's ears. "Do you know how much preparation that spell requires? How much time and magical power? Now I'm going to have to start again—just as soon as I've dealt with you two."

He came toward them, and as he walked, he changed. He grew taller, tall enough that his head almost touched the low ceiling. His very ordinary hair vanished like smoke, his eyebrows, too, leaving him completely bald, and his face became long and hollow. His brown eyes turned the color of polished amber, swarming with black flecks.

Not-Boswell raised a hand and sketched a spellshape in the air.

"Get down!" yelled Peter, and he shoved Brine flat as magic flared. In the enclosed corridor, the effect was like a star exploding. Peter shouted and stumbled back, half-blinded by the flash. He grabbed hold of Brine as she scrambled up, and they both ran, screaming, for the stairs.

Voices and clanging metal sounded from below. Peter looked back over his shoulder at the man who wasn't Boswell. He stalked toward them. Three pieces of starshell dangled like charms from the chain in his right hand, and long shadows spread from his feet, slowly swallowing the corridor.

Brine stumbled to a halt, staring. Peter hauled her out of the way a second before the magician raised his right hand and blasted a hole in the ceiling. This was Tallis Magus all over again, except a thousand times worse.

This time, though, Peter didn't leave Brine and run. Even while every thought screamed that this was his stupidest idea ever and he was going to die, he stepped between her and the magician. Magic was his field. Like Cassie had the *Onion* and Brine had her books. He had to do something.

Not-Boswell looked at him, the bare places where his eyebrows should have been rising in surprise. "You're a brave boy," he said. "Brave and exceptionally stupid."

Peter clenched his fists, his whole body trembling, and put his hand in his pocket for his starshell.

Then a scrape of steel disturbed the air behind him. He turned his head with difficulty.

Cassie O'Pia strolled up the last few steps to join them. A sword swung idly in each hand, and there was a dark patch on her shirt that might have been blood.

"Kids," she said quietly, "when I say 'run,' I want you to run as if Marfak West himself was on your tail." She looked over Peter's head at the man who stood watching her. "Which," she added, "isn't as much of an exaggeration as you might think."

Peter's knees buckled. Marfak West was dead—the sharks had eaten him.

But he didn't look very dead.

Marfak West raised his hands. Cassie raised her swords. "Run!"

CHAPTER 8

Oh, her hair is as red as the sun in its bed,
Her eyes are as blue as the waves.
All girls long to be her, fair Cassie O'Pia.
All men long to live as her slaves.

For she's swift and she's strong and, though I may be wrong,
She is all that your heart could desire.
For one chance to see her, fair Cassie O'Pia,
A man would walk naked through fire.

(From THE BALLAD OF CASSIE O'PIA,
Verses 14–15, Author Unknown)

The air around Peter sizzled. He stood for one second more, then he grabbed Brine's arm and ran for his life.

Brine tugged back against him. "Peter, wait. That can't be Marfak West—he's dead."

"Do you want to go up there and tell him?" Peter flattened himself into the wall as Ewan Hughes charged up the stairs past them, pursued by guards. Ewan's hair was on fire, but he didn't seem to have noticed. Peter started down the stairs again. For once, Brine followed without arguing.

Shouts and clashes of weapons rose to greet them. Above them, another explosion rocked the tower. They clattered down the last few flights of stairs and ran headlong into a group of guards who were on their way up. Peter couldn't see anything beyond waving limbs. Panic drove him on, and possibly Brine pushing from behind. He squeezed between armored legs, thankful for once that no one seemed to think he was worth bothering about.

He emerged to see Tim Burre and Trudi fighting a path to the doors. Trudi had a meat cleaver in one hand and what looked like a leg of mutton in the other, and she was using both with equal efficiency. Peter slipped into the gap behind them. His mind was numb. Marfak West. The fact that the magician was alive at all wasn't really a shock—the stories about him were too terrifying to end in defeat and death. But he'd always assumed Marfak West had escaped and was terrorizing some other part of the world far away. Not anywhere near *him*.

A guard loomed, sword raised. Peter ducked, and Trudi took two quick steps back and muttoned the man in the back of the head. Red droplets splashed across Peter's face. He hoped they were from the meat. He wiped them off on his sleeve.

Brine clutched at his shirt from behind. "Peter!"

Light flashed at the top of the stairs. In a daze, Peter saw Cassie O'Pia come tumbling down. Ewan Hughes was on her heels, the back of his head still smoking, and behind Ewan came a shape so dark and twisted it made Peter's eyes ache. He tried to shout a warning, but the sound never came. Or maybe it did, but the noise of the ceiling exploding drowned it.

There followed one of those long, curious pauses that seemed almost peaceful compared to what had gone before. Everyone lay staring at one another while the dust settled in a gray drift. Then they all—pirates, guards, even Baron Kaitos—picked themselves up and ran for the door.

The starshell pieces twitched in Peter's pocket. The air was filled with magic, and they were absorbing it fast, but Peter didn't have time even to think about using them. The fleeing crowd swept him along after Brine, and he burst through the doors into bright sunshine. He kept running until he was across the courtyard and out of the main gates. Pausing, he rested his hands on his knees, gasping in air, his chest and throat on fire.

The baron's tower was swaying. One of the turrets fell off and demolished a nearby tree.

The tower creaked, shuddered, and settled with a noise of rumbling stone. The baron couldn't possibly pretend it wasn't leaning now. The top of it looked as if it were trying to see around a corner.

"I don't think the baron is going to be happy," said Brine, panting for breath next to him.

Peter straightened up and attempted a grin. "I don't know.

The world's first-ever leaning tower. He can charge people to come and look at it."

Cassie skidded to a halt beside them. "Come on, you two. We're getting out of here."

Peter and Brine looked at each other. Peter shrugged. Stay here with an angry, ex-dead magician, or go back to the *Onion* with pirates who'd tried to sell him. It showed how bad things were that the pirates were the better option.

►┅┼┼┼╞

C assie whooped as she slid down the last rocky slope onto the deserted beach. The rowing boats stood together, untouched. The news-scribe was still sitting on his rock. He had plenty to write about now, Peter thought.

"Well, that could have been worse," said Cassie. "Though I think we may have overstayed our welcome here. Let's go."

The soft crunch of footsteps on sand stopped her. They all stopped, then turned slowly.

Marfak West wore black, head to foot, and, unlike Baron Kaitos, black suited him. His bald head shone with the gleam of reflected magic. His midnight chain mail glistened, and his sable cloak undulated softly around him. Where he trod, little ripples spread out as if the sand was trying to get away from him.

The news-scribe scooped up his gull and fled. Peter would have followed, but his legs weren't working. He felt like he'd shrunk to the size of a beetle and Marfak West could crush him with one finger. Why had he ever thought he could stand in the magician's way? What could any of them do?

"Die!" shouted Ewan Hughes and leaped at Marfak West. The magician flicked his wrist, and a little ball of light shot from his hand to strike Ewan in midair, flinging him across the beach and into the boats. Ewan lay there, groaning.

Cassie stepped forward. "Your quarrel is with me. Let the others go."

Marfak West shook his head. "Strangely, Captain, I have no interest in our so-called quarrel, not anymore. I want the *Onion*."

Cassie's knuckles whitened on her cutlass hilts. "Over my dead body."

"I always like it when people say that," said Marfak West. He advanced on them, step by measured step.

Brine tugged Peter's arm. "Do something."

Peter started to shake his head, then turned, met the full force of her glare, and learned that Marfak West was not the last word in terror after all. His face burned. Nodding, he edged his hand into his pocket and curled his fingers over his two scraps of starshell. Their magic buzzed against his palm. Peter did one of the few things he could do well. He drew an arrow in the air and pulled, trying to jerk the starshell from Marfak West's hand.

It was like trying to drag an island. Peter's muscles strained. A brief flash of surprise crossed Marfak West's lashless eyes, and he laughed. "Do you really think you can use magic against me?"

"Leave him alone," shouted Trudi. It was enough to deflect the magician's attention for a moment. Peter's thoughts scrambled into another shape. He braced himself, then—instead of trying to pull the weight of magic—he reversed the spellshape, threw all his strength against it, and pushed.

Every action has an opposite reaction, Boswell said, which is why you should never throw magic at magic. Peter remembered that too late. His magic collided with Marfak West's and rebounded. His starshell pieces exploded to nothing in his hand. The force threw him backward, a hot pain skewered his right palm, and he sprawled, gasping, in the sand, seeing everything in flashes. Marfak West stumbled. Cassie crashed into him. Everyone else ran about, their mouths opening and shutting, making no sound.

Peter's ears popped painfully.

". . . boats!" shouted Cassie. Tim Burre swept Peter up and dumped him in the nearest one. Ewan Hughes struggled in beside him and grabbed a pair of oars. Brine scrambled in at the back as Ewan began to row.

"All right?" asked Ewan. Peter nodded. The movement didn't make his head fall off after all. He opened his hand and stared at a small, perfectly round, charred spot of skin in the middle of his palm—the only part of him that didn't hurt. A few specks of starshell still clung to his skin—all that remained of the two starshell pieces. Peter picked at the flecks with his fingernails. So much for trying to hide the fact that he was a magician.

Orange fire arched overhead: Marfak West's last attempt to

stop them. Ewan rowed faster, taking them out of reach. Then, somehow, they were alongside the *Onion* and ropes were uncoiling into their eager hands. They scrambled up and fell, gasping and bleeding, onto the deck. Ewan Hughes helped Brine to her feet and winked at her. "That was close," he said.

And then a giant purple tentacle rose out of the sea and grabbed him by the throat.

CHAPTER 9

Starshell provides the magic, but how it is used depends on the skill of the magician. An unskilled magician is wasteful—think of a child drawing shapes with a thick pen. But a great magician is like a skilled artist painting with a fine brush. With the tiniest amount of magic, he can perform wonders.

(From ALDEBRAN BOSWELL'S BIG BOOK OF MAGIC)

Brine yelled as Ewan Hughes flailed frantically, almost chopping off his own head in his attempts to get at the tentacle that was simultaneously throttling him and dragging him off the deck.

"Octopus!" cried Cassie, leaping past Brine to attack. Her blade swung, embedding itself in rubbery flesh. She wrenched it free and struck again, and the tentacle uncurled and sprang back into the sea with the speed of a rope being released.

Ewan Hughes collapsed to his knees, scarlet-faced and coughing.

"What's the plural of octopus?" he croaked.

Cassie calmly wiped slime off her cutlass. "Octopuses, I think. Or octopi. Why?"

Something wet tapped Brine on the shoulder. She spun away, barely in time as a tentacle snatched at her. "Um . . . ," she began, but no one was listening. They were all too busy staring.

The *Onion* bobbed amid a forest of tentacles. They swarmed in from every side, swollen and shiny, their greasy colors groping in blind hunger at the edge of the deck. The sea between the ship and the shore boiled red, purple, and green with living creatures. And, out in the bay, striding across the backs of them all as calmly as if he were taking a stroll along the beach, Marfak West came walking.

Brine's mouth turned dry. "He's not really doing that, is he?"

"It appears that he is," replied Cassie, chopping at more tentacles.

A crab landed on Brine's head. She jumped and shook it off. This was impossible. Absolutely, completely, totally impossible.

Marfak West continued walking. The light surrounding him flickered. "He's running out of magic," said Peter. He turned to Cassie. "We can fight him. Even the most powerful magician in the world is only as good as his starshell. When he runs out of power, he'll be helpless."

Brine doubted that, but she looked around for a weapon. All she could see was a bucket. She snatched it up and retreated toward the mainmast, trying to stay out of the way of the writhing tentacles. The deck was fast becoming as slippery as one of Trudi's frying pans.

Marfak West rose unsteadily into the air and landed on the

edge of the deck. Brine heard herself moan in fear. Peter bumped into her—for once, she was glad he was close by.

Marfak West raised his hands. Magic flickered.

"Get him!" yelled Cassie. The pirates all charged together, apart from Tim Burre, who fell over the cat. Brine took a look at the severed tentacles around her, and an idea formed. It was a mad idea, but no madder than anything else that had happened already. She bent and began stuffing tentacles into her bucket.

"What are you doing?" asked Peter.

"This."

She threw the bucket at Marfak West.

It stopped before it reached him and fell to the deck along with most of the tentacles, but some of them kept going and hit the magician with wet slaps. He picked a tentacle off his shoulder and flicked it away.

"I know what you're thinking," he said. "You're wondering how much magic I have left. I've been using it so fast I might have run out already. On the other hand, I might have enough to smear you all over this ship." He turned and, for a second, his gaze met Brine's. "Well?" he asked. "Are you willing to risk it?"

Brine shrank back against the mast, her heart pounding.

Then Marfak West snapped his fingers. "Come here, magician," he said, and Brine realized with guilty relief that he wanted Peter, not her.

Peter took a jerky, unwilling step forward. Brine caught his arm and tried to pull him back. Rob and Ewan ran at Marfak West. Rob's clothes suddenly sprouted flames and he went down with a hoarse cry, and Ewan stopped and keeled over as if he'd run headfirst into a wall.

Then a flash of cream fur dashed across the deck. Stray magic sparked from Zen's whiskers. The cat skidded on octopus slime but kept running, and Brine saw what Zen had noticed: a particularly juicy tip of tentacle sticking out from underneath the magician's left boot. Octopus: his favorite. The cat reached it, seized it, and pulled.

Marfak West stumbled, his arms flying up in the air. A bolt of magic took out half the crow's nest. The startled cat snatched the tentacle and fled. The magician stepped back; his heel caught the slime trail, and he skidded, then sat down heavily.

Every pirate within reach jumped on top of him. A blinding flare of magic threw six of them straight off again, but the others kept hold.

Cassie crossed the deck, looked at the dripping cutlass in her hand, and rested the tip between the magician's twitching shoulder blades. "Surrender or die," she said. "Or both, if you like."

━━━━━━━

An hour later, the deck was scrubbed, Zen was asleep in Brine's lap, snoring off the biggest seafood feast of his life, and the crew were gathered around the mainmast watching Marfak West. The magician had been stripped of every last speck of starshell and was bound to the mast from his hips to his shoulders with so many ropes a hurricane wouldn't have shifted him. Brine still didn't want to go near him. Even magicless and bound, Marfak West didn't seem like a prisoner to her, and the way he smiled at the crew suggested that he regarded them not as his captors but as a captive audience.

No one else seemed to notice. Cassie sat on an upturned bucket, her cutlass in one hand and Marfak West's starshell in the other. Empty of magic, the three pieces were dull gray, dangling from their golden chain. Peter kept trying not to look at them and was being rather too obvious about it.

Brine leaned across to him. "I don't think you should be allowed any more starshell. You keep breaking it."

He rubbed at his hand. "It wasn't my fault. You were the one who told me to do something."

"You can't do anything without blaming me, can you?" asked Brine. It was a relief to be arguing with Peter again. It reminded her that at least one thing in the world was still the same.

"Do we get to throw the magician overboard now?" asked Ewan Hughes.

Cassie shook her head. "No one's throwing anyone overboard." Her gaze flicked back to Marfak West. "Yet," she added. She picked at the edge of her cutlass, flicking reddish scraps onto the deck. "I must say you're looking remarkably healthy, considering that the last time we saw you, you were dead."

Marfak West's lips curled. "Did you really think I would die so easily?"

"Really? Yes." Cassie grinned at him and slid her cutlass back into its sheath. "But we can't wait to hear all about the dramatic escape, so do carry on gloating."

Marfak West leveled his stare at her. "Gloating is for fools who don't feel important enough. And you, Captain, are the biggest fool alive. You didn't see me die. You saw the *Antares* sink, and you sailed away to spread the news that you'd defeated me. But, while the eight oceans celebrated your victory, I clung to the wreckage of my ship. I hung on for days, surviving on rainwater and seaweed. Flesh-eating crabs gnawed all the toes from my left foot, but I held fast. Little by little, my starshell revived, and as my power returned, I drew together the last, smashed timbers of the *Antares* and made a raft." He paused. "And then I enslaved a thousand squid to tow me across the ocean."

Ewan Hughes gave a disbelieving snort. "You've had four years to come up with a story, and that's the best you can do?" He got up and pulled off the magician's left boot.

The foot, as Marfak West had claimed, was entirely toeless.

"You'll pay for what you did," Marfak West promised Cassie quietly.

"That seems to be reasonable grounds for tossing you to the sharks," said Cassie.

"Be my guest." He made several unsucessful attempts to squash his foot back into his boot. "Kill me, and lose your chance to uncover the greatest treasure in the world. Every word I spoke on Morning is true. Magical North exists. Boswell's real great-grandson told me everything just before he died."

"He died?" Brine echoed, aghast, and regretted speaking as Marfak West turned his head toward her.

"Of course he died," he said. "I killed him." His gaze seemed to go right through her. "Where do *you* come from?" he asked.

Even though he was tied up and helpless, the way he looked at her, with sharp recognition, made Brine shiver. He knew, she thought. Marfak West already knew where she was from, and he just wanted her to confirm it. She wet her lips. "Where do you think?"

"It's none of your business where she's from," said Cassie, cutting her off. She nodded to Ewan, who stuck his hands between the ropes around the magician's chest.

"If you're looking for the map," said Marfak West after a moment's fruitless rummaging, "you'll find it in my trouser pocket. The map won't help you, though—it's just a rough guide. The exact location of Magical North exists only inside my head."

"Want me to cut it off and take a look?" Ewan asked Cassie with a grin. No one else smiled. Ewan found the map and passed it back to Cassie. She opened it across her knees but didn't look at it; her gaze remained fixed on the magician.

Brine suppressed another shiver. Marfak West was playing with them. Anyone with any sense—which excluded most of the people sitting around her—could see it. If he wanted to sail off after Magical North, there were plenty of ships that would be far easier for him to take control of. He was up to something, but what?

Marfak West knows who you are, a voice said in her mind. Brine tried to ignore it.

Cassie traced a finger across the top of the map. "Once a

year on Orion's Day," she said. "That's less than two months away."

"If you're saying you can't do it . . . ," taunted Marfak West.

Everyone swiveled in Cassie's direction. She sat, head bowed, lost in thought over Boswell's map. When she looked up, she was smiling—a bright sword blade of a smile. The same smile Brine had seen when Cassie decided to take them to Morning. It was a smile that said she'd made up her mind and no one was going to change it. Putting the map aside, she got up and crossed the deck to Brine and Peter.

Brine held her breath. Here it came—the harsh telling-off for hiding the fact that Peter was a magician. Brine didn't know what the punishment would be, but she guessed it would involve a lot of deck-scrubbing.

But Cassie just stood for a moment, saying nothing, then she dropped the starshell chain into Peter's hands.

"As of now," she said, "you're the ship's magician."

Brine's mouth fell open. Those three pieces of shell were worth more than the *Onion*, and Cassie had handed them over as if they were nothing.

Peter nodded as if he'd been expecting this. He didn't look entirely happy as he folded the chain around the starshell pieces. Something inside Brine sank a little bit, too. If Peter was the ship's magician, where did that leave her?

Cassie turned away from them. "As for him," she said, pointing at Marfak West, "untie him. Then lock him in the brig."

CHAPTER 10

BARBECUED OCTOPUS

Collect up as many giant octopus tentacles as you can find—
one per person is usually enough. Rub them well with salt and
pepper and leave them to dry in the sun for an hour. Rinse thor-
oughly. Barbecue over a hot fire until black on the outside and
just done and still pink inside.

(From COOKING UP A STORME—
THE RECIPES OF A GOURMET PIRATE)

Night fell. The *Onion* sailed on at a steady pace. Not toward
anywhere in particular yet, but away. Away from Morning
and Baron Kaitos, and if that direction happened to take them a
little bit north, everyone agreed it was entirely coincidence.

Brine lay in her hammock, wondering how anybody could
sleep. Everything felt far too normal, and it was completely
wrong. They had Marfak West in the brig. *Marfak West.* Thief
and murderer and magician, Cassie's deadliest enemy, and he
was chained up in the lower hold. Just a few layers of wood

between Brine and him. Marfak West, who seemed to know where she'd come from. Yet here she lay, listening to people snore as if none of the past day had even happened.

Peter's voice drifted out of the darkness just above her. "Brine, are you awake?"

She shook her head. "I'm not talking to you."

"That's a surprise. What have I done this time?"

Brine didn't answer. It would sound too petty to admit she was annoyed because he was the ship's magician and she was still the ship's nothing. She'd been nothing all her life. Wasn't it time she got a turn at being somebody?

Peter's hammock wobbled as he rolled over to look down at her. "Brine, come on, you've got to help me. You heard what they all said about magicians before, and now everyone's expecting *me* to do magic. I can't. Not the sort Cassie will be wanting."

"You don't even know what sort that is," said Brine, but she, too, had the feeling that Cassie wouldn't be content with Peter pushing and pulling things. She sat up. "I don't see what I can do about it. No one listens to me."

"They should. You're the one who's always coming up with plans."

"Am I?" She forgot she was supposed to be annoyed for a moment. She slid out of the hammock. Her head was thumping. "I can't sleep. I'm going for a walk."

"Don't go too far. You'll fall in the sea."

"Very funny."

Brine climbed the ladder to the deck. The night sky loomed

over her, deep blue and huge with stars. Wood, wind, and sail hummed together. She turned her face northward, easily picking out the bright light of Orion amid the constellations. What if Marfak West was right and she could stand at Magical North and see the whole world? It wouldn't matter what he knew about her then; she could find out for herself. She imagined the whole world spread like a map before her, with her home clearly marked. Wouldn't that be worth the journey?

Turning, she saw Cassie standing at the helm. She was back in her old clothes, and with her hair cloaking her face, she almost merged into the night. Even the emerald around her neck looked more gray than green in the moonlight.

For half a minute, the two of them watched each other across the deck, neither saying a word. Cassie had saved Brine's life twice and tried to sell her once—and Brine had no idea what the pirate was going to do next.

Cassie lifted a hand in greeting. Brine hesitated, then walked over to join her.

"Look," said Cassie, pointing. "The constellation of Orion. The first set of stars to be born, they say, though I don't know how they can tell. You see the three stars that make up the ship's mast? Did you know the top one is also called the *Onion*? It's not a single star at all, some people say, but hundreds of them, layer after layer, all nestling one within another."

Brine said nothing. Cassie pointed again. "If you look to the left a bit, you can see my constellation. Cassiopeia—the keeper of secrets."

There were so many stars Brine wasn't sure which ones Cassie meant, but she nodded anyway.

"Did your father really lose you in a game of cards?" she asked. She thought about all the stories she'd heard about Cassie. They couldn't all be true—there were too many of them.

"It wasn't cards." Cassie's hand dropped down to the emerald around her neck. "It wasn't my father, either. My brother challenged a man twice his size to a duel. He lost, unsurprisingly, and he offered me to the man in exchange for his life. I wasn't supposed to have any choice in the matter. That's the kind of island I lived on." Her gaze drifted back to the stars. "I pretended to go along with it and then, on the evening of the wedding when everyone was drinking, I picked up everything I could carry, stole a boat, and rowed away. There were no fights with giant octopuses, no mutant sea monsters—well, not many. All the rest is exaggeration."

Brine shook her head. "No it's not. All the rest is story."

Their gazes met, and for a moment, they both smiled.

Cassie O'Pia, the keeper of secrets. It suited her, Brine thought. Stories were just secrets in reverse, really. You hid something important inside a load of words where no one could ever find it. She wondered whether the story Cassie had just told her was any more true than all the other ones. It didn't seem to matter. The story wasn't even about Cassie O'Pia; it was about every boy or girl who'd ever wanted to run away from home and look for adventure. People needed stories, and stories needed people like Cassie. What was it Aldebran Boswell called it? Symbiosis. Two things making each other stronger.

Brine looked down and concentrated on drawing a pattern with her finger on the deck rail. "I have no idea where I come from," she said. "I was found at sea with a piece of starshell around my neck, and I've never been able to remember how I got there. I became a magician's servant, but I'm allergic to magic—the stuff makes me sneeze. When I tried to change things, Peter and I ended up stranded. If you hadn't come along, we might have died. Even when I thought I'd met a descendant of Boswell, he turned out to be Marfak West. I'm unlucky: That's all I am. If I stay on board the *Onion*, I'll probably end up sinking her."

She paused, waiting for Cassie to laugh. Either that or believe her and throw her overboard.

Cassie did neither. "Luck's a funny thing," she agreed seriously. "It changes more often than the sea and never does what you expect. Take the *Onion*'s last captain. He survived a fight with a mutant octopus only to die of food poisoning after eating barbecued tentacle. What sort of luck is that?"

Brine rested her chin on her hand.

"I wouldn't worry about it too much," said Cassie. "Let the future take care of itself. Anything may happen yet."

It dawned on Brine then, quick as the blink of a star, why Cassie was out here on her own. "You don't know what to do," she said.

Cassie laughed. "Brine, I never know what to do. That's

what floating about on an ocean does to you—you can't plan ahead. The weather changes, and your carefully timetabled fortnight of marauding is put on hold while you make emergency repairs." Her voice fell away, and a small frown creased the skin between her eyes. "I've got my worst enemy locked in the hold. If our positions were reversed, Marfak West would have killed me without a thought, and I wouldn't have blamed him. We sank his ship. The *Antares* was the only thing he loved in the world. He won't rest until the *Onion* is at the bottom of the ocean." Her frown deepened.

"But despite all that, you think he's telling the truth," said Brine.

Cassie turned her emerald round and round on its chain. "Actually, I know he's telling the truth. That's what makes it so complicated. When I thought he was just some scientist's great-grandson, I didn't believe a word of it. But Marfak West doesn't lie—not about the things that matter—and he doesn't make mistakes, either. If he says Magical North exists and only he knows where it is, then I believe him. I don't trust him, of course. He's not telling us everything, and he'll turn on us the first chance he gets." She paused and smiled. "But imagine the stories if we succeed."

Brine looked up at the stars. The topmost star of Orion shone with a steady white light. Today was the eighteenth day of the month of Tench. Orion's Day was only six weeks away, when the sun would set over Magical North and their chance would be gone for a whole year.

Cassie's grin flashed in the darkness. "Not many people get to have stories like ours, Brine. We're lucky. Very lucky indeed." She yawned loudly. "Now, get some sleep. We've got a long voyage ahead."

Brine felt herself smiling back. She liked the way Cassie said *we*, the unspoken assumption that Brine was part of the crew now. There weren't many people in the world who could kidnap you, try to sell you, then carry on as if nothing had happened—more than that, to sweep you along with them so you were almost glad everything had happened that way.

"One other thing," said Cassie as Brine turned to go back across the deck. "I need you to do something for me."

Brine nodded eagerly. This was it: her chance to be useful after all.

"Keep an eye on Peter," said Cassie. "We're going to need him, and I don't want anything happening to him."

It felt to Brine as if the deck had just dropped from underneath her. Of course, it was bound to be Peter who really mattered, not her. He was the one with all the talent. All she had was her stupid allergy to magic.

Cassie either didn't notice her change of expression or didn't care. She gave Brine a clap on the shoulder and pushed her in the direction of the hatch.

Brine waited awhile longer, then went back to bed. Peter was asleep, which was annoying because she'd have enjoyed ignoring him if he were awake. She squirmed into the hammock under his and lay there. She wasn't going to worry about it. Magic was boring, anyway, and Peter could look after himself. No way was she going to keep an eye on him.

The *Onion* sailed on, watched by a million, million uncaring stars.

►····┼┼┼●

Dawn flooded the sky in a turmoil of pink and blue. Far away, other sails skimmed the horizon while, closer, dolphins played around the ship, their slender bodies glistening like silver. The crew crowded together on deck to eat breakfast, talking quietly. Ewan Hughes never quite let go of his sword, Brine noticed, and several of the others kept staring at the deck as if they could see through the planks to their unwelcome guest in the brig below.

Trudi sucked the last piece of shrimp from a skewer. "What do you want to see when we get to Magical North?" she asked. "What does it mean, anyway, seeing the whole world? Is it like a map? Do we get to fly over the world and see everything, or what?"

She looked at Peter as if she expected him to know the answer.

"It's no use asking him," said Brine. "He's only an apprentice magician, really. He doesn't know a lot."

Peter's cheeks reddened angrily, but Trudi's thoughts had already moved on, and she didn't notice. Her face took on a dreamy, faraway look. "I wouldn't mind seeing my ex-husbands again. They've probably all married other people by now, but you never know."

"Ex-husbands?" asked Brine. "How many have you got?"

Trudi blushed. "Three or four. They only loved me for my cooking."

"When I get to Magical North," said Bill Lightning, "I'm going to look for my kids. The youngest one will be twelve by now."

Tim Burrc sighed. "I knew a girl once, back in the west. I always wondered what became of her."

Ewan laughed. "And while you all are standing around looking at the world, I'm going to be picking up gold. Even if I have to fill my boots to the brim and walk back barefoot." He turned as Cassie came out on deck. "What about you, Captain? What do you want to see when we stand on Magical North?"

Cassie smiled, but something in her eyes looked strained. "I haven't said we're going there yet."

"The *Onion*'s been sailing north since yesterday," said Ewan. "Northish, anyway. And I can't help noticing that a certain magician is still alive in the brig. If we're bound for Magical North, you might as well tell us."

Cassie looked down at the deck. Her expression changed: a sudden release of frown lines as if she'd just gotten rid of something that had been troubling her. She clapped her hands. "Gather round, everyone. We are going to make a plan."

Ewan blinked. "A plan? Since when do we have plans?"

"Since we needed them," said Cassie crisply. "Marfak West

will turn on us, but we beat him once before, and we can do it again. As long as we keep his starshell out of his hands, he can't use magic, and that makes him almost helpless. That's the first part of the plan." She paused, as if waiting for someone to disagree. No one did. "Right," she continued, "our trading in Morning didn't go quite as well as we'd hoped."

"You're telling me," muttered Ewan.

Cassie ignored him. "So," she continued, "we still need supplies. We'll stop off at a few islands and see what we can do. And then I want to know exactly what we're getting into, and there's only one place, short of the inside of Marfak West's head, where we might be able to find out."

The crew groaned. Zen let out a little mew.

"Barnard's Reach," said Ewan. "I knew it."

CHAPTER 11

They say there are three kinds of people in the world: those who listen to stories, those who tell them, and those who make them. Barnard's Reach is home to a fourth kind: those who keep them. The library island is little more than a jut of land at the southern mouth of the Gemini Seas. It is accessed only by appointment, and never at all if you are a man—the libraries are for women only. There, the Book Sisters collect and record everything that happens in the world. Nobody knows what drives them to spend their lives in the company of books, but when a story begins with "they say," you can bet your boots "they" came from Barnard's Reach.

(From ALDEBRAN BOSWELL'S BOOK OF THE WORLD)

For the next week, the *Onion* zigzagged her way north between islands. At each one it was the same: They stopped, Cassie did a lot of talking, and they sailed on, taking with them an extra barrel or crate of dried goods while the islanders scratched their heads and wondered why they'd just traded a whole load of valuable supplies for a bucket of slightly old chopped octopus.

Gradually, the days grew longer and colder. Peter was used

to Minutes, where the seasons followed the same pattern every year and you always knew what time of day it was by the position of the sun in the sky. Everything changed so much faster at sea that he wasn't even sure what the time was anymore, never mind the date. He knew he ought to be practicing magic, but everywhere he went on board, at least two members of the crew seemed to end up watching him, sometimes with grinning anticipation as if they expected him to do something spectacular any minute, but more often with stares as sharp as a cutlass point. Not so long ago, Peter had believed that getting a spell wrong in front of an audience was the worst thing that could possibly happen. Now he'd found something worse: getting it right and being stabbed by superstitious pirates.

The three pieces of starshell caused their own problems. They were too big to carry around all the time. Marfak West may have done it, but he must have had pockets lined with gold or something. Peter was afraid of breaking them if he kept them in his pocket, but he had nowhere safe to leave them. He'd tried taking them off their chain, and just carrying one piece, but that still meant he had to find somewhere for the other two. In the end, he kept all three wrapped in a bundle of rags hung up by his hammock, and he checked on them several times a day to make sure they weren't eating their way through the cloth. It wasn't ideal, but it was the best he could do.

Meanwhile, to his annoyance, Brine was looking more and more like a member of the crew. Coming back on deck one day after checking on the starshell, Peter saw her halfway up the rigging. She was wearing borrowed trousers, the legs rolled up to fit her, and her wiry hair was tucked inside a yellow cap.

"Hi," said Peter, looking up at her.

"Hi, yourself." She slid down off the rigging to join him. "Did you want something?"

"No, I . . ." He didn't know what to say; he just knew that he needed to talk to someone—someone who wouldn't look at him like he was some sort of exotic new species. He scuffed a foot back and forth. "Cassie's determined to take us north, then."

"I guess so." She flashed a grin at him. "It's exciting, isn't it? We're seeing the world at last. And we'll get to see the libraries at Barnard's Reach."

"*You'll* get to see the libraries," said Peter. "They don't allow men, remember, and I'm pretty sure boys count as men."

"Oh. Sorry, I keep forgetting."

She didn't sound sorry. She sounded pleased, as if she was glad she'd found something she could do that he couldn't. Peter turned away from her and looked up at Tim Burre, who was clinging to the top of the mainmast, mending the crow's nest. "What do you think about Marfak West?" he asked.

"I don't know. You're the magician—you tell me."

Peter didn't know whether she was serious or not. He decided to pretend that she was. "I think he's leading us into a trap. He's supposed to be the world's most powerful magician, and yet he wasted all his magic and let himself be captured. Why?"

"Maybe he wants to stand on Magical North and look for starshell," said Brine. "I don't know. Why don't you go and ask him?" She took her cap off and put it back on the wrong way round. "You worry too much. Cassie knows what she's doing. Just practice your magic and leave the rest to her."

Practice magic. That was easy for Brine to say. The only practice Peter had ever done was copying spellshapes over and over, hoping he'd get enough of them right that Tallis Magus wouldn't hit him.

"Maybe if you helped . . . ," he began tentatively, but then Ewan Hughes shouted to Brine across the deck.

"Got to go," she said. She ran to join Ewan, leaving Peter standing alone. A few minutes later, Brine and Ewan were practicing sword-fighting together. Peter put on a face that was supposed to say fighting was far too dull for magicians to bother with and scratched at the black spot on his palm where the starshell had burned him. The skin seemed to be healing over, but it looked like he was going to have a permanent mark there.

". . . And then you twist like this," said Ewan.

Peter got up and slid away unnoticed by either of them, which felt unfair. People ought to notice him: He was a magician.

He hadn't entirely decided where he was going—just somewhere he could get away from everyone. He climbed down the ladder to the mid-deck, but he could hear Trudi banging about in the galley, and she was bound to come out and ask him to help. For a moment he stood, then he opened the hatch to the lower deck and climbed down.

A faint rasping greeted his ears as he groped his way between the packing crates. It sounded like handfuls of shells being rubbed together. Then he saw the iron cage at the back of the hold, and he realized what the sound was. Marfak West was laughing.

The magician was so tall that, sitting upright, his head wasn't far from the top of the cage. His wrists were chained in front of him and his ankles were chained together, but he managed to look as if he'd chosen to sit like that and the cage and chains just happened to be around him.

Peter edged closer. Marfak West stopped laughing and sniffed loudly.

"Do you know you stink of fish?"

Peter scowled. "Mock all you like. I'm not the one in a cage."

"Are you sure about that? There are more cages than ones made of bars." Marfak West stretched, making his chains rattle. The black flecks in his eyes drifted in slow circles. Common sense told Peter to leave now. But if he left, it would look like he was afraid, and for some reason, he didn't want Marfak West to think he was a coward.

For at least a minute, they looked at each other. Eventually, Marfak West shifted position. "I presume you're not here to inquire after my health."

"Why are you doing this?" asked Peter. The words blurted out, as if of their own accord. "Why do you want to go to Magical North at all, and why like this? Aren't you embarrassed to be Cassie's prisoner?"

"Not really," the magician said. "This ship is taking me where I want to go, and while the rest of you are running about on deck getting hot and annoyed, I can wait here and sleep. I'd say this was a far better arrangement. Apart from the catering." He smiled. "As for what I want with Magical North, what do you think?"

Peter scratched his hand. "Some of the crew are saying you want to look for starshell."

"That's not a bad plan. Is that what you think?"

Peter paused a moment. "No. I don't think so. It might be a good plan for someone else, but it seems . . . it seems too small for you."

Marfak West dipped his head. "You know what they say about me—my soul is twisted. Magic has corrupted me, and I corrupt everything I touch."

The space around Peter seemed to grow darker, and colder. His feet carried him back a step. "They say a lot of things that aren't true."

"So they do," agreed the magician. "Stories are told by the victors, after all. The heroic crew of the *Onion* defeated the evil magician. That's how it usually goes." He sat back. "No one ever tells the story of how my pioneering work—work that would have benefited all humanity—was cut short by marauding pirates. And all because I had the misfortune to possess something that Cassie O'Pia can never have."

"What was that?" asked Peter, forgetting for a moment that he was supposed to be afraid.

"Infamy. It's like fame, but more so." Marfak West wrapped

his arms around his knees and gazed steadily ahead. "That's the thing with stories: They don't just need a hero, they need a villain. Cassie wanted to be a hero, and so she needed to find a villain to defeat. But the good thing about being a villain is that everybody thinks they know you. They put you in a little box marked 'Evil,' and they never expect you to do anything that isn't bad. And that, believe it or not, gives you a great deal of power—the power to surprise." The flecks in the magician's eyes drifted inward, making his pupils appear huge. "The answer to your question is yes, by the way. I'll teach you magic."

Peter's throat turned to sandpaper. The thought had been there in his head all along; he just hadn't dared give words to it. Words made it too real, too possible. He backed away so fast he bumped into a packing crate.

"Why?" he asked. "I'm on Cassie's crew. I'm one of the people who believe you're evil. Why would you teach me anything?"

Marfak West studied his fingernails. "Who knows? Maybe it's because I really am evil and I'm locked in a cage with nothing to do but cause whatever harm I can." He regarded Peter steadily. "Or maybe because knowledge—especially magical knowledge—should be passed on, and you're the only one I've met who has any inclination to learn." He eased his boot off and massaged his toeless foot. "You can't perform magic without starshell," he said. "Next time you come, bring a piece."

Shaking his head, Peter stumbled away through the maze of crates and climbed the ladder up the decks. Did Marfak West think he was that stupid? The moment Marfak West got his hands on starshell, he'd mind-control everyone and take over the *Onion*.

But, said a voice in his head, *if Marfak West wanted the* Onion, *he could have taken her back at Morning.* For now it clearly suited him to be a prisoner.

Marfak West was a murderer. The name of nightmares.

But he was a magician, and Peter needed to learn magic, before Cassie found out how little he could actually do.

He emerged onto the main deck and stood blinking in the sunlight. Cassie was at the helm, teaching Brine how to steer. If either of them had noticed Peter then, he might have joined them. He might have forgotten all about Marfak West. But neither of them did. He stood and watched. Cassie looked like an ordinary fisherwoman, with her hair tied back and her skin burned from the sun. Nothing heroic about her. Peter shook his head. He'd seen her fight. She'd rescued them from the sea. She'd saved their lives.

But she'd also lied to them, tricked them, and tried to sell them. What sort of a hero would do that? And now she was taking the whole ship on an impossible quest just because her worst enemy had challenged her to stop him if she could.

Another thought struck him: If the stories about Cassie O'Pia weren't true, maybe the stories about Marfak West weren't, either.

CHAPTER 12

Marfak West is dead. Finally defeated by Cassie O'Pia and the valiant crew of the *Onion*, his ship sunk beneath the icy green waters of the Gemini Seas. And yet, even amid the celebrations, some are saying the magician must have escaped, that evil of his magnitude never dies.

(From BARNARD'S REACH CHRONICLE OF THE EIGHT OCEANS)

Two more days went by. Brine was surprised to find how much she was enjoying life on board the *Onion*. Compared with keeping house for Tallis Magus, it was as easy as a crab sandwich. She wondered where that saying had come from. Trudi had tried to make crab sandwiches one day, and by the time she'd cut them all into little crab shapes, the bread had disintegrated. She'd given up, pushed the whole lot into a pot, and called it seafood trifle. Tim Burre had eaten his portion, but mainly because Trudi had been sitting next to him. The rest of them had scraped their plates overboard when Trudi wasn't looking.

Still, life on board *was* easy. Or rather, Brine thought,

pausing halfway through coiling a length of rope, she was probably working harder than ever, but it was different. Maybe because no one treated her like a servant anymore. She followed orders, but so did everyone else. The only thing she missed was Magus's library, and then only sometimes. The *Onion* was, after all, on its way to the biggest library in the whole world.

She tried not to think too much about Barnard's Reach, because every time she did, her hands shook with excitement and she dropped things. Or if the libraries came into her dreams at night, she woke up and couldn't get back to sleep again for impatience. Besides, she had plenty to learn right where she was. She'd already learned how to tie twenty-three kinds of knots, and she knew the signs that the weather was about to change. She was starting to recognize the constellations and understand how people could navigate by them. All the things she'd read about in books and dreamed of doing were now coming true.

The only downside was Peter. He hung about the ship, looking as miserable as wet seaweed, and just being around him was enough to make Brine feel depressed. She wasn't even sure how to talk to him. Back on Minutes, they'd spent most of their time fighting, but so much had changed since then that when she thought back, their arguments seemed petty and childish. She didn't really want to argue with him anymore, but she wasn't sure what to say instead.

She was glad this morning that he wasn't around. This morning the wind was behind them and the *Onion* raced on as if eager to get this journey over with. Brine didn't want anything to spoil it.

"You're becoming a sailor," Ewan Hughes told Brine as she sat on deck mending ropes. The approval in his voice brought a warm flush of color to her cheeks.

"How long before we reach Barnard's Reach?" she asked.

Ewan gazed into the wind. "Two or three days, depending on the weather." He didn't seem to share Brine's eagerness to get there, but of course he wouldn't be allowed on the island, being a man.

"Does it bother you that they don't let men in the library?" she asked him.

Ewan shrugged one massive shoulder. "Not really. Men shouldn't be around books. It encourages them to think too much, and when men start thinking too much, they become dangerous. Reading is women's work. Women and magicians."

Brine couldn't imagine anyone not wanting to read. "What about Aldebran Boswell? He was the greatest explorer who ever lived."

Ewan considered. "You're saying if I learn to read, I might sail off the top of the world and never be seen again?"

"No, I'm saying that you can . . . I don't know. Learn new things, use your imagination." She ground to a halt. "Never mind," she sighed.

Ewan grinned at her and stood up. "That's the spirit. Now, speaking of learning new things, how would you like to learn to break a man's arm in two easy stages?"

For the past two days, Peter had been trying to work up the nerve to venture back down to the lowest deck. Boredom did it in the end—two days of nothing but sea to look at, and if one more person had said wasn't it nice how Brine was fitting in, he'd have punched them.

Marfak West was lying on his side in his cage, snoring softly. Peter shifted from foot to foot. The fragile weight of the magician's starshell dragged at him. He took the piece out and looked at it, standing well back from the cage. He'd brought the smallest of the three pieces, and even that seemed a terrible risk.

Marfak West's eyes flickered open. Peter jerked his hands behind his back. "You're not having it."

"Well, of course I'm not. The moment starshell touches my hand, I shall seize control of the *Onion* and murder everyone aboard."

Peter swallowed the lump in his throat. Marfak West grinned at him. "You really can't take a joke, can you?" He sat up and stretched. "I'm glad you came back, by the way. I've met precious few people in my life with any talent for magic."

Peter sat down, trying to hide the fact that his legs were wobbling. Now that he was here, he found that he didn't know what to say.

"Magic," continued Marfak West, "is the hardest thing in the world to master. Very few people can even sense it, let alone use it." He rested his chin on his fingertips. "Tell me about yourself, Peter. When did you find out you had the talent? Are your parents magicians?"

No one had ever shown the slightest interest in who Peter was. He sat up a little straighter. "No, they both work on fishing boats. Tallis Magus—my old master—came to the village looking for an apprentice. He had a piece of starshell with him, and I was the only one who could feel magic in it. My parents handed me over to him without a word. It was like they couldn't wait to get rid of me."

"Ignorant people are always afraid of magic," said Marfak West. "It's not their fault they don't know any better. I found my first piece of starshell when I was about your age. I didn't have anyone to teach me, so I taught myself. I experimented, putting the magic into different shapes, finding out what worked and what didn't. I was lucky."

"I suppose so," said Peter doubtfully. Marfak West didn't seem to be the sort of person who'd rely on luck.

The magician's eyes glinted. "Do me a favor, will you? When you disagree with me, say so. Luck had nothing to do with it. Do you think I just happened to spot a piece of starshell? Or did I spend every free minute searching the beaches for the stuff? And then, when people found out what I could do and tried to stop me, did I meekly give up all my dreams of being a magician, or did I fight back?"

"I'm guessing you fought back," said Peter, torn between fascination with the story and fear that this conversation was sailing into whole oceans that he really didn't want to explore.

Marfak West nodded. "If you want to be a magician, you have to fight. That's the first rule. Everyone will want your power, but nobody will want you."

Peter's heart sank. It all seemed like a lot of effort for nothing. "Why bother, then?"

"Because of the second rule." A smile crawled across the magician's face. "Magic makes you better than them. Never forget that."

Peter felt himself smile back. He held the starshell piece in his cupped hands and watched the magic swirl across the surface. Better than Cassie? Better than Brine? That wasn't true. Marfak West was only saying what he thought Peter wanted to hear. Peter didn't know why, but if the magician was willing to teach him magic, why not go along with it? Just as long as he remembered that he was dealing with a liar.

"So," he said, looking up, "are we just going to sit here and talk, or are you going to teach me some magic?"

>-++||||●

Brine was already wishing she hadn't offered to teach Tim Burre to write.

"No, hold the pen like this," she said, correcting his grip for the twentieth time. "Let the tip rest between your fingers, and move it slowly."

Tim copied out the first two letters of his name and paused. "I'm not sure I like all this drawing shapes. It's a bit too much like magic."

"It's nothing like magic," Brine sighed. "You're making letters, not spellshapes. Just think what you'll be able to do when you can read, all the things you can learn. You know what they say—knowledge is power."

Tim's brow wrinkled. "That definitely sounds like magic. You're not a secret magician as well, are you?"

"Me? No. I'm allergic to magic." Anyway, the whole practice of magic was starting to feel a bit boring to her. All the rules you had to learn, and the endless memorizing of spellshapes. It was annoying that Peter got all the attention for it, but did she really want that sort of attention, anyway? She'd much rather spend time on the main deck, watching the world as she sped through it, than holed up in a corner studying spellshapes.

Tim handed the pen back to her. "I better get back to work. You, too—I think Trudi wanted help in the galley."

Brine left him to it. She saw Cassie watching her as she crossed the deck and waved. She shouldn't blame the pirates for not wanting to learn. They didn't need to read and write—they needed to know how to tie knots and steer a ship by the stars and a hundred other things that letters on pages weren't necessarily going to help with. It was just that when she finally felt she was starting to fit in somewhere, her ability to read and write made her different, and she didn't want to be different anymore.

She wondered where Peter was. He'd understand.

Trudi put her head out of the galley as Brine came past.

"Have you seen Peter?" asked Brine.

"No. Do you want to help make butter?" She held up a jar

of off-white liquid, which Brine presumed had once been milk. "You have to keep shaking it until it goes solid."

Brine took the jar and gave it a shake. "Trudi, can you read?"

Trudi beamed at her. "Of course I can. I can write, too. I keep a recipe book."

She dumped a sheaf of papers on the table. Brine read the top couple. "They're . . . interesting. Can you really make jelly out of strawberry jam and eels?"

"You can, but no one will eat it." Trudi looked at her closely. "Are you all right? You don't have to help if you don't want to."

"No, it's fine. I wasn't doing anything else." Brine kept shaking the jar and saw a few flecks of yellow appear. She grinned. "Look at that—it's working!"

Another day passed. Peter sat in front of Marfak West's cage, trying to persuade a piece of starshell to rise out of his hand. The shell was almost empty. Peter could feel the last scraps of magic fluttering, but they didn't want to come out.

"You're trying too hard," said Marfak West. "You need to coax the power out, not force it. If you push too hard, you'll lose control of it altogether. Like that," he added, as the shell shot off Peter's hand and landed inside the cage right at the magician's feet.

Peter gasped, and his heart almost stopped. Marfak West reached down, retrieved the shell, and handed it back through the bars with a mocking bow. "I told you," he said, "if I'd wanted to take the *Onion,* I'd have done it already."

Peter polished the shell on his shirt, trying to cover up the fact that his hands were shaking. His heart, making up for its moment of inactivity, pounded at twice the normal rate. The scar in the center of his right palm burned.

"The bigger the starshell, the faster it draws in magic and the more it holds," said Marfak West, returning to the lesson as if nothing had happened. "Break that piece in half, and each half would hold less than half its original amount. Don't break it in half, by the way. That would be a really stupid thing to do."

Peter put the shell down carefully. "I know all this. When are you going to teach me some new spellshapes?"

Marfak West shook his head. "Spellshapes don't matter. They're just the rules. Once you truly understand magic, how it moves, how it feels in your hands, you can make it do anything. You'll be able to create your own rules. Try again. Don't think of a shape, just think of the starshell lifting up out of your hand."

Peter still felt shaky. He balanced the starshell on one hand and held his other hand over it.

"There's nothing special about magic," said Marfak West. "Magic is just another form of energy. The ability to use it is what's special, and that comes from you, not the starshell."

The starshell quivered, then rose up off Peter's hand. He caught it gently in his other hand and felt the last of its magic quietly disperse.

Marfak West applauded. "Well done."

Peter's cheeks flamed. He knew that Marfak West was a liar, that—as usual—he was only saying the words Peter wanted to hear. Yet, somehow those two words of praise meant more than all the years with Tallis Magus.

Later, Peter climbed the ladder to the main deck slowly, lost in a confusion of thoughts, most of which came down to a single word—*why?* Why was Marfak West doing this? Why was he on board, why Magical North?

He had the bad luck to bump into Brine as he came out on deck. She sneezed, paused, and gave him a sharp look. "Have you been playing with magic?"

"Of course I have," he said. "You told me I should practice, didn't you?" He set his face into a scowl and shoved his hands into his pockets. The starshell piece was empty, but he imagined he could feel a spot of magic buzzing against his palm, like a trapped fly. He'd had enough of this—enough of her playing at pirates with the crew, enough of her telling him what to do.

"How can you be sure Cassie won't try to sell us again?" he asked. "We don't know anything about her apart from what she's told us. How do we know it's not all lies?"

Brine opened her mouth and snapped it shut again. "Get lost, Peter," she said. She brushed past him and walked away to join Cassie and Ewan.

Peter felt a stab of jealousy as he watched the three of them laugh together. How come Brine was suddenly so good at making friends with people? Especially these people. He brushed his hair back. *Ignore her*, he thought. *You're better than her.* He waited a moment for his heartbeat to return to normal, then strolled out on deck as if nothing had happened.

CHAPTER 13

Information is truth, and truth demands respect. It is not our job to judge the stories of the world, to decide which ones are worthy of saving and which should be lost. The many rules of Barnard's Reach ensure that all information is handled with equal care. The first task of a new Book Sister is to follow the rules until they become part of her. Until she can't do anything except follow.

(From THE RULES AND REGULATIONS OF BARNARD'S REACH,
VOLUME I: INTRODUCTION)

"Land ahoy!" shouted Tim Burre.

Brine jumped up eagerly. She couldn't see land. The sea ahead was shrouded in mist. If she stared hard, she could just make out the shapes of other ships. She watched them, wondering why they looked so familiar, until she realized she was seeing reflections of the *Onion*.

"Mirrormist," said Cassie, joining her. "They say it's caused by magic condensing when it hits cold patches of sea fog. The Book Sisters have turned it into a defense. If anything hostile tries to come through, the mist will thicken and make it impossible to pass. Fortunately, we're not hostile."

Brine heard the snap of rope and turned to see Ewan Hughes untying a rowing boat. "You're not going to try selling me again, are you?" she asked suspiciously.

"Of course not," said Cassie. "The Book Sisters wouldn't allow it, anyway. They have rules against that sort of thing."

"They have rules against everything," muttered Ewan.

Cassie ignored him. "Three people should be enough. Trudi, you can read a bit. Let's do me, you, and Brine."

Brine looked around for Peter, but he was nowhere to be seen. Hiding belowdecks, probably, because he wasn't allowed on the island, she thought. Back on Minutes, she'd always been the one who was left out of everything. She remembered how that felt.

"Brine, are you coming?" asked Cassie.

She'd have to talk to Peter when she got back. She climbed down into the boat.

►⊢╫╫╉✦

It had been so long since Brine had set foot on land that when she stepped out of the rowing boat onto the beach, she felt as if the ground were swaying underneath her. Cassie and Trudi didn't seem to notice—they were more used to it, Brine supposed. She looked around. She couldn't see any libraries—only gray cliffs with birds nesting on every ledge.

"Where—" she started to ask.

Trudi hushed her. "Keep your voice down. They say the whole island is made of glass, and any sudden noise will shatter it."

"Who says?"

Trudi looked up at the cliffs and the circling birds. "I don't know. Just *they.*"

Cassie started toward a path that zigzagged up along the cliff face and began climbing, far too fast. Brine felt oddly deflated as she followed. She'd spent the past week imagining soaring towers made entirely out of books, but so far there was nothing to see but rocks and birds.

Admittedly, there were a lot of birds. They were everywhere, from black seamartins with flashes of yellow on their wings to the giant atlas gulls, whose feathers looked like a map of the world. The constant beat of wings was only drowned out by the even more constant sound of shrieking and cawing. Trudi was eyeing the nearest ones, and Brine knew she was imagining them boiled in pastry.

More birds scattered as they reached the top of the path. Cassie paused and rested her hands on her knees, breathing hard. A wooden sign stood to perfect attention before them.

Welcome to Barnard's Reach, Home of Knowledge.
Please Follow the Rules.

Just behind it, a much larger sign read:

These Are the Rules

1. No admittance without appointment.
2. No men admitted ever.
3. No shouting.
4. No talking.
5. No whispering unless strictly necessary.
6. Do not run.
7. Do not walk on the grass.
8. Do not disturb the birds.

There were more rules, but Brine couldn't read them. The writing became smaller and smaller farther down the sign, as if the writer had realized she was running out of space.

Cassie straightened up. "We're here." She sounded like she'd just run a hundred miles. She gave the sign a kick. "Ahoy, there!"

Brine winced, but the island failed to shatter like glass. It seemed that story, at least, wasn't true. "There's no one here," she said uneasily.

"Don't worry," said Cassie. "They're just hiding." She looked around, then strode off in what appeared to be a completely random direction. But a few seconds later, she stopped and kicked something that made a metallic clang—a door in the hill.

It looked as if someone had dropped it there by mistake—a polished iron door, set in the side of the hill. A single streak of bird dropping marked one corner, and judging by how spotlessly clean the rest of the door was, Brine guessed that someone would be out soon to clean it off. There was no door handle, but an eye slot about three-quarters of the way up squeaked open.

A pair of brown eyes appeared on the other side of the slot, blinking rapidly behind thick spectacles.

"D-do you have an appointment?"

"We're pirates," said Cassie. "We don't do appointments."

The eyes blinked some more. "You can't visit the libraries without an appointment. It's the rules." The slot began to shut. Cassie stopped it with the tip of her cutlass.

"We don't do rules, either."

Brine calculated that it would be about two seconds before Cassie ran out of persuasive arguments and tried something more direct and cutlass-based. She squeezed in between the pirates and the door. "Hello," she said. "My name is Brine Seaborne, and these are my friends, Cassie O'Pia and Trudi Storme. We'd like to make an appointment to visit the library in ten minutes' time. May we do that?"

The eyes widened at the mention of Cassie's name, then bobbed up and down in a nod. Brine thought she heard a squeak of relief. The slot in the door snapped shut.

Brine counted to ten, then knocked. The slot opened again.

"Hello," said Brine. "My name is Brine Seaborne. My friends and I have an appointment. We may be a few minutes early."

Bolts slid back inside the door.

"How did you do that?" asked Trudi.

Brine cast her a smile. "When you've been a servant as long as I have, you learn to get around the rules."

The door opened. Brine thought she was looking at a heap of clothes, but then she realized there was a person inside them. A girl, a year or two younger than she was. A small thin face was just about visible behind masses of heavy, dark brown hair and a pair of glasses the size of clamshells.

"Please come in," said the girl. Her glasses wobbled perilously. She spoke in a voice that was a fraction above a whisper, and she gave the impression that she thought even that was too loud.

They clattered inside, and the door whispered shut behind them. A single lantern on the wall was losing a valiant battle against the dark. All Brine could see was a spiral staircase leading down into a vast, deep hole.

"Where's the library?" she asked.

Their guide started down the stairs.

>+++++++

In the past two weeks of wondering what the library looked like, Brine's imagination had never even come close to this. An underground stairwell descended through spirals of books and, every thirty steps or so, a room opened out, most of them so narrow there was barely space between the bookshelves they all contained. Every so often, Brine caught sight of figures in brown robes, their feet making no sound as they walked. One of them pushed a small trolley full of books and was carefully putting them all away. Brine paused to watch but the nervous librarian guide hurried her on.

"How far do these stairs go?" asked Brine.

"Shhh."

They continued down past several more rooms, then their guide stopped. A sign on the wall said READING ROOMS. PLEASE BE SILENT. A robe hung on the wall next to a door. "What brings Cassie O'Pia to the towers of knowledge?" it whispered.

Brine jumped. The robe stepped away from the wall, and a pair of thin hands reached up to push the hood back, revealing an equally thin face, pale and starved of sunlight.

"I am Ursula," whispered the librarian. "Assistant Keeper of Books: Geographical Exploration and Poetry, Seventh Grade. There is nothing here for you. Please leave."

Cassie shook her head. "We're not here as pirates. We're looking for information. What do you know about Magical North?"

Ursula stared at her while the seconds slid silently by. The librarian knew something, Brine thought. She recognized the look on Ursula's face—half-guilty, half-wary, as if she'd just been caught doing something wrong.

"Also," added Cassie, "my young friend here would like to see the books."

Ursula switched her stare to Brine. Brine tried to appear casual, as if she visited libraries all the time.

"Very well." Ursula frowned. She gestured to the girl who'd brought them down. "Tom Girl, take the young lady on the visitors' tour."

Tom Girl's glasses bounced as she nodded.

"I'd rather stay," said Brine. Much as she wanted to see the library, she knew that the moment she was gone, Cassie was going to start talking about Magical North, and she didn't want to miss anything. Cassie waved her away. Sighing, Brine followed Tom Girl back up the stairs.

CHAPTER 14

A magician must always take care to apply the correct spellshape. Magic is naturally dangerous, and containing it within spellshapes makes it safer to use. Never completely safe, but safer. It is extremely dangerous to deviate from the accepted shapes.

(From ALDEBRAN BOSWELL'S BIG BOOK OF MAGIC)

Ewan Hughes had sent Peter to clean the galley while Trudi wasn't around. Instead, Peter had crept back down to the bottom of the ship. He was beginning to wish he hadn't bothered. Marfak West seemed irritable today, or maybe it was Peter himself. He'd practiced with the starshell until he could draw magic out of the pieces, lift things up, put them back down, and keep a small magical light burning for ages. He should have been pleased, but somehow it had all started to feel a bit boring.

"I thought you were the most powerful magician on the planet," said Peter, lifting a pair of large, wooden crates into the air with a quick gesture. "How about teaching me some proper magic?"

Marfak West's eyes glittered. "You *are* learning proper magic. How many people do you know who can levitate packing crates?"

Peter set the crates back down.

"Real magic—magic that does not depend on spellshapes—takes practice, and practice takes time," said Marfak West. "Don't think you can start rushing things, because you'll fail. And, believe me, when you're handling the raw power of magic, you do not want to fail."

Peter hadn't come to be lectured at. He'd only come because it was better than scrubbing the galley. If he were Marfak West, he wouldn't be sitting in a cage wrapped in chains. He'd break out, take over the *Onion* and do . . . well, do something other than just sit there.

"Then what's the point of spellshapes?" he asked. "Why did Tallis Magus make me spend years learning them if you don't need them?"

"Because Tallis Magus is like most magicians—timid, rule-bound, and not actually very good at magic. Spellshapes are a shortcut, allowing someone like him to cast more powerful spells simply by learning the right shape. They're useful occasionally—you interrupted one back on Morning, you'll remember—but for people like us, they can become a cage. Rely on spellshapes, and you'll never go beyond what you can memorize and copy."

Peter hadn't missed the way Marfak West said "people like us," as if he and Peter were on one side and the whole world on the other. He wasn't sure he liked the idea, though the notion of using magic without spellshapes was interesting. "The stories say you can turn people into fish," he said. "What's the point of turning people into fish if you can't even get out of a cage?"

"The stories, as you know, are a load of rubbish," said Marfak West. "I did not turn people into fish. I conducted a one-off experiment in enhancing ordinary people with the more useful abilities of sea creatures. The ability to breathe underwater, for example. All of my subjects were volunteers. I didn't force anyone against their will, and, in any case, the experiment failed."

This was more interesting than levitating starshell or crates. Peter sat forward. "What happened?"

"Cassie O'Pia happened, what do you think?" Marfak West flapped a hand irritably. "The big hero who destroyed my life's work. My volunteers all fled into the sea when she sank the *Antares*, and I was left with nothing. If anyone had bothered to ask what I was doing instead of charging in and sinking my ship, human evolution could be a thousand years on by now."

"Evolution?"

"Adaptation. Progress. Where do you think people are going to live when we run out of land? It will happen, you know. Think of those tiny islands where fishermen live on the edge of starvation. Think of Morning—all the rich people building towers because there simply isn't enough land for them all."

Peter had thought that Baron Kaitos just liked high towers.

"One day," said Marfak West, "mankind will have to take to the seas to survive, and if we leave the process to luck, most of us will starve before we grow our own gills. I was trying to speed things up, to give us a fighting chance when the time comes. But no, I am the evil magician, and I must be stopped."

"If you don't want people to treat you like an evil magician, you could maybe, you know, not act like one," suggested Peter.

Marfak West glowered and didn't answer. Peter grinned recklessly. "Do you know why people sing songs about Cassie O'Pia and you never get a mention? It's because she talks to people. Everyone knows what she's doing all the time." He sang, "Marfak West, Marfak West, don't know what he wanted, but he tried his best."

Marfak West's eyes flashed. Peter stopped singing, cold fingers of fear crawling up his back. He'd gone too far. All the same, something inside him felt ready to snap. "It's not my fault," he said. "What am I supposed to think if I only ever hear Cassie's side of the story? Why do you want to go to Magical North? If it even exists, which I doubt."

"Magical North exists," retorted the magician. "So does the treasure. You're welcome to them both—I have other plans. You're thinking of Magical North as the end of the journey. It's not—it's only the beginning."

"What's that supposed to mean?" asked Peter.

"You'll find out." Marfak West turned his face away. "I thought you were here to learn. What do you want to try next?"

Brine walked between shelves that were bowed with books, her chest ready to explode with excitement.

"The library is built out of a natural cave system," said Tom Girl. "The cellars at the bottom are at sea level, and they're always cold. Our oldest books are stored there so they can be kept at the right temperature. Then, going up to ground level, we have libraries for separate subjects. This section is all geography."

Brine reached up to take a book off a shelf and stopped as Tom Girl squeaked in protest. Several older Sisters turned and frowned at the noise. It struck Brine then that Tom Girl was the only young person she'd seen in the library. She turned to ask her about it, but Tom Girl was also looking at her curiously.

"What island are you from?" asked Tom Girl softly. "You're not from the Columba Ocean."

Brine found herself dropping her own voice to match. "Technically, I'm from Minutes in the Atlas Ocean. But really I don't know. I was found at sea."

"Oh. That's interesting."

Brine didn't feel like talking about it. "Not really. Why do they call you Tom Girl?"

Tom Girl shrugged and rearranged her hair over her face. "It's what they call a girl who keeps acting like a boy."

"I don't get it," Brine said.

Tom Girl sighed. "Clumsy, loud, and stupid. It's supposed to be a joke, my mother says." She didn't sound like she thought it was very funny.

"Your mother?"

"Ursula. Assistant Keeper of Books: Geographical Exploration and Poetry, Seventh Grade. That's why they let me stay here, because of her." She sighed again. "Come on." She led the way up to the next floor and into a room full of small wooden cages. Most of them held bored-looking seagulls.

"Here's where we keep the messenger gulls," said Tom Girl. She opened a box full to the brim with narrow cylindrical containers. "We received news last week that Cassie O'Pia destroyed Baron Kaitos's tower on Morning."

"She did, sort of. There was a bit of a fight and . . ." Brine wasn't sure how much she should say. "Wouldn't it be easier if some of you went out to gather the news yourselves?"

Tom Girl gasped and let go of the box lid. It fell back with a crash. A Book Sister rushed through the door.

"Sorry," said Brine, "my hand slipped. I should go and find Cassie. She'll probably have gotten herself into trouble by now."

Tom Girl slipped between her and the door. "Do you want to see the science library?"

>→++|||●

The science library was almost back at the top of the stairs. Brine was wheezing by the time they arrived. She gazed around the room while she waited for the tightness in her lungs to ease. An old woman sat at a table in the center, watching sand trickle through a giant hourglass.

"That's how we keep time," whispered Tom Girl. She led Brine out of earshot of the Sister, who was already frowning at them. "It takes exactly sixty minutes for the sand to go through the glass, and then you turn it over. You're not allowed to read or do anything else, because you might miss the moment. It's usually my job, that and waiting by the door in case we have visitors. They won't let me work with the books anymore—not since I dropped one."

Brine couldn't imagine anything more boring than turning a glass over once an hour, especially doing it surrounded by books she wasn't allowed to read. Not even working for bladder-faced Penn Turbill would be that bad. She stood for a while and watched the Book Sister look at the glass. Something was trying to click into place in her mind, and she couldn't quite get it. "How long have you lived here?" she asked.

Tom Girl shrugged. "All my life. Just over ten years. My mother came here when she was expecting me."

"When she was expecting you? But how did she know you'd be a . . ."

The Book Sister turned the hourglass. Brine's thoughts turned upside down with it.

And there it was. *Click.*

CHAPTER 15

There is no such thing as secret knowledge. This is why people will spend years clutching a secret to their breast only to throw away every last word of it when a passing stranger asks a question. This is how it should be. What is the point of knowledge if nobody knows it?

(From ALDEBRAN BOSWELL'S BOOK OF SCIENTIFIC KNOWLEDGE)

Ursula sat upright on a wooden chair at a table full of books, holding another book in her hands. The walls were lined floor to ceiling with shelves, but Ursula's was the only chair in the room, so Cassie and Trudi sat on the floor.

"They say," murmured Ursula, "that Aldebran Boswell visited Barnard's Reach before setting off for Magical North."

Cassie wished the librarian would speak up a bit. She had to lean forward to hear.

Ursula opened the book with a little creak of pages. "Boswell was the only man ever to have been allowed on the island, and even then, he wasn't allowed in the library. He had to stand outside. But in the months that followed his visit, he sent his journal by seagull, page by page, to the Head Keeper of Diaries. All the pages were carefully collected together and preserved, though few have been able to read them."

"Is it in code?" asked Trudi.

"No. Just very bad handwriting." Ursula turned a page. "What would you like to hear about first? The storms of the dead? The freezing winds and monsters of ice? Or the invisible man-eating bears, or the birds whose song can charm you into the sea to your death?" She shut the book. "Go home, Cassie O'Pia. Tell the world you found Magical North if you must. They'll believe you."

Cassie met her gaze. "I won't believe me."

"You are a fool," said Ursula. "Boswell died trying to find Magical North. What makes you think you can succeed? You'll die, too—you and all your crew."

Trudi looked uneasy. "No one's going to die," said Cassie. She held out her hand. "We'll take the book."

Ursula wrapped her arms around it. "No book leaves the library. It's the rules."

Cassie put a hand to her cutlass.

And then the door crashed open and Brine charged through, dragging Tom Girl behind her.

►⊶┼┼┼╉⊱

A disguise spell?" Marfak West repeated. His forehead wrinkled as if he was lifting his nonexistent eyebrows, but he shrugged and nodded. "Why not?" He stood up in his cage. He was too tall to stand straight, so he bent over at the shoulders. "The spell is similar to mind control—you're making people see something that's not there. The tricky part is keeping the spell going. You can fool one person for a short time quite easily, but fooling a lot of people most of the time takes real dedication. The starting point of the spell, however, is to fool yourself. Imagine who you want to be. Picture yourself as that person. Hold that picture in your mind. Then let the magic come out of the starshell, and as it does, let your picture slide over you, like you're putting on a cloak. Do you understand?"

Peter frowned. "Yes."

"Liar. You haven't got a clue what I'm talking about." Marfak West sighed. "Don't worry about getting it right. Don't look at your hands, just feel the magic merging with the picture in your mind. Magic wants to be used, remember. All you have to do is nudge it in the right direction, and it'll do the rest by itself."

Peter wished Marfak West would just show him the spellshape. He cupped the starshell piece in both hands and tried to concentrate. "What will happen if I get it wrong?" he asked nervously.

"Nothing," said Marfak West. "Nothing at all. The magic will scatter harmlessly. You'll waste it, but who cares?"

Tallis Magus had always made dire threats about what

would happen if Peter got a spellshape even slightly wrong. Peter felt himself relax. Instead of worrying about what he was doing, he watched the magic uncoil from the starshell and spread up his arms as if he were wearing it. He completely forgot he hadn't actually thought of a disguise.

"Not bad," said Marfak West as the magic dispersed into the air. "Now do it again and picture the disguise. Don't think too hard about it, just do it."

Peter's hand grew warm. This time, he felt the spell slide over him and stay there. He looked up, grinning. "Like that?"

Marfak West studied him. "That's an interesting choice of disguise."

Anything else he might have said was drowned out by Ewan Hughes's voice. "Peter! Are you down here? The answer had better be no."

The pirate came stamping between the packing crates. Peter quickly dropped the disguise and turned to face him. "It's all right," he said. "I'm just guarding the prisoner."

"The prisoner's in a metal cage. He doesn't need guarding." Ewan Hughes pushed Peter behind him. "If I catch you anywhere near the boy again," he threatened, "I'll break both your arms. And then your neck."

"I could hardly prevent the boy from visiting," said Marfak West. "As you have pointed out, I'm in a cage."

Peter snorted and turned it into a cough. Ewan Hughes rounded on him. "And if I catch you here again, I'll break your legs. Let's see how well you climb down here if you can't walk.

Come on now, move." He put a hand on Peter's shoulder and marched him away.

Ewan kept the pressure on his shoulder until they reached the ladder to the mid-deck. Peter shoved him away. He was shaking—not with fear, but with rage. Who did Ewan think he was, bursting in on his practice time and threatening him? Even though the starshell was back in his pocket, Peter felt magic coiling into his hand, ready to lash out.

Ewan stepped back. "Peter," he said, dropping his voice, "I know you're a magician and cleverer than the rest of us. Cassie said we had to leave you alone to practice, and I trust her. But that man"—he jerked his head back—"is rottener than a moldy stink-fish. He'll tell you what you want to hear and betray you later just for the fun of it. It's best not to give him the chance. You understand?"

Peter hung his head. The starshell dragged down on his pocket like a rock. The weight of a whole world that he wasn't allowed to explore. "Cassie told you to leave me alone?"

Ewan nodded. "She didn't want us loading you with extra work. Though if I'd known what you were doing, I'd have had you scrubbing the deck until you were too tired to think. What were you talking to him about, anyway?"

Progress. Evolution. The fact that Marfak West might have been trying to do something good after all. "Nothing," said Peter. Nothing that Ewan would understand. "Don't worry," he said. "I'll stay away from him."

"Good man."

But as Peter climbed the ladder, Marfak West's voice echoed between his ears. *Interesting choice of disguise.*

It wasn't interesting at all. Peter knew he'd only picked it because he had no imagination, because he could only picture something if he knew what it looked like, and Marfak West had been sitting right in front of him. It was natural to go for the only thing he could see. He didn't want to be Marfak West. He didn't even want to be like him. Not one bit.

This island is one big lie," said Brine. "All your rules, all your talk of truth, and you're all liars." She barely registered the book in Ursula's hands or the fact that Cassie had her sword halfway out. "It was right in front of me, and I almost didn't see it. Tom Girl is what you call a girl who acts like a boy. You were expecting a baby when you came to Barnard's Reach, weren't you? Only they don't allow men on the island. Or boys—not even baby boys."

"Brine," Cassie began, "this really isn't the right time—"

Brine shook her head. "Just look at Tom Girl. Look at her. . . . Look at *him.*"

The room fell silent so fast it was like someone had turned a switch. Everyone stared. Tom Girl turned scarlet.

Ursula sat back down. She looked like she was about to crumble away. "I had no choice," she whispered tremblingly. "I needed somewhere to go. I came here, and the Sisters took me in. I was sure my baby was going to be a girl. When Tom Girl—"

She faltered. "When Tom was born, I loved him from the moment he opened his eyes. I couldn't abandon him, and yet I couldn't keep him." She paused and drew in a shuddering breath. "I did the only thing I could. I pretended that Tom was a girl. I raised my son as a daughter."

CHAPTER 16

Barnard's Reach began as a single collection of books put together by a merchants' guild. The written word, however, has a power of its own, and soon the guild established the first library collection with the purpose of collecting and storing knowledge from all over the world. Without knowledge, we cannot take our next step in this world.

(From THE RULES AND REGULATIONS OF BARNARD'S REACH, VOLUME 3: HISTORY)

For what seemed like an age, nobody spoke. Tom Girl retreated into her—no, into his—robe until Brine could see only the tip of his nose poking out. "You must have known," said Brine. "You couldn't not know a thing like that. There are differences." She felt herself blushing. "Obvious differences."

Tom bobbed his head. "Of course I knew." He shot an apologetic glance at Ursula. "Sorry, Mum, but we live on an island full of books. With pictures. It wasn't that hard to work out."

Ursula turned pale. "You never said."

"Of course I didn't. I know the rules. And everyone else kept pretending, so it was easier to go along with it. I knew it would get sorted out one day."

Ursula walked to Tom and wrapped her arms around his shoulders. "The stories are true about you, Cassie O'Pia: You always bring trouble. Take your friends and leave."

"Will you give us Boswell's book if we go?" asked Cassie.

"No," said Ursula, Tom, and Brine all at the same time.

"You can't take books out of the library," said Ursula. "It's the rules."

"Never mind the book!" shouted Brine. "We're not leaving without Tom." Belatedly, she registered what Cassie had said. "That's *Boswell's* book on the table?"

"The book won't do you any good," said Ursula. "Only I can read it."

Tom bit his lip. "I can read it."

And there was the answer, shining in front of them. Some people would have loved to live in a library, but Tom was quite obviously not one of them. Clumsy, loud, and stupid, he'd said—but it wasn't because he was a boy. It was because you had to walk silently here, careful not to disturb a single book. Maybe he'd find he didn't belong on the *Onion*, either, but at least he'd have the chance to find out. A chance was better than nothing.

Ursula tightened her grip on Tom until she was in danger of choking him. Tom said nothing, but his eyes behind his spectacles were wide with longing.

Cassie cleared her throat. "Brine, the *Onion* is a pirate ship, not a playground. I wasn't planning on filling it with children."

"You said you never plan," said Brine. "You wait to see what happens. Well, this has happened. What are we going to do about it?" Her heart beat hard. "Tom can read Boswell's book for us. And he can write up the voyage—the whole story of how we sailed to Magical North and back. Someone once told me not many people get to have stories like ours. What's the point of having a good story if no one gets to hear it?"

Cassie frowned, her gaze becoming thoughtful. Then she smiled her bright, familiar smile, and Brine relaxed.

Cassie sat down on the edge of the table. "Speaking of stories, Brine, did you know that many centuries ago, men and women lived on Barnard's Reach together? They were famous as explorers and adventurers. Then it all stopped."

Ursula tightened her lips, her arms still tight around Tom. "A Book Sister's duty lies in the library, not in the world."

"The reason was seasickness," said Cassie. "Their Head Collector of Manuscripts had it so bad she threw up if she even saw a boat. Rather than just admit it and stay behind while other people went exploring, she decided everybody should stay on the island and extend the libraries. And because some of the men refused to destroy their ships, she sent them all away. All the book collectors became book keepers. The Head Collector destroyed all the records so nobody else would know, but I know. Because four hundred years ago, the *Onion* belonged to Barnard's Reach. It was one of the ships that wasn't destroyed. The story has been handed down with her. That's the secret of these libraries—one woman with more stubbornness than sense."

Tom wriggled. "Mum, please."

"This is your home," said Ursula. "You don't even know these people."

Tom flicked a glance at Brine. "You don't have to know someone long to know what they're like. Brine saw who I was right away."

Ursula released him and pulled a cord by one of the shelves. "If you leave Barnard's Reach, you won't ever be allowed back, you know. Do you really want that? You need to forget all this nonsense. Captain O'Pia, you will be escorted out now. Please leave quietly."

Brine heard footsteps outside. Quiet footsteps, but lots of them. Then the door opened and Book Sisters crowded in. Some of them held swords. They gripped them stiffly, as if they'd learned how to fight by reading about it.

Ten librarians against two pirates. Brine hoped Cassie and Trudi wouldn't hurt them too badly. But then the ranks of Book Sisters parted and another woman walked into the room. She was dressed in a library robe like the others, but while everyone else walked almost silently, her shoes had heels that clicked on the floor. Brine fought the urge to stand up straight and push her hair back neatly.

Ursula took a step back. "Mother Keeper, I was just—"

"Be silent," snapped the Mother Keeper. She folded the hood of her robe back with thin hands. She had a sharp and pale face, framed with yellow hair, and her lips, painted pink for some reason, were set in an angry line. "These people don't have a proper appointment. They should never have been allowed in. Take your daughter and go to your room. I'll deal with them."

Ursula bit her lip. Brine could see the struggle in her face. If she obeyed the Mother Keeper, she'd have to keep the lie going forever. But if she told the truth now, she'd lose Tom, maybe forever.

"Come on, Tom Girl," whispered Ursula.

"Stop!" shouted Brine. Her voice surprised everyone, including herself. The Mother Keeper's sharp frown told her she ought to keep out of this, and she almost agreed.

Almost, but not quite. She snatched Boswell's book from the table where it lay and held it up by the corners. "We're leaving," she said, "and Tom's coming with us. Stand aside, or the book gets it."

Books: the one thing the librarians cared about more than the rules. Cassie gave a grunt that sounded suspiciously like laughter. Brine took a step toward the door, and the Sisters edged back from her.

The Mother Keeper stopped her. "Yes, destroy the book," she whispered. Her voice was as thin as a paper cut. "Aldebran Boswell's last journal. The record of his voyage to Magical North, and there is only one copy in the whole world. Rip it up, then. Tear out the pages. Destroy that piece of knowledge forever."

Brine looked down at the book. Boswell's name was on the front cover. Inside, thin scrawling handwriting, almost unreadable, and drawings of maps covered the pages.

Her hands trembled. Boswell's own book, in his own writing. Cassie gave her an encouraging smile; Trudi just looked confused. Tom met her gaze, and she saw the hope die in him. He nodded slightly to show he understood. He wouldn't have been able to damage a book, either, especially not that one.

Brine shut her eyes and tore out the first page. The thin paper came away with a little stab of sound that echoed the sudden pain at the back of her throat.

The Mother Keeper screeched. Brine held up the severed page. "There are plenty more where this came from. Shall I go on?"

"Get back," the Mother Keeper whispered to the Sisters. Slowly, they sheathed their swords and shuffled away from the door. Brine gripped Boswell's book on either side of the spine.

"We're leaving," she said. "If you try to stop us, this book is confetti. Tom, if you want to come, you have to come now."

She walked through the door between the murderous gazes of the Book Sisters, with Cassie and Trudi on either side of her. Tom hopped from foot to foot in a fury of indecision. Then, as the door started to close, he squeaked, "Sorry, Mum," and dashed through after them.

><<<+++++≈

They clattered up the stairs, Brine walking backward and holding Boswell's journal up by the corners. It seemed to grow heavier by the second, so that her arms were trembling by the time they reached the iron door at the top. She stepped through backward into sunlight and lowered her hands with a moan of relief. She couldn't believe what she'd just done.

"That made for a change," said Trudi cheerfully. "Cassie trying to talk us out of trouble, and Brine resorting to violence."

Brine felt empty inside, as if she'd torn something out of herself along with the book. She slid the ripped-out page back inside the cover and handed it to Tom. "You can mend it, can't you?"

He nodded, his eyes wide. "No one's ever threatened a book for me before."

Brine smiled back, feeling better.

"Well," said Cassie, "that could have been worse." She looked a little queasy as she gazed down the steep cliff path to the boat. Trudi set off first, and Cassie followed. Tom came last, dragging his feet now that the chance to leave the island had become a reality.

They reached the bottom, and Cassie let out a long breath that sounded like she'd been holding it all the way down. "I'm sure your mother meant well," she said. "She only wanted what was best for you."

Tom shrugged. "It doesn't really matter now," he said in a tight little voice. "I doubt I'll ever see her again." He lifted his glasses to rub his hand across his eyes and sniffed.

Cassie gazed into the distance, watching the birds circle over the cliff. A few minutes ago, they'd been hurrying to get away, yet long minutes passed and still Cassie didn't move. Brine wondered what she was looking at and then she spotted a figure high above them and she understood.

"Well," began Cassie at last, "let's—"

"Tom!"

It was a real, actual shout. The call echoed off the cliffs, sending birds screeching for cover. Ursula ran down the cliff path awkwardly, partly because her robe kept wrapping around her legs and partly because she was clutching several objects to her chest with both arms. She slid to a halt at the bottom and thrust them at Tom. A birdcage containing a pair of black and white gulls and a bag large enough to hold several books— and judging by the corners that pushed through the cloth, that's exactly what it did hold.

"I've brought your things," she said. "And messenger gulls, in case you want to write home."

Tom flung his arms around her. Cassie put her hand on Brine's shoulder and steered her off to wait by the boat.

"Thank you," said Brine.

"For what?"

"For this." She felt her eyes prickling as she looked at Tom and Ursula. Nobody on Minutes would have hugged Brine good-bye. Only Tallis Magus and Penn Turbill knew she'd left, and they wouldn't care for long. Cassie was the first person she'd met who'd really cared about anyone. "And for everything else, too," Brine added. "Even though you tried to sell me and Peter. You meant well."

"I usually do," said Cassie. "That's the problem." But she looked a bit misty-eyed.

Ursula drew away, then hugged Tom once more and ran back

up the path. He stood and watched her go. When she'd reached the top, he straightened his shoulders, pushed back the hood of his robe, and gathered up his things. He walked to the boat and clambered in, holding the birdcage in front of him like a shield.

Brine's throat burned. If it weren't for her, Tom would be safe in the library right now. They could have walked out and left him—maybe they should have walked out and left him. But here he was, leaving home, leaving his only family to join the *Onion* on a voyage that might end in disaster. Now Brine knew what Cassie felt like, never sure what was going to happen next.

The boat rocked gently as they pushed away from land. Tom immediately turned green and threw up over the side. He refused to let go of the birdcage, though. He wouldn't even let go of it when they climbed the rope ladder back onto the *Onion*.

Peter came running and stopped when he saw Tom.

"Peter, this is Tom," said Brine. "He's a librarian. Tom, this is Peter. He's a magician."

Tom's mouth dropped open. "Really?"

Peter flushed. "I'm still learning. Why are you wearing a dress?"

"It's librarian uniform," said Cassie crisply. "Right. Brine, you're in charge of Tom. Tom, you're in charge of reading Boswell's book. And . . ." She caught Ewan Hughes's gaze. "And Peter," she finished, "you're in charge of coming with me—right now."

CHAPTER 17

BOILED SEAGULL PIE

Take two seagulls per person and boil overnight wrapped in old
socks. When done, pick the meat off the bones and return to the
cooking pot with lots of water, rum, and whatever vegetables
you can find. Cover the pot with a thick layer of pastry and set
over the fire for four hours. The pastry will still be raw in the
middle, but if you put a slice on the plate and spoon the filling
over the top, nobody will notice.

(From COOKING UP A STORME—
THE RECIPES OF A GOURMET PIRATE)

Peter's stomach dropped through the deck. Cassie knew. The
thought echoed in his head. She knew about his visits to
Marfak West. She'd probably guessed he'd been learning magic
from him. He followed her to the far side of the deck, his footsteps slow and heavy. Glancing behind, he saw Brine taking the
birdcage from Tom and Tom running back to the side of the
ship with his hands over his mouth. Peter might have been
curious about Tom if it weren't for the fact that Cassie was
waiting.

He straightened. Deny everything. He'd never talked to Marfak West, he'd never been near him, he'd never even heard of him.

Cassie turned to face him. Her fingers played with the emerald around her neck. "I owe you an apology," she said.

"I've never—" Peter began. He stopped. "Pardon?"

Cassie dropped her hands to her sides. "I was counting on the fact that one magician would be drawn to another. I was also counting on the fact that if Marfak West thought you were sneaking down to see him against my orders, he'd be more likely to talk to you. But I forgot how young you are, and how good Marfak West is at twisting the truth. And, of course, I couldn't tell the rest of the crew what was going on in case they said anything to you."

Peter wished he knew what she was talking about. "Am I in trouble?"

"Of course you're not in trouble. I used you to get information out of Marfak West, and I shouldn't have. I'm sorry."

This was even worse than being in trouble. Cassie wasn't furious with him, she wasn't going to punish him, but she'd used him. Without saying a word to him first, without even thinking about what he might want. It was just like Marfak West had said—people will all want your power and nobody will want you.

No. Marfak West is a liar. He twists the truth.

But hadn't Cassie just done that, too? Peter dropped his gaze. If Cassie had used him, at least it meant she thought he could be useful. It wasn't much to hold on to, but it was better than nothing.

"So has he told you anything?" asked Cassie.

Did she really think she could just apologize and then expect him to tell her everything? Peter shifted from foot to foot. "He's been teaching me magic. He offered, and it seemed like a good idea to go along with it."

"Of course it did," agreed Cassie. "I've got a feeling things are going to become a lot more difficult from now on. We'll be crossing the Gemini Seas next—that's where we sank Marfak West's ship. Whatever else he wants, he certainly wants revenge for that."

Magical North was just the start of the journey, Marfak West had said, but he hadn't said what was going to come next. The words stuck in Peter's throat. Marfak West deserved nothing from him, but did Cassie deserve anything more?

"What are you going to do?" he asked. He was half-afraid she'd give up on the voyage altogether, turn south, and send him back to Minutes. The moment the thought was in his head, he knew that, no matter what else, he didn't want to go back.

Cassie didn't say anything. Peter looked up at her and she smiled. "If Marfak West wants us to go north, whatever is there must be worth having, and I'm going to make sure we get it before he does."

"But Marfak West isn't looking for Magical North," said Peter. The words felt heavy in his mouth, as if he'd become a traitor by saying them. Cassie's gaze turned curious and Peter felt his cheeks burning. "He told me. He believes it exists, and all the treasure, but it's not what he wants. And I don't think he wants to stand on Magical North and look for starshell, either."

Cassie nodded as if he'd told her something she'd already guessed. "Thank you," she said. "I think it's better if you stay away from him for now, but keep practicing your magic. I've a feeling we're going to need you before this is over."

"I'll do my best." He tried to match her smile. "As long as you promise not to try to sell me again."

"It's a deal," said Cassie. "To tell you the truth, I'm glad that didn't work out. I thought I was doing you a favor, finding you a safe home, but we're all going to be a lot safer with you on board."

She ran back to join the others. Peter watched her pull Brine aside. Whatever she was saying, Brine didn't seem to like it. Good, he thought. He sat down on the deck and took the starshell piece out of his pocket. He thought about the pirate captain who'd tricked and used him, and about the magician who might try to kill him, and he didn't know which one of them he should distrust more.

He sighed when he saw Brine and the new boy heading his way. Tom was clutching that stupid birdcage again. They'd want to talk to him, and he didn't feel like talking to anyone right now, especially not Brine. And the way Tom kept staring at him was already annoying, and the boy had been on the ship for less than ten minutes.

Peter walked away to the deck rail and leaned against it, hoping Brine would take the hint and go away. She didn't, of course.

"What did Cassie want?" she asked.

Peter shrugged. "Nothing. Just talking about magic." He jerked his head at Tom. "Does he know we have Marfak West on board?"

Tom nearly dropped the birdcage. "Marfak West? But he's dead. The stories—"

"That's the thing about stories, you see," said Peter. "They're all made up. Marfak West is alive, he's here, he's locked up in the brig, and he's going to show us the way to Magical North. If he doesn't murder us all first," he added with a grin.

Tom's face turned so white Peter thought he was going to fall down. He felt a flush of triumph. He bet Tom had never expected this when he'd left his safe library to go adventuring.

"Stop being horrible, Peter," said Brine.

"I'm not being horrible. I'm being realistic. If you're going to go dragging people along on this voyage, they deserve to know what they're getting into." He turned on Tom. "And you can stop staring at me like I'm something special just because I can do a bit of magic."

Tom dipped his head. "I'm not," he said in a low voice. "I was staring at you because you're a boy, and I've never seen another boy before. They didn't allow them on Barnard's Reach."

Peter didn't know what to say to that. It felt like a hard, angry knot inside him had suddenly begun to unravel.

"Though being a magician sounds amazing," said Tom.

For some reason, this made Peter laugh. "I'm only an apprentice, really." He took the birdcage out of Tom's hands.

"We should find somewhere safe for this. What do messenger gulls eat?"

"Fish. And seaweed. And old rope—anything you give them, really."

The three of them walked back across the deck together. Anyone watching might have thought they were friends.

By the time they'd found somewhere to hang the birdcage (moving Zen out of the way about twenty times) and Peter had shown Tom around the top two decks of the ship, Peter was beginning to like having a new person on board.

They sat down to eat as the sun was setting. "I've never eaten boiled pie before," said Tom politely. Peter doubted anyone had ever eaten boiled pie before, and not many people seemed to be eating it now.

Ewan Hughes wandered over to them, carrying a bundle of clothes and a pair of scissors. "Thought you might like to lose the hair and get into some trousers," he said to Tom. "You don't need to look like a girl now that you're out of the library."

Tom retreated on his bottom. "I don't look like a girl. I look like me, and I want to stay that way." He tucked his hair inside his robe and put his hands over his head protectively, as if he thought Ewan was going to cut all his hair off there and then.

Ewan's eyebrows rose in surprise, then he laughed. "Why not," he agreed, sticking the scissors through his belt. "If you can't be yourself on board the *Onion*, then where can you?"

Tom smiled in relief, but he kept a wary eye on Ewan as the pirate went back to join Cassie. Brine pulled Tom to his feet. "Come on, you can help me clear up. Are you coming, Peter, or have you got practicing to do?"

She asked casually, as if it were perfectly normal to invite him to join in. Peter started to shake his head, then thought better of it and nodded.

He enjoyed the next hour. Gathering up plates, sweeping away bits of soggy pie crust that people had tried to hide when Trudi wasn't looking. Some of the crew even pointed out bits he'd missed, as if he was normal and not a magician they wanted to stab with cutlasses. Then, when they were done, Brine taught Tom how to climb into the hammocks and they lay there, seeing how far they could make them swing, until they heard Cassie shouting.

►┄┼┼┼●➤

"We are going to find Magical North," said Cassie when everyone was gathered round. "We don't just have science on our side, we have magic—and we have Boswell's book. Tom, what does Boswell say about the next part of our voyage?"

Tom blushed as everyone turned to look at him, then produced Boswell's book from a pocket in his robe. The torn-out first page had been tucked neatly in front. "*The fifth day of Balistes*," read Tom. "*Today we left Barnard's Reach and turned north.*" He paused, reading on silently, smoothing each page down as he turned it. "They sail for a while. Nothing much happens. *The twelfth day of Balistes. We left the Gemini Seas behind us and entered uncharted waters. The crew have named this place the Sea of Sighs. The storms came upon us suddenly. Thunder first, then lightning, and finally the wind.*"

Tom glanced up from the book. "*The wind was full of the voices of the dead,*" he finished.

The mainsail flapped, making Peter jump. He looked out at the perfectly calm sea. "What comes next?"

Tom bent his head back over the book. "*Two crewmen jumped overboard to their deaths. I thought I saw the spirits of my own father and mother, dead these twenty years. The first mate saw such terrible sights that he still refuses to speak.*" He turned a page and looked up. "That's it. The next bit is about a monster made of ice."

Peter shivered. The crew looked around uneasily as if they expected ghosts to start rising from the deck. Tom slid the book inside his robe and sat with his arms wrapped around himself.

"Which way, Captain?" asked Ewan Hughes.

Peter knew what the answer would be. Cassie walked to the helm. "North. And look out for storms."

CHAPTER 18

Magic is a naturally occurring energy, and it flows in a north-
erly direction. This may explain why more starshell is to be
found in the Gemini Seas than anywhere else. Legends of magical creatures—dragons, unicorns, merfolk, and so on—are
often set in the far north. Of course, the far north has never
been explored, so the legends have the extra advantage that no
one can dispute the existence of such creatures there.

(From ALDEBRAN BOSWELL'S BIG BOOK OF MAGIC)

As if the weather were determined to prove Boswell wrong,
the seas remained resolutely calm for the next few days. The
Onion surged through clear blue waters, and the cold air held
barely a trace of wind and certainly no sign of a storm. Brine
found it was easy to forget about ghosts, easy to believe that
Boswell had exaggerated the whole thing. Peter seemed happier,
too, staying up on deck with her and Tom, and once he even
joined in a sword-fight practice with Ewan. Brine was pleased.
She wondered if most of Peter's bad temper before had been
because of all the time he'd had to spend with Tallis Magus. He

was certainly a lot easier to get on with now; at times she even caught herself liking him.

Then, on the seventh night, Brine woke with Peter shaking her.

"You were shouting in your sleep," said Peter. "What were you dreaming?"

Brine sat up. "I don't know." A few last images fled. An island full of trees, a boat, and then she'd been a shooting star, streaking halfway across the world. She rubbed her eyes, trying to see in the dark underdeck, and wondered why everything appeared to be swaying more than usual. "Where's Tom?"

"Asleep. It appears he can sleep through anything." Peter's voice was tight and nervous. He was holding all three of his starshell pieces, and a faint glow came off them, just enough to see by. He must have been practicing, Brine thought. She hadn't known he could do that.

Peter lifted his hand higher, and she saw his face. He looked more than nervous—he looked afraid. Brine slid out of her hammock. "What's going on?"

A low growl shook the ship. It was followed three seconds later by a crack that sounded like the *Onion* had split in half and a flash of light that turned the cabin white. The remaining crew were out of their hammocks in an instant. Tom woke with a yell and fell out of his.

"It's just a storm," said Brine. "No need to panic." But she heard the edge of panic in her voice as she said it.

Cassie came sliding down the ladder. "All hands on

deck—except you three. Stay down here until we tell you it's safe. It's only a storm. It could be worse."

"Told you," Brine told Peter. She tried to smile, but her face felt rigid with fear. Her heart thundered as loudly as the storm. She backed against the side of the cabin as everyone headed for the ladder.

Tim Burre was the last one up. "Try not to worry," he said. "We'll be fine." He slammed the hatch shut behind him. A moment later, lightning flared in streaks around the edges.

Tom's birds set up a mad squawking in their cage. Something sharp latched on to Brine's ankle and she yelled, but it was only Zen trying to climb her leg. She pulled him off and held him close, burying her face in his warm fur as the ship rocked. She felt sick. Tom crawled into a corner, and she heard him retching, but she didn't dare move to see if he was all right.

The floor suddenly bucked and threw her off her feet. Zen raked his claws down her cheek, broke free, and ran. A low wind moaned. Brine felt an answering moan rise in her own throat. Long shadows skittered across the walls as the wind sighed again.

Tom wrapped his library robe around his head. "It's the voices of the dead. We're all going to die."

Brine rubbed her hand over her cheek and felt blood where Zen had scratched her. The dead didn't have voices. It was only the wind. The wind groaning and sighing through every tiny crack in the ship, filling her ears until she thought she could hear voices calling her name. "Don't be silly, Tom," she said loudly, to drown the voices out. They only moaned louder. The

Onion tipped backward. Something crashed to the deck overhead. Brine bit back a scream. What was happening up there?

They all slid as the *Onion* rolled forward again. Brine grabbed hold of a trailing hammock. "Peter, do something."

"Like what?"

The wind shrieked. Another crash suggested something large had just broken. At this rate, the *Onion* wouldn't last long. If they stayed belowdecks, they'd drown.

"Wait here," said Peter. He began to crawl to the half-open hatch that led down to the lower deck.

The lower deck, where Marfak West was waiting.

Brine's heart almost stopped. She grabbed Peter's ankle. "Hold on!"

"We have to stop the storm," he shouted over the noise of the wind. "I can't do it. Have you got any other ideas?"

Brine didn't. Reluctantly, she let him go. He lifted the hatch and slid through. Brine followed him down, with Tom right behind her.

Packing crates lay everywhere. Some of them had smashed open, and their contents had spilled out across the floor. Peter took a cautious step forward and allowed his starshell light to fill the space.

Tom shouted in fright.

Marfak West stood in his iron cage and watched them. The ship lurched and tumbled, but he didn't move, not even when a crate hit the cage and shattered.

"Tom," said Peter with a grin, "meet Marfak West."

Tom's glasses fell off.

The magician's eyes glinted with amusement. "Pleased to meet you, too. By the ship's behavior, I take it we have entered a storm. Has the wind begun to howl like the souls of the dead yet?"

Wind shrieked through the hold. "Good," said Marfak West. "We appear to be heading in the right direction. Now, if you'd like the *Onion* to survive, the three of you will do exactly what I say. You, girl, go and tell Cassie to steer the ship directly into the storm."

Brine's breath stopped dead in her chest. "You've got to be joking."

"Do it," said Peter.

She shook her head fiercely. "I'm not leaving you down here with him." It struck her as odd that she was worried about Peter's safety when it would be far more dangerous up on deck right now.

Peter peeled his gaze away from the magician in his cage and turned to face Brine. "I'll be all right. Just do it—please."

He'd never said please before. Then again, he'd never asked her to do anything before. It was always her telling him what to do. Brine's mouth was too dry to speak. *Trust me*, Peter's eyes seemed to be saying, and she found, to her surprise, that she did.

"Be careful," she said. She turned and ran, before she could change her mind, and climbed back up the ladder.

The wind blew Brine off her feet as she emerged on deck. She struggled back up and clung to the mast, gasping. The air was so thick with spray she could barely see. Above her, the mainsail flapped as if it were trying to tear free. Broken ropes snapped to and fro.

She shouted, but the wind tore her voice away. A wave crashed right over her. The clouds above crawled with green lightning. Brine caught a sudden glimpse of figures out on the sea, and her heart bumped. The spirits of the dead—but no. Ghosts didn't exist. She looked around wildly, trying to find Cassie.

"Look out!" cried Bill Lightning, stumbling past her. A rope snapped and whipped across his face with a crack. He reeled, his nose flattened.

Find Cassie. That was all that mattered. Brine let go of the mast and crawled on her hands and knees. The *Onion* plunged down and she slid, screaming. For one moment, she thought she'd be tipped straight into the sea, then her feet caught in a net and she came to an abrupt stop that almost jerked her legs out of joint. She lay sobbing for breath.

The air cleared for a second, and she saw Cassie at the helm. Brine cried out in relief, kicked away the net, and staggered back to her feet. "Cassie! Sail into the storm!"

Cassie couldn't possibly have heard, but she turned.

"Into the storm!" Brine yelled again.

A pair of arms lifted her up from behind. Squirming, she saw Tim Burre.

"What are you doing out here?" He slung her over his shoulder and started back toward the hatch. Brine struggled.

"Cassie!"

The *Onion* shuddered, every rope thrumming. Slowly, battered by sea and wind, she began to turn around. Brine clung to Tim Burre upside down while the storm screamed in her ears. The sky, if it was possible, became even blacker.

The *Onion* dipped sharply, then dropped as if the sea below her had disappeared. Everything hung still for a moment. Brine drew in breath to scream and stopped, her mouth hanging open.

The wind fled, whining like a kicked dog. The sails hung limp. The sea gave one final heave and lay still.

One by one, the pirates picked themselves up, staring.

"That's something you don't see every day," said Trudi.

Clouds still surrounded them and lightning crackled in ghostly patterns, but the sea was calm. It was like looking up at the sky from the bottom of a well.

Tim Burre let Brine go, and she slid to the deck. "What the—" he began.

He got no further, because Peter climbed out of the hatch, and right behind him was Marfak West. The magician's arms were loaded with chains, but he didn't seem to mind them. He stood, observing the cloud banks and bursts of lightning with interest.

Brine sat there, staring. When Peter had said to trust him, she'd had some vague idea he'd stay belowdecks with Marfak West and deal with the storm from there. She hadn't thought he'd let the magician out of his cage. A brief hope that Peter wasn't that stupid and that Marfak West was mind-controlling him died as she saw Tom scrambling out behind them.

"This wasn't my idea," said Tom.

Marfak West smiled. "He's telling the truth. If it were up to him to have ideas, we'd all be doomed. Fortunately, your magician had more sense."

Everybody started shouting.

"Be quiet," snapped Cassie. "Ewan, put your sword away. Tom, stop trembling. Everything is under control." She turned to Peter, her eyebrows raised. "I'm assuming it is?"

He nodded, scarlet-faced. "I unlocked his cage with magic. I didn't know I could, but it worked. He says he can guide us out of the storm."

"He's lying," said Ewan. "If he knew the way through the storm, he's had plenty of time to tell us already."

Marfak West gave an irritated sigh. "How was I supposed to tell you anything when I was locked in a cage by myself and you frightened away my only visitor? I'm telling you now: We're at the very heart of the storm. From here, there is one safe path out. If you miss it, the storm will overwhelm the *Onion* and we'll sink. But stay here, and all we can do is sail in circles until we starve. Believe me, I have no wish to drown or starve with you."

"Throw him overboard," said Rob Grosse. "We don't need him." The crew muttered in agreement.

Cassie looked down at the deck. "Peter will guide us," she said. "Marfak West will help him, and I'll be standing right behind. If you try anything except get us safely out of here, magician, I'll cut your head off. Do you understand?"

Marfak West gave a stiff nod. "Peter, come with me." He stalked to the helm. Peter shot Brine a helpless glance and followed. She wanted to go after him, but it felt like her feet were stuck to the deck and she couldn't move. It wasn't Marfak West's doing, but her own body refusing to obey her. She watched as Peter joined the magician at the helm and Cassie and Ewan took up positions behind them.

"This is a big mistake," said Tom.

Brine nodded. She couldn't speak. And she couldn't help noticing that Peter didn't shrink away from Marfak West like everyone else did. In fact, he stood closer to him than to Cassie, as if Cassie was the one Peter didn't trust, and the magician, the vilest man in the whole world, was an old friend.

CHAPTER 19

Ghosts do not exist. I can say this confidently, after much research. I have killed many people, and none of them have come back to haunt me.

(From ADVENTURES IN MAGIC AND SCIENCE:
THE RESEARCH AND EXPERIMENTS OF MARFAK WEST)

It's a basic finding spell," said Marfak West. "I'm sure you know the spellshape for that one. Use it if it helps, and simply picture a way out of this storm."

Peter could have done without the word *simply*. This was impossible. He didn't know what he was looking for or how to picture it. The heavy warmth of the starshell pieces usually made him feel better, but instead his stomach churned so fast he thought he was going to throw up. He squeezed his eyes shut, trying to imagine he was back on Minutes, on solid ground. Anywhere but here, with everyone watching him as if they expected him to fail.

He jerked magic clumsily from the starshell and tried to curl it round into a circle. *This had better work*, he thought. *If it doesn't, Ewan Hughes is going to throw me to the sharks.* If Cassie hadn't stepped in, the crew would probably have thrown Marfak West overboard already by now, and Peter with him.

And yet, for some reason, Cassie *had* stepped in. Peter wondered why. He cast her a quick, worried glance. The magic slipped from his fingers and scattered. Cassie couldn't have seen it, but she smiled at him, her sword held firmly at Marfak West's back.

"You can do it," she whispered.

Peter drew in a breath. Cassie didn't like this any more than the rest of the crew, but she was giving him a chance. A simple finding spell. Right. He knew what the spellshape looked like. He held his wrist and turned his hand around. Brine sneezed and retreated as a circle of bright magic formed in the air. Peter stared through the ring of magic and imagined a path cutting through the storm, the clouds parting on either side of the ship and clear sky above them.

Nothing happened.

"It's no good," said Peter as the spellshape wavered and crumbled. "I can't imagine something I haven't seen. It just doesn't feel real."

Marfak West growled in frustration. "Of course it doesn't feel real. It *isn't* real, not the way you're doing it. Ask yourself, here and now, what do you want most?"

Magical North. The thought sprang into Peter's head. He wanted to stand at Magical North and see . . . not the world, but the future—*his* future. Would he ever be a good magician, would he ever stop feeling so out of place? Would he become a hero or a villain, a Cassie O'Pia or a Marfak West?

"There's nothing more real than what you're feeling," said Marfak West.

His words flashed through Peter's mind, as bright as magic. Everything Peter wanted, the answers to all his questions, lay on the far side of this storm. As soon as the thought had left him, he knew which way they had to go, as clearly as if he could see the path right in front of him. He held the starshell gently and felt a faint tug in return. "Left," he said, hoping he was correct.

Cassie's fingers dug into his shoulder. "Full speed to the left!"

▸⊶┼╂┼●

B rine sat and watched as Peter gave directions. The wind tugged at her clothes, whispering around her while, above the mainmast, a twist of light turned the clouds violet.

"It's a natural phenomenon caused by static discharge," said Tom. "Nothing to worry about." He was looking away from her as he spoke, so she couldn't see his face, but she guessed it was roughly the same shade of gray as the sea.

"Hello, Brine," said the static discharge.

The voice was like lightning across her vision. Brine yelped.

There was no such thing as ghosts. She knew that for a fact. You lived and then you died and you stayed dead. It was the world's way of making room for new people. *It's a trick of the storm*, she thought. She tried to say so, but she couldn't manage more than a squeak. That didn't seem to bother her parents, who both smiled at her.

Brine wasn't sure how she could tell they were her

parents—she just knew. Her father was tall, dark-skinned, and handsome. Her mother was shorter, with crinkly black hair that crackled with stray lightning. Brine's head felt like it was about to explode. She got up slowly and walked away from Tom. He didn't notice: His gaze had already drifted into the distance.

"You're not real," she said to the ghosts of her parents.

"Of course we are," said Brine's father. "Otherwise we wouldn't be here. It's good to see you looking so well. We did worry that you wouldn't survive."

"Maybe you should have thought about that before you put me in a boat and sent me off to die," said Brine angrily. She didn't care if they weren't real. She'd been saving this argument up inside herself for a long time. "Why did you do it?"

Her mother wiped away a tear. "We had to. It was the only chance we had of saving your life."

Brine shook her head. This wasn't real—it couldn't be. "You're only saying that because it's what I want you to say. You're only in my head."

Her father held out his arms to her. "We're here. We've come to take you home."

That was all Brine needed to hear. She started forward, but a pair of arms grabbed her round the middle. The ghosts of her parents vanished back into the sea. Brine yelled, kicked, and heard a familiar yelp of pain behind her. She swung round, her fists raised, and stopped when she realized she was staring straight into Peter's face.

"What do you think you're doing?" she shouted.

He dropped his gaze and pointed.

Brine looked behind her. She was right on the edge of the ship. Another step would have taken her overboard.

"It must have been good, whatever you were seeing," said Peter.

"Not really." She stumbled past him and leaned against the mast, her legs trembling. The *Onion* had slowed almost to a stop, and around the deck, the crew were stirring as if they were just waking up and weren't sure where they were. Marfak West waited at the helm, an impatient frown on his face.

"If you've quite finished rescuing your silly friends," he said, "we have a job to finish."

Peter's cheeks flushed.

"You'd better do it," said Brine. "We should get out of here." She reached for him as he turned to go. "Thanks," she added.

Peter cast her a smile and went back to Marfak West. Brine's knees gave way, and she slid down onto the deck. She hadn't really seen her parents, she knew. The storm had affected her and made her see what she wanted to see. The only part of it that was real at all was when Peter had dropped everything to save her life.

Tom joined her, looking shaken. "Sorry," he whispered.

"It's not your fault. What did you see?"

"Lightning, and some shapes that looked like birds, only bigger, and one of them breathed fire at me like a dragon." Tom scratched his nose, frowning. "Then I saw you walking to the edge of the ship, and Peter ran and grabbed you. I don't think Marfak West was very happy."

Brine rested her head on her knees. "I thought I saw my parents, just for a minute." She heaved a sigh.

"You'll find them," said Tom.

"I know. When we get to Magical North. I'll look for them, find out where they are now. Then I'll go and find them in person."

"I can help," said Tom. "Barnard's Reach has all the stories of the world collected together. They're bound to have something about people being abandoned at sea."

It was nice of him to offer. "Maybe," said Brine. She didn't add "I hope so," because hoping for something seemed to be the quickest way to make sure it never happened.

The *Onion* continued onward as Peter guided them. A short time later, the wind picked up, but it seemed to be urging them on now instead of knocking them from side to side. A patch of pale light appeared on the deck—real, pure sunlight. The crew cheered. It was ragged and exhausted, but a cheer nevertheless.

▶┅┼┼╟╾

Peter heard the cheers, but he didn't take his gaze off the starshell, not until the clouds broke and the *Onion* burst through the far edge of the storm into sunlight. Only then did he lower his hands and look around. Brine and Tom were sitting by the mainmast. Trudi was trying to bandage Bill Lightning's broken nose, while Rob Grosse and Tim Burre cleared away severed ropes. For all the attention the crew paid Peter, he might as well not have been there.

Cassie sheathed her cutlass. "Well done, Peter." She left him with Marfak West and went to check on Bill.

"Get used to it," said Marfak West. "They'll pull you out when they need something, but they'll never trust you. Your magic makes you better than them, and they know it, so you'll never be one of them." He turned toward Ewan Hughes, who was approaching, his face like thunder. "Don't you agree, Mr. Hughes?"

Ewan seized the magician by the arms. "I wasn't listening. You're going back in your cage, where you belong."

Marfak West met Peter's gaze as the pirate pulled him away. "See what I mean? They're afraid of what we might do together, so they have to keep us apart. Don't worry, though—they'll want us both again soon enough. We haven't reached the sea monster yet."

Peter turned his back on him, trying to pretend he didn't care that all the crew were talking but no one was talking to him. He hoped Marfak West was joking about the sea monster, but he had a nasty feeling that Marfak West didn't tell jokes. He pushed through everyone to the side of the ship and stood, feeling slightly sick. He tried not to notice how the rest of the crew avoided looking at him, and how Rob Grosse and Tim Burre started whispering the moment he turned his back. Marfak West was right—he was never going to fit in, not really, and it was about time he got used to it.

Someone touched him on the shoulder, and he turned and saw Brine. She looked different, and it took him a moment to work out why—she was smiling at him, smiling as if she actually like him. Then she sniffed and stifled a sneeze. "That was really brave when you grabbed me," she said. "Stupid, but brave. We could have gone off course, back into the storm."

"I didn't really think about it." Peter kicked the edge of the deck. The empty hollow inside him began to fill up with the slow realization that maybe he did have at least one friend on board, after all. He didn't want to think about it; he didn't want to think at all. He wanted everyone to be wrong—that was what he was trying not to think, and, typically, the effort of not thinking about something brought that thing straight into his mind. Once, Marfak West was just a name in a story and the name had scared Peter so much he couldn't sleep at night. Not anymore. Now Peter thought he understood the magician a little, and even liked him a little. And that one thought scared him more than the name *Marfak West* ever had.

CHAPTER 20

You can sail at your leisure to seek out great treasure
But I've got a better idea.
Stay home in your bed and dream gently instead
Of a wonder called Cassie O'Pia.

Her beauty exceeds all that anyone needs,
Her eyes set the morning aglow.
For one chance to see her, fair Cassie O'Pia,
A man would walk naked through snow.

(From THE BALLAD OF CASSIE O'PIA,
Verses 184–185, Author Unknown)

The *Onion* sailed through waters that were definitely choppy, but not in a violent, deliberate way. It was more like the sea was giving a nudge now and then to remind the crew it could still capsize the ship if it wanted to. Peter wondered if he could give the sea a shove back and decided it was best just to let his starshell recover for now.

The days continued to lengthen, and the temperature dropped

as they traveled, the sun taking permanent cover behind the clouds. A few times, Peter spotted whales following the ship, and the wind sharpened until it cut through several layers of clothing. Cassie loaned Brine a sweater, and Ewan Hughes gave Peter an old coat that was much too big but did help keep the cold out.

At last, the air became so cold and dry that it hurt to breathe, and all the crew were fighting to get under the remaining blankets. The sky faded to a ghostly green that never changed or grew dark. Flashes of brighter colors twisted overhead from time to time.

"The Stella Borealis," said Tom, looking up at them. He sat on an upturned bucket, writing. "Northern starlight. Boswell called it the Magus Borealis because he said it's caused by magic flaring off the world into the sky."

Peter hooked another bucket round and sat down next to him, huddling into his coat. Tom, in contrast, seemed to be sitting up straighter every day. He'd stopped hunching over as if he was afraid he'd touch something and break it, and his voice, though still quiet, had lost the library whisper.

Peter put his hands in his pockets. He'd wrapped the three starshell pieces up together. They were regaining magic faster than he'd anticipated—an effect of being so far north, he guessed—and the cloth around them was already starting to fray. Soon, he'd have to find another bunch of rags to wrap them in.

"What was it like growing up in a library?" he asked Tom.

Tom thought a moment. "Imagine that you live in a place where you're not allowed to run or talk or play. Now imagine that you've only got old ladies for company."

Peter imagined and shuddered. Tom nibbled the end of his pen. "Stories are full of people who are the odd ones out when they're growing up but turn into heroes. I used to pretend that I was a magician and one day I'd find some starshell and save the world."

"It's not that great being a magician," said Peter. "Back home, I had to do all the jobs Tallis Magus didn't want. And copy out spellshapes—a lot. I was on my own, apart from Brine, and she was only the servant." He shifted uncomfortably, remembering how he'd ordered her around. "You can see if you're a magician if you like," he offered. He took the starshell out of his pocket. "You just have to hold the starshell and try to feel the magic inside."

Tom snatched his hands back. "Thanks, but I think I'm going to be a news-scribe instead—one who travels the world."

Peter didn't blame him. Sometimes he wished that he'd never put his hand on starshell and found out what he could do. And sometimes it seemed to be the only thing in the world that mattered.

He saw Ewan Hughes approaching, and he groaned inwardly. A few of the crew had stopped what they were doing and were casually edging closer, too.

What now? "Whatever it is," said Peter, "it isn't my fault."

"It's not that," said Ewan. He kept his hands behind his back. "The thing is, me and the crew noticed how you don't have anywhere safe to keep your starshell, and . . . well. We got together and made something for you."

He thrust a box out at Peter.

Peter blinked at it. He reached out and took it, still believing this was a trick. Lifting the lid, he saw that the inside was lined with gold and silver coins, all hammered flat and overlapping like fish scales.

"We all chipped in," said Ewan. "We made it bigger than you need, too. You know, in case you find any more starshell."

A warm feeling spread in Peter's chest. The crew were all looking at him, and Peter spotted something in their faces he hadn't seen before. A certain pride and a wary respect. Had that been there all along, and he'd just never noticed? The warmth in his chest spread up to his cheeks.

"Uh, thanks," he said.

"You're welcome." Ewan stood for a moment, frowning as if he wasn't quite sure what else he should say. Peter's shoulders sagged in relief when the pirate walked away. He put the starshell pieces in the box, laid their gold chain on top of them, and closed the lid. He could still feel the magic in his fingertips. "Have you ever wished," he asked Tom, "that people would just want you for who you are and not for what you can do?"

"I don't know," said Tom. "I can't do much."

"That's not true. You're good at finding things out—and writing them down."

Tom reached for the inkpot.

"Are you writing this conversation down?" asked Peter.

Tom's cheeks colored. "I'm supposed to be composing a first-hand account. I want to record everything."

"It's all right. Write what you like." Peter looked around and saw Brine standing on her own at the front of the ship. Once, he'd thought she was only Tallis Magus's servant. How could he have thought Brine was only an anything? He stood up. "I just need to . . ." He wasn't sure what he needed to do, but Tom was already engrossed in writing again.

Brine was watching the sea through a telescope. She lowered it when Peter joined her and gave him a curious look, halfway between a smile and a frown, as if she wasn't sure what he was going to say or whether she was going to like it.

"The crew gave me a present," said Peter, holding up the box for her to see.

Brine nodded. "I saw. Are you all right? You don't look well."

"I think so. I . . ." He took a breath. "I wanted to say sorry."

Brine's face filled up with surprise so fast that Peter almost laughed. He tucked the starshell box under his arm and pushed his hands in his pockets. "I should have been nicer to you. I never thought before what it must have been like not knowing where you came from, and then ending up as Magus's servant. I could have helped more." He gave a rueful grin. "Though you weren't the easiest person to live with. Remember when you used to throw things at me?"

"You deserved it." Brine returned his smile. "On the other hand, I do keep dragging you into trouble, and you've never thrown anything at me for that. Truce?"

"Truce," he agreed.

They shook hands. Peter heaved a sigh. "I hope the crew aren't too disappointed when they find out what a bad magician I am."

"They won't find out," said Brine. "Because you're not a bad magician. You're a lot better than you think. Tallis Magus never let you do anything. All you did was copy out boring spellshapes. And how many spellshapes did Tallis know by heart, anyway?"

"I don't know. Twenty or thirty, I guess. He usually got me to look them up."

"There you are, then. He was, what, fifty years old, and he knew thirty spellshapes? That's less than one a year. It's no wonder you weren't learning a lot. You had a useless teacher."

That was exactly what Marfak West had said, but when Brine said it, it sounded true. "I'm still only an apprentice, though," he said, "and now I have no one to teach me."

"I'm not sure you need anyone." Brine frowned. "You know that doctor on Minutes who painted seascapes? He didn't have to think about every tiny movement the brush was making—he just knew how he wanted the waves to look, and he made it happen. Back in the storm, when you were guiding the ship, you looked like an artist painting with magic. Like you knew exactly what you were doing."

If he had, it had been thanks to Marfak West, Peter thought, but he felt lighter, as if some weight he'd been carrying around had just lifted. "Marfak West isn't looking for Magical North," he said. "There's something else there that he wants."

Brine's frown deepened. "Does Cassie know?"

"Yes, I told her. She thinks we'll be able to beat him when the time comes."

"If Cassie thinks so, I'm sure it'll be all right. We can trust her."

Cassie was standing at the helm. She waved when she saw Peter looking. Peter waved back. The fact that she'd first tried to sell him and then to use him to spy on Marfak West didn't seem to matter so much now. Blaming Cassie for anything was a bit like blaming the wind for blowing.

"We'll find Magical North," said Peter. "We'll find your parents, we'll defeat Marfak West, and people will sing songs about us all over the eight oceans."

"According to Boswell, we have to get past the sea monster first," Brine said.

Peter grinned. "After the ghost storm? It'll be easy."

"Ice ahoy!" shouted Ewan Hughes.

>·····⫲⫲⫲●

The sea couldn't freeze—it was impossible. Peter knew it for a fact. There was too much water, and it was full of salt, which melted ice. But, possible or not, the way ahead was busy with jags of pure white, taller than mountains. Peter stood and watched them move. They swayed like the coils of a great sea monster, a thousand times more terrible than the Dreaded Great Sea Beast of the South.

Tom leafed through Boswell's book. "Boswell talked about ice. First the Sea of Sighs, which we've done. Then you have to find your way past the sea monster. Then there's a tunnel leading up to a cavern. He must mean down to a cavern." He looked up. "I guess this is the sea monster."

"How can ice be a monster?" asked Trudi.

Flat plates of ice floated all around, gently drifting out of the way as the *Onion* nosed by. A black-and-white bird popped out of the water and scrambled onto one of them, staring at the ship with orange eyes. Peter stared back. If birds could shrug, this one did—dismissively.

"*The northern seas are home to many strange creatures,*" read Tom. "*Some of them are said to taste like chicken, although most of them will eat you first. Beware the birds, and look out for invisible bears.*"

"Invisible bears," said Cassie. "We've fought bears before. It could be worse."

Peter wished everyone would be quiet so he could think. With every second that passed, the *Onion* was taking them closer to Magical North. The end of the voyage for Cassie and the start of Marfak West's plans. Peter had a nasty feeling that when Cassie and Marfak West clashed, he was going to be caught right in the middle. He took his starshell out of its box and held it up. The three pieces glowed with amber magic.

"Can you put that away?" asked Brine, sneezing. Peter did, but he could still feel the pieces prickling impatiently. He watched the ice draw closer. Great lumps of it bobbed up to the *Onion* as if they were curious about the unexpected presence of a ship. No one spoke, and now Peter wished someone would, just to break the silence. Cassie stood with a rigid frown of concentration on her face as she eased the *Onion* into the spaces that still contained water.

Another black-and-white bird slid off the ice into the sea with a little plop. It was followed by a bigger splash that could have been anything. Peter looked back and saw a tail break the surface of the water in the distance. If whales and birds could survive in this sea, it couldn't be too bad. But the ice was now closing in behind them. Peter watched it drift into the ship's wake. Any one of the pieces was big enough to crush the *Onion*.

"You do know that very soon we won't be able to turn back," he said. "Even if we wanted to."

Cassie stared straight ahead. "The *Onion* never turns back. The stars will fall out of the sky before we accept defeat."

"Stars can't fall," said Tom. "They're balls of burning gas and rock, thousands of miles across. If one of them fell, we'd all know about it." He looked up, caught Cassie's gaze, and blushed. "Though not for long," he added.

Eventually, the ship came to a halt against a semicircle of sparkling, frozen pillars. The only way on was through a corridor of green water barely wider than a rowing boat.

Cassie let out a sigh that billowed white on the frozen air. "Well, everyone, this is it," she said. "It's time we let our friend out of the hold."

CHAPTER 21

I had hoped that after crossing the Sea of Sighs the worst would be behind us, but it appears I may have been wrong. This morning we spied glistening coils in the distance: the body of an enormous monster made entirely of ice.

(From ALDEBRAN BOSWELL'S JOURNAL OF STRANGE ADVENTURES IN THE YEAR OF DISCOVERY)

Brine's heart gave an involuntary leap as Marfak West walked out on deck. The magician's hands were chained behind him, and Ewan Hughes prodded him along with a cutlass. Several others drew their swords, but Marfak West ignored them all as he passed. He nodded to Peter, who stared down at the deck, his expression blank.

"We're here," said Cassie, tucking her hair back inside her hat. "What now?"

Marfak West gave her a look that Brine could only have described as frozen. "Boswell's monster. A beast made of ice and snow but perfectly capable of crushing this ship to splinters." His smile showed exactly what he thought of the prospect. Brine edged closer to Peter and noticed that Tom was doing the same.

"Don't worry," murmured Peter. "He can't do anything while I have his starshell." He didn't sound too sure of himself.

Marfak West walked to the rowing boats and gave one of them a kick. "If you try to take the *Onion* any farther, you'll lose her," he said. "A small boat, however, will be able to navigate between the ice floes. I know the way. I can guide you. The sun will be setting on Orion's Day soon, so I suggest we leave now."

"No," said Ewan. "He's lying. He wants us to leave the *Onion* so he can steal her."

Marfak West stood like a statue. "How exactly am I supposed to steal the *Onion* if I'm in a rowing boat with you?"

"You'll think of something," growled Ewan. In two steps, he was across the deck, his cutlass at the magician's throat.

Cassie grabbed Ewan's wrist. "We didn't bring him this far just so you could jab holes in him."

Ewan stood rigid. Brine held her breath, her heart pounding as the pirate scowled. Her palms were damp.

Slowly, Ewan lowered his cutlass.

Brine's shoulders sagged, and she knew then from the sudden bitterness at the back of her throat that it wasn't fear she'd felt—it was eagerness. She'd wanted Ewan to do it. She had wanted to see Marfak West die, and if Ewan had cut his throat, she'd have cheered. It wasn't the nicest feeling to know you'd approve of a murder, even the murder of Marfak West. Brine didn't dare look at him in case he guessed what was in her mind.

Cassie, apparently oblivious to the turmoil inside Brine, turned to face the rest of the crew. "Here's the plan," she said. "Ewan will stay here and captain the *Onion*. I'm going to take one of the rowing boats and find Magical North. And you can stop gloating, Marfak West, because my sword will be at your back the whole time. If you even think about betraying us, I'll cut your heart out. Any other volunteers?"

The pirates looked at their feet, the ice, and the sky, anywhere but at one another. Brine wondered how many of them had wanted Ewan to kill Marfak West just then.

"I'll come," said Peter, sounding as if there was nothing he wanted to do less.

Brine raised her hand. "If Peter's coming, so am I."

"And me," said Tom. Brine shook her head at him, but Tom's chin jutted stubbornly. "Why not? I'm almost as old as you, and I'm supposed to be writing all this down. Cassie, tell her."

Brine expected Cassie to say no. Instead, as Cassie looked at Tom, her expression changed from reluctance to acceptance. "We're not going to find Magical North by force of arms," she said.

Brine's mouth fell open. "He's only a child!"

"So are you," said Cassie. "Do you want me to leave you behind?"

Brine shut her mouth quickly. Cassie scanned the crew. "I'll take one boat with Marfak West, Peter, and Brine. Bill, you're in the second boat with Rob and Tom. We'll take one of Tom's messenger gulls with us. If the sun sets and you don't hear from us, I order you to leave. If we don't make it back, there's no reason to assume a rescue party will do any better." She smiled her bright sword-blade of a smile. "Now, come on. Get to it."

They prepared quickly. Cassie loaded a few supplies into a bag. Tim Burre found a wooden box and lined it with fur so there was just enough room for one of Tom's messenger gulls to sit inside. Brine didn't take anything. There didn't seem much point. If they succeeded, they wouldn't need it. And if they failed . . . but no, she wasn't going to think about that.

"Good luck," whispered Trudi. She pressed a spare bottle of ink into Tom's hand and a piece of dried haddock into Brine's. "In case the gull gets hungry."

Ewan Hughes's face was grim. "Cassie, this is madness. I say lock the magician back in his cage, and you and me take a boat to have a look around."

"And how will you and me on our own find Magical North?" Cassie asked him.

Ewan scowled and turned away.

Cassie sighed. "Then we're all set. One last thing—Peter, give Ewan the starshell."

Ewan swung back around. Peter gaped.

"Marfak West is only dangerous if he can do magic," said Cassie. "If he can't get his hands on starshell, he can't do magic, and therefore it's a lot safer to be around him."

She sounded like she'd been thinking about this for a long time and, actually, Brine thought, it wasn't a bad idea.

"But without starshell, I can't do magic, either," Peter pointed out.

Cassie put a hand on his shoulder. "And what magic will you use to stop Marfak West if he steals your starshell?"

Marfak West cleared his throat. "Technically, it's *my* starshell. You stole the pieces from me."

"Shut up," said Cassie. "Peter, I'm sorry, but the starshell stays here. You can stay with it or leave it behind."

For a moment, Brine thought Peter was going to stay, but he sighed and handed the box of starshell pieces to Ewan Hughes. "Look after it," he said.

Ewan nodded, glowering. He was still glowering as the pirates let down the boats and climbed into them. As far as Brine could tell, he was still glowering when they moved away and the towers of ice hid the *Onion* from her sight.

▶⇥┼┼┼┼●

No matter where you were on the eight oceans, sitting in a boat always felt the same, Brine thought. The scenery might vary, and the weather, but the creak and splash of oars, the gentle rocking of wood beneath your legs, the knowledge that this thin shell of wood was the only thing between you and drowning— these were always the same.

Cassie rowed steadily, keeping her eyes on the *Onion* for as long as they could see it. Brine watched her and wished she knew what Cassie was thinking. She also wished that Marfak West would sit still. He kept wriggling on the narrow bench, and every time he moved, he made all his chains rattle. It was starting to get on Brine's nerves.

"Go straight on," said the magician as Cassie veered to one side. "There's a gap just behind you."

The ice glided past. From a distance, it had all looked very much the same shade of white. Close up, it glittered, and the colors varied from pure, brilliant silver through shades of green and turquoise and even patches of muddy yellow. And it creaked. Louder than the creaking of timber in a storm, and with the added excitement of sudden, sharp cracks that made Brine jump, expecting vast sheets of ice to come crashing down on top of them at any moment.

"Look," said Peter, pointing as a black-and-white bird stuck its head out of the water. It blinked its round orange eyes at them. Brine wished she had some fish to throw.

"Keep away from it," snapped Marfak West. If Brine hadn't known better, she'd have said the magician sounded afraid.

"There's another one," said Peter.

"And another," added Cassie.

Three birds hopped onto the ice and began to sway. A faint humming filled Brine's ears. Cassie sang as she rowed, and Brine sang along. It was strange: They were surrounded by ice, she could see her breath freezing, and yet she felt warm. A bead of sweat trickled down her back. Her gaze slid to the water. Cool, inviting.

Marfak West threw the bailing cup. The birds gave a surprised squawk and vanished. In an instant, the pressure fell from Brine's mind. She sagged forward. "What was that?"

Cassie turned her head. "Whatever they are, they're back. And—how sweet—they've brought friends."

"Row!" yelled Marfak West. His voice startled Cassie into action. She hauled at the oars. The boat moved sluggishly. Brine saw bird-shaped specks sliding across the ice. She was ready for the humming this time, but not for the volume of it. The force almost threw her out of the boat. Through the ache in her ears, she was vaguely aware that Cassie had stopped rowing and was mopping her face; Peter was undoing his coat. Brine looked across to the other boat and saw Bill Lightning standing up. Tom grabbed him round the knees.

"What nice birds," said Cassie dreamily, getting to her feet. "I think I shall go for a swim."

Marfak West shouted a stream of words Brine didn't understand. Her mind filled with harsh shrieks, then sudden, wonderful silence. She slid down into the bottom of the boat. A pair of large weights landed on top of her. After a few seconds, she realized they were Cassie and Peter.

They all sat up. The birds had gone. Tom gave them a wave from the other boat. Brine rubbed her head and groaned.

Cassie drew her sword and put it to Marfak West's chest. "What did you do?" she demanded.

He gazed back calmly. "You really must stop thinking I'm trying to kill you. It is quite tiresome. I talked to the birds.

I explained how we would turn them all into casserole if they didn't leave us alone, and I sent them away. You don't need magic for that, just the right words."

Brine remembered the sea creatures he'd summoned at Morning. Her mouth was dry. "You sent them away? Where to?"

A thin smile crawled across the magician's face.

CHAPTER 22

She fought giant bats and an island of rats,
And slew the dread beast in its lair.
She conquered the plague, saved us all from the grave,
The buccaneer extraordinaire.

(From THE BALLAD OF CASSIE O'PIA,
Verse 200, Author Unknown)

Ewan Hughes had been worried ever since Cassie and the others had left the *Onion*. Now, having had nothing but ice to look at for nearly an hour, he was bored as well. It was not his favorite combination. He sat below the mainsail, listening to the ice creak and trying not to think about what might be happening to the rowing boats.

Zen wound around his ankles, mewing, then tried to climb his leg. Ewan bent down. "Something you don't like, puss?" The cat purred and wriggled up inside his coat.

"Come and look at this," called Trudi.

Holding Zen steady, Ewan strode across the frosty deck. A little man in a dinner suit loitered on a nearby plate of ice. Ewan blinked, and it turned into one of the black-and-white birds. "What's it doing?" asked Ewan. "And why don't its feet freeze?"

Trudi scratched her head. "Maybe they're pretend feet." She leaned over the deck rail. "It swims like a fish but it's got feathers like a bird. Who's a cute fish-bird, then?"

The fish-bird slipped and almost fell, flapping its arms in comic circles to stay on its feet. A collective "awww . . ." rose from the deck.

"There's another one," said Tim Burre, pointing. The crew all turned. Sure enough, another black-and-white figure was making its laborious way across the ice. Ewan Hughes saw another one bobbing in the water. All three of the birds—no, all four of them, all six of them, all eight . . . all *lots* of them— turned to face the *Onion*, watching intently with round orange eyes.

"It's almost as if they're trying to tell us something," said Tim wonderingly. "Does anyone have any fish I can throw?"

>+++++#€

Peter's whole body ached with cold. Marfak West sat cross-legged opposite him. His face looked sharp and eager, honed by the wind and the cold until he seemed more like an ice statue than a man. *Magical North is just the beginning*, Peter thought. His hands felt wrong without starshell to hold. His fingers kept clutching at nothing.

A lone fish-bird ducked under the boats and emerged

beyond them. Something white lumbered by on the ice high above, but when Peter blinked, it vanished. He scraped his hair back out of his eyes. This was ridiculous. He didn't even know why Cassie had brought him along—he should have stayed behind on the *Onion,* where he could at least do something. He hadn't liked Cassie's assumption, either, that Marfak West could steal the starshell from him any time he wanted. Although she was probably right, which made it worse.

"Stop!" shouted Marfak West.

Cassie hauled on the oars as a whole section of ice crumbled away and slid into the sea right ahead of them. Tom's rowing boat bumped into theirs, sending them dipping and lurching before they steadied. Peter clutched the edge of the boat, gasping for breath. For a moment, he thought he was going to fall into the freezing sea. Brine pulled him back.

"I don't like this," she said. "What if the ice isn't the sea monster after all? What if there's a real, actual sea monster waiting just around the next corner?"

"Can you please stop talking about monsters?" said Peter, his stomach still lurching. He hated that they had to rely on Marfak West to guide them. Marfak West, who had plans they knew nothing about.

A low growl made Peter jump. *Just the ice.* The sound died away with a final snarl, and silence returned. Peter sat on his hands to keep them still and pretended to enjoy the view.

It was hard to keep track of time when everything looked

so much the same, but he reckoned they must have rowed for another hour, taking it in turns while Marfak West gave directions. Then, ahead of them, the sea narrowed into a point. A few large flakes of ice broke away as Cassie bumped against a snowy ridge, and that was it. No more water. The ice was a single, unbroken sheet.

Bill Lightning pulled up alongside them. His broken nose was covered in a thin layer of frost. "What's happening now?"

"Nothing." Marfak West stepped out of the boat. "We've run out of sea. Now we walk."

►·++︱︱︱●➤

Ewan Hughes had a headache. A throbbing pressure behind his eyes that felt like his brain was slowly expanding. He rubbed his forehead. The pressure increased.

Fish-birds surrounded the *Onion* on all sides. They stood in rows on the ice and bobbed in the water, their orange eyes fixed on the ship. As Ewan watched, another one joined the crowd, sliding in silently at the back. Ewan turned his head, blinking. His eyes stung with shards of ice. And either the *Onion* was swaying from side to side or the birds were.

"Go . . . away . . . ," muttered Trudi. Her lips barely moved. Ewan waved a hand in front of her face, and she didn't even blink. The fish-birds all rattled their flippers, making a sound like icicles in a high wind. A subtle tremor ran through the hull of the *Onion*.

No one moved. No one was going to, either, thought Ewan. His vision blurred.

"What a lovely day," said Trudi beside him. "I think I shall take a bath." Something inside Ewan's head echoed that he really should consider joining her.

Then Zen stuck his claws in Ewan's earlobe. The shock of pain splintered the pressure on his mind. He gasped, seeing for the first time the fully massed ranks of fish-birds. They stood on every piece of ice, motionless apart from an occasional flap of a black flipper, all staring.

One of the crew climbed up onto the deck rail and launched himself off with a shout. Ewan yelled and grabbed a rope, too late. Fifty black-and-white birds slid into the water. A scream rose up, then the sound of fifty sharp beaks tearing at flesh. Ewan's stomach turned over. Trudi staggered past him, her arms waving. Ewan grabbed her and shook her until her eyes cleared. Two other pirates were trying to escape overboard. He leaped for them and hauled them back by the legs.

"Tie yourself to the mast!" he shouted at Trudi. "Tie everyone else as well. Masts, rail, anything that won't move." He grabbed a piece of rope and looped it around his own waist. The birds all turned in his direction. The urge to fling himself off the *Onion* would have been overwhelming were it not for Zen's claws raking his face. Ewan wrestled his gloves off and managed to tie the rope to the mast before his hands went numb. Another pirate was poised to jump. Ewan took a couple of running steps and brought his fists together on the man's head, knocking him unconscious.

"Fine!" Ewan yelled at the birds. "You want me to go mad, I'll go mad. *But you're not going to like it.*"

Seven people stood in a place where people had probably never stood before. Peter felt he should have more of a sense of achievement at the fact. It wasn't that long ago, after all, that he was Tallis Magus's apprentice and had never left the islands of Minutes. Yes, and he would happily go back there and be a nobody for the rest of his life if it meant getting out of this place. He shielded his eyes from the never-ending sunshine and looked around for landmarks. There were none.

Marfak West eased his shoulders in a circle. "I suppose you wouldn't care to unchain my hands now?"

Cassie drew her sword. "Correct. I wouldn't care to. This is where you start earning your keep. Which way?"

Marfak West couldn't possibly know, Peter thought. Even if he'd memorized the location of Magical North as he'd claimed, he had nothing to guide them by. The ground sloped away, gently rising until it merged into the sky. Every direction looked the same to Peter.

Tom and Brine huddled beside him. Tom clutched the box holding the messenger gull under his coat. The bird hadn't made a sound since they'd gotten into the rowing boat. Peter hoped it was all right.

Marfak West surveyed the ice, his expression unchanging. "This way," he said after a moment.

Bill Lightning shook his head, teeth chattering. "He's lying. He wants to freeze us all."

"Maybe I do," agreed the magician. "But I'd prefer to do it after we reach Magical North. You forget, I have devoted years to studying Boswell's last voyage. The ice plains have grown since then, and Boswell arrived by a slightly different route, but he had no clear idea of what he was looking for, and I do. Peter, try to feel the magic around you. Does it seem stronger in any direction?"

Peter automatically put his hand in his pocket for his starshell before remembering Cassie had left the three pieces with Ewan back on the *Onion*.

Brine turned her head and sneezed. Peter grinned. "He's right. That way."

They walked in single file, Marfak West leading the way with Cassie just behind him. Rob Grosse and Bill Lightning brought up the rear. Peter had expected the ice to be slippery and was surprised to find that it wasn't. The snow formed a powdery, perfectly dry layer underfoot.

"How much farther?" asked Bill Lightning.

Marfak West turned his head. "We'll get there before you freeze to death, don't worry."

The snow up ahead shifted. Peter blinked and shook his head, trying to get his vision straight. When everything was the same shade of ghostly white, it was far too easy to imagine ferocious creatures crouched in the snow, waiting to ambush them.

Tom stopped walking. "What was that?"

"It's nothing," said Brine.

A crackle of Stella Borealis twisted the sky out of shape. "Don't look now," murmured Cassie. "But you might all want to turn and look."

A deep-throated growl shook the ice.

>++++H+E

The *Onion* swayed from side to side in a slow dance. Fish-birds were everywhere: bobbing on the sea, perched on the peaks of ice that rose higher than the *Onion*'s mast. Most of the crew lay unconscious. The ones who were awake strained madly at the ropes that bound them. From their mouths came the same word: "Cruel, cruel, CRUEL!" It rose into a chant that bounced between icebergs, filling the sea with the flat sound of misery.

This was the birds' doing, thought Ewan. "I'm cruel?" he shouted at the birds. "You're the ones trying to eat me." A rope stretched from his belt to the mast behind him. A fish-bird pecked at his feet. Ewan swung his sword and sent the thing wheeling back into the sea. Another one immediately hopped in to take its place. Ewan wiped sweat from his face. This was hopeless; the birds were as implacable as the ice. How did you fight ice?

The answer flashed through him: fire.

He looked around, cursing himself that none of the lanterns were lit—no need for them when the sun didn't set. He jumped over a fish-bird, kicked another one out of the way, and snatched a lantern and flint. Fish-birds swarmed at him, and he didn't have time—or hands—to fight them. They surrounded him, pecking at him with sharp beaks. Ewan hissed in pain, almost dropped the flint, but kept striking until he saw sparks leap. Two more fish-birds started to peck at the rope that held him secure to the mast.

Cruel, cruel, cruel.

Ewan lit the lantern and hurled it out onto the ice, right into the middle of the largest group of attacking fish-birds.

The oil exploded. Shards of glass and little bits of black and white shot up in a shower. A second later, the ice raft emptied as all the surviving fish-birds belly-flopped into the sea.

Ewan fell to his knees, sharp agony flaring through his senses, hotter than the lamp flame. Tim Burre broke free from the mast and stumbled toward the deck rail. Ewan grappled him down, muttered an apology, and hit him with his cutlass hilt. Tim's eyes rolled back as he sagged unconscious. His lips began to move, murmuring the same word over and over again. *Cruel, cruel, cruel.*

Ewan launched himself across the deck for another lamp.

"As you can see," he yelled, "I have plenty of these." That wasn't true, but he hoped birds couldn't count. He brandished the lantern threateningly. "Let my friends go, or I might be forced to throw another one." He drew his arm back. A thousand orange eyes slowly turned their gaze away from him. Not a bird moved.

"Ewan," said Trudi, "what are you doing?"

Ewan turned to see the crew waking up. He breathed a sigh of relief and put down the lantern. Then, all around the *Onion* came a flurry of wings, a rattle like the sound of a thousand bird claws unsheathing together. The air filled with a heavy black-and-white hail. Fish-birds, throwing themselves off the higher ice shelves, crashing onto the deck. One of them bounced off Ewan Hughes's head and lay stunned; others stood up and began waddling forward.

Ewan paused a moment, then yelled and charged them all.

Black, feathered bodies slithered away beneath his cutlass. A curved beak tore a gash out of the back of his hand. A bucket rolled past and a cream paw shot out of it, swiping a bird around the ears and retreating. Another pirate disappeared overboard, screaming. The *Onion* itself was gradually disappearing under a weight of black-and-white bodies. Ewan Hughes wondered just how many of them the ship could take before the deck gave way and they sank.

What a stupid way to die, he thought, and for a moment he was glad that no one would survive to sing songs about this.

CHAPTER 23

I have written previously that many legends of magical creatures are set in the far north. It is strange how the legends fail to
mention the magical creatures that actually do live in the northern icelands. However, I imagine that anyone who meets one of
these creatures is likely to die instantly, thus losing the oppor-
tunity to begin a new legend.

(From ALDEBRAN BOSWELL'S JOURNAL OF STRANGE
ADVENTURES IN THE YEAR OF DISCOVERY)

E veryone scrambled for cover that wasn't there. Brine, not
knowing whether to run or hide, spun round on the spot.
Eight paces away, a monstrous furry creature, white as the snow
that surrounded it, appeared in the act of taking its paw away
from its coal-black nose.

"Bear!" shouted Cassie and whipped out her sword.

"Bare what?" asked Bill Lightning.

The bear let out a roar that sent them stumbling backward,
put its paw over its nose, and vanished again. The pirates
regrouped in a semicircle. Brine drew her sword and gripped
it hard to stop herself from trembling. She'd practiced enough

with Ewan Hughes, she reminded herself. She wasn't completely helpless. Even if she felt like she was.

"Invisible bears," whispered Tom. "Boswell was right."

The bear reappeared a few paces away. It leaped at them, and Cassie O'Pia jumped to meet it. They clashed with a snarl and a scrape of claws on steel. Cassie danced away, her coat torn. The bear dropped back to the ground and paced in a slow circle, sniffing the air. Evidently, it wasn't used to its food fighting back.

It disappeared again, and Peter gave a sigh. "It's gone."

There was the heavy sound of a giant bear walking invisibly on three legs. "Look out!" shouted Tom. He crashed into Peter as the bear struck. Brine screamed. Tom stumbled and fell. The bear's claws slashed through his coat, smashing the wooden box Tom still clutched. The gull flapped free and flew away, shrieking in terror.

The bear reared up on its hind legs. Tall as a tree with claws like swords—claws that could slice right through you. Brine opened her mouth, but she couldn't make a sound; her chest felt like it was solid ice. Her fingers lost their grip on her sword, and it fell, useless, into the snow.

Then Rob Grosse and Bill Lightning were in front of her, driving the bear back to where Cassie was waiting with a sword in each hand. She slashed quickly and spun away. The bear howled, dropped to all fours, and vanished again. This time, spots of blood marked the ice.

"Didn't you once fight ten bears with a lobster claw and a dishcloth?" Peter asked Bill.

Bill kept his gaze on the snow. "Don't know who told you that."

Brine snatched up her sword. Marfak West was watching them, his usual superior smile on his face. Brine wanted to drive her sword right through him. "Tell it to go away," she shouted.

He shrugged. "Sorry. I only do sea creatures."

The bear blinked back into visibility behind Cassie. She dropped flat as a huge paw smashed through the air just above her head and vanished again.

"It has to put its paw down to attack," said Tom. "And then it becomes visible. That's its weakness—it can't attack while camouflaged."

"It's not much of a weakness," Cassie shouted back, stabbing at empty air. "This is useless. We can't kill something if we can't see it."

Brine watched the ice. A tiny red smudge appeared a few paces away. She tensed, gripping her sword, then screamed and stumbled as the bear reappeared standing on three legs, its front paw already raised to strike.

"Duck!" shouted Tom. Something flashed over Brine's head and hit the bear's flank. Droplets spattered out, forming a dark constellation against its snow-white fur.

The bear put its paw back over its nose, but this time everyone could still see the ink splatters.

"After it!" shouted Cassie. The pirates charged in pursuit. The bear turned back to meet their swords and, faced with several sharp points, changed its mind about attacking. It whined softly, dropped back to all fours, and slunk away.

Peter slapped Tom on the shoulder. "Well done," he panted.

Tom beamed. "Mum always said the pen was mightier than the sword," he said. But then his smile faltered, and he turned away to begin gathering up wood and feathers from the snow.

"She'll fly back to the *Onion*," said Brine. "She's safer than any of us right now." She tried not to think about the fact that their one means of contacting the *Onion* was gone and they were standing in a frozen wilderness with only Cassie O'Pia to rely on. Worse than that: Cassie O'Pia and Marfak West.

The *Onion* was so full of feathers it looked like the inside of a pillow. The crew, all wide awake now, fought for their lives. Ewan Hughes stabbed and slashed, trying to stay out of the way of sharp beaks and even sharper claws. A group of birds were pecking through the rope that held Tim Burre to the mainmast and, as fast as Ewan fought them away, more slipped in behind him to take their place. A beak raked his leg, gouging out a stinging furrow. The birds fought with one thought in their minds— *meat*. Ewan felt it every time a hungry gaze fell on him. He fought back grimly, without hope, yet something inside him wouldn't let him give up. Even if he was the last man left alive, while he had breath in his body, he'd fight on.

"Something's wrong," said Trudi.

Ewan unhooked a fish-bird from his buttocks. "I know. We're being eaten alive by cute birds."

Trudi shook her head. "Not that. I mean something else is wrong."

The *Onion* shivered. All the fish-birds stood still, their heads cocked sideways. Ewan backed off a couple of steps, his sword still up. Blood dripped from the back of his hand.

A tremor ran through the sea. It was gone in an instant, too quickly to know what it was or whether he'd only imagined it.

The next tremor was definitely not imaginary. The *Onion* jolted. Ewan staggered, a surge of terror shaking him from head to foot. But he wasn't the only one who was afraid. For a second, the birds stood motionless, every feather standing on end, as if frozen rigid with fear. Zen hissed and tried to climb Ewan's leg, shredding the few parts of his trousers the fish-birds hadn't already destroyed. Then, as if one of them had given a signal, every bird rushed, pushing and shoving, off the deck. The sea around the *Onion* churned with a thousand splashes, then was suddenly still.

The deck was empty. So were all the ice floes.

Ewan frowned. His chest hurt, and he looked down and saw blood on his shirt. He couldn't remember how that had happened. There were gashes all up his legs, too. They'd heal, he thought, but what had happened to make the birds all flee? He turned to look at Trudi.

She gave him a worried smile. "Cassie will be back soon," she said. "She'll know what to do."

A gull cried overhead. As it dropped down toward the ship, Ewan saw the message canister on its leg and his heart leaped. He held out his hands, and the bird flopped awkwardly into his grasp. It was trembling with cold, exhaustion, and fear. It blinked once at Ewan before a last shudder ran through its frozen body and its eyes clouded.

Ewan undid the little canister on the gull's leg and eased out the strip of paper inside. It was blank.

Every cut on Ewan's body throbbed. He turned the paper over, as if this would make words miraculously appear.

"Let me see," said Trudi. Ewan shook his head and passed it to her. Her face fell.

Ewan couldn't look at her. Slowly, he crossed the deck, picked up a square of torn canvas, and wrapped up the gull's body as carefully as if he were tucking it into bed.

That was it, then: Cassie wasn't coming back. He repeated it to himself three times and still couldn't make himself believe it. Yet the fact that the bird had returned without a message could only mean one thing: Something bad had happened. Ewan didn't know what, but he was certain that if they stayed here, they were all going to die.

"Raise the anchor," he said heavily.

Trudi's eyes widened. "What about Cassie?"

"We'll come back for her." He didn't know whether he meant it or not. He hoped he did.

Another tremor ran through the sea. The *Onion* jolted.

Without another word, Trudi cut the rope that still tied her to the mast and ran to help wind in the anchor.

There was not a fish-bird in sight, and Ewan Hughes felt more afraid than ever.

▶┅╫╫╍◖

Peter was freezing but he was too tired to shiver. He tried to remember how long they'd been walking since the bear attack, but it was impossible to tell because the light never changed and everywhere he looked was the same hazy white. They could all go color blind here, he thought, and never know. He glanced back at the little group of fish-birds waddling along after them and shook off a halfhearted urge to find some water and throw himself in. The birds didn't seem too interested in attacking them anymore. They probably wondered what this group of stumbling, wingless things were doing dragging themselves across the snow.

"Must"—Tom spoke between gasps—"write—this—down. Long-term effect of magical exposure on wildlife."

"There must be magic in the air," said Cassie as Brine sneezed. "Can you use it?"

Peter shook his head. He didn't tell her he'd already been trying. He couldn't just pull magic out of thin air. He needed to hold it in his hands. He needed the starshell, and the starshell was back on board the *Onion* with Ewan Hughes. A drop of melting ice ran down Peter's nose. He wiped it away and walked on. Every time he raised a foot, it felt heavier. He wondered what would happen when his feet became so heavy he could no longer lift them off the snow.

Any minute now, he thought, he was going to sit down. Just for a little while. Any . . . minute . . .

He paused, looking down, a frown cracking the ice on his face. "What's happening to the ground?"

The ice looked different, less white and more amber, as if there was magic buried so deeply he couldn't feel it.

Tom stumbled into him. Cassie stopped. "That's it—we're turning back. Even Magical North isn't worth dying for."

"Who said anything about dying?" asked Marfak West. "We're here." He stamped hard, then bent his knees and jumped.

Cracks ran across the ice. With a roar like a bear, the ground gave way.

CHAPTER 24

A person passes through seven distinct stages when falling to his death. One's whole life does indeed pass before the eyes. Sensation is amplified as the screaming brain tries to cram in every last scrap of information before the universe turns forever dark.

(From ADVENTURES IN MAGIC AND SCIENCE:
THE RESEARCH AND EXPERIMENTS OF MARFAK WEST)

Ewan Hughes was the first to see the ocean darken. A ship-sized patch of sea off the starboard side, rapidly turning the color of ink. The pirates edged closer together in the middle of the deck. The *Onion* moved sluggishly, bumping between icebergs.

"Faster!" yelled Ewan, though it didn't do any good. The sails flapped once or twice and gave up on the effort. The dark patch of sea raced closer and abruptly disappeared beneath the *Onion*.

The ship sat still for a second, then something slammed into her hull from below. The pirates yelled, and the ones who weren't still tied to various things grabbed hold of one another, which wasn't a lot of use, as it only meant they all slid together. The cage with Tom's surviving messenger gull rocked on the mast where it hung. Zen ran in circles beneath it until the deck tipped a little more and he dug his claws into the planks and hung on.

Then, as quickly as it had started, the sea slapped them back flat. Groaning and bruised, everyone tried to get untangled from everyone else.

"That was clo—" began Trudi.

A jet of spray arched across them and hit the mainmast. The ship rocked. Ewan Hughes grabbed for a trailing rope and missed. Luckily, the *Onion* chose that moment to tilt back the other way, or he'd have been tossed into the sea. He scrambled back to his knees and stayed there, his mouth wide open.

A vast blue-gray head rose out of the water right ahead of them, and an eye the size of a planet regarded them indifferently. Ewan Hughes drew himself to his feet. All fear drained out of him: This was beyond fear. At least the fish-birds had made the fight seem personal.

The whale sized up the entire ship in a single look. A mouth opened, wide enough to swallow the *Onion* whole. Thought flooded back into Ewan's brain.

"The anchor!" he snapped.

He ran to it. Tim Burre grabbed hold, too, and together they threw it. It bounced off the whale's head and made a hole in the deck.

Ewan swore, but the whale vanished. For a second, Ewan allowed himself to believe they'd beaten it. He ran to the side of the ship and peered over. A shadow in the water shrank, then rapidly expanded. Ewan Hughes had less than a second to register the fact that something enormous was going to hit them before a tail burst through the icebergs. It paused overhead for the space of a heartbeat and crashed down, catching the *Onion* on the port side.

The ship skipped sideways like a pebble on a pond. Everywhere, ropes snapped free. Tim Burre tried to haul the anchor out of the deck but couldn't move it. Then the great blue tail swung around. It missed him—just—but came back a moment later and flicked the *Onion* up in the air. They landed with a prow-shattering jar. Waves washed across the deck. Trudi lost her hold on the mainsail and slid, screaming. Tim Burre forgot the anchor and ran after her.

"Hold on!" he yelled.

"What do you think I'm doing?" Trudi's expression changed. "Tim, look out!"

A shadow fell across the deck. The whale loomed over them, its tail thrashing the waves into yellow foam. Spray and ice filled the air. The mainmast cracked and toppled.

"Tim Burre!" shouted Ewan.

It was too late.

Trudi rolled free, but the mast gave a sickening crunch and fell right where Tim Burre was standing. He disappeared into the deck with a cry. And all around, pirates screamed and wood began to split as the *Onion* sank lower into the freezing ocean.

Peter had thought that falling to his death would be different than it turned out to be. There wasn't enough time even to begin thinking, and the only part of his life that flashed before his eyes was the split second in which he screamed and grabbed a chunk of ice, which snapped off in his hands. That moment seemed to go on forever, though. He didn't even notice he'd stopped falling until a pair of boots kicked him in the head and Brine's voice said, "Ouch."

Peter lay still, waiting for his thoughts to catch up with him. His companions sprawled around him, groaning. Tom's glasses hung off his face in pieces. The others had scrapes and bruises. Marfak West should have come off worst, with his hands chained behind his back, but he was the first of them to sit up.

"Where are we?" asked Peter, coughing. He struggled upright, looked around, and gaped in astonishment.

They were at the edge of an underground cavern so big the other side was lost in shadow. Sunlight flooded in through the jagged holes everyone had made when they'd fallen, and glittering spears of ice hung from the remaining ceiling. The middle of the cavern was a perfectly oval lake of dark blue water, but to reach it—and this was the part Peter was having the most trouble taking in—you'd have to clamber over an entire mountain of shiny, glittering treasure.

The floor was not so much paved with gold as buried beneath it—heaps of coins so deep you could plunge your arm in up to the shoulder and still not touch the bottom. Necklaces coiled in piles like snakes. Bracelets, rings, and earrings spilled out of decaying sacks. Discarded rainbows of emeralds, rubies, and sapphires lay in swathes.

"How could so much treasure end up here?" asked Rob Grosse.

Marfak West kicked a breastplate aside and stood up. "Nobody knows. The fact is, it's here. I promised you treasure. Help yourselves."

The pirates needed no more encouragement. They whooped and ran at the golden piles. Bill Lightning ripped open a sack of coins and started stuffing them into his pockets. Cassie picked up a sword with emeralds in the hilt and swished it.

"It's raining diamonds," shouted Rob, tossing handfuls of them in the air.

Peter watched them all uneasily. They were behaving perfectly normally, he supposed. This much treasure ought to be exciting. But he couldn't shake off the feeling that it was only bits of metal and stone, and none of it really mattered. He edged back to join Brine, who was trying to put Tom's glasses back together. "I don't like this," he said.

"Me neither." She turned her head. "What's Marfak West doing?"

The magician was picking his way across the piles of treasure to the lake in the center. "Peter," he called. "Come and have a look at this."

"Don't," Brine said. Peter brushed her hand aside.

"It's all right." He crossed the treasure to join Marfak West.

The lake was frozen over, but Peter could see water moving beneath the thin layer of ice. He put his foot on it, and cracks spread. Marfak West pulled him back.

Peter gasped, realizing the magician was no longer chained. "How did you do that?"

"Practice," said Marfak West. His voice was coldly mocking.

Across the cavern, Cassie noticed what was happening and started forward. "Let the boy go. Now."

"Make me." Marfak West's hand closed around Peter's wrist. "You really are completely stupid," he said conversationally to Peter. "You don't know the first thing about power or how to use it." He forced Peter's hand up over his head. "You don't even know, for example, that you have a piece of starshell embedded in your hand."

Peter experienced a moment of ice-cold shock, then the center of his palm blazed with heat and magic flooded out. Amber light flashed across the cavern. Necklaces writhed like snakes around Cassie's feet and tripped her. A suit of armor fell on Rob Grosse. Bill Lightning's sword twisted in his hand and stabbed him through the foot. Tom squeaked out a battle cry and prepared to charge, but the coins on the floor shimmered and opened up like quicksand, swallowing him and Brine.

Marfak West wrapped an arm around Peter's throat, half choking him. "Stay where you are, or I'll break his neck," he threatened needlessly, as everyone was too entangled in treasure to move.

Peter felt the last of the magic drain from his hand. His palm turned cold. Marfak West grunted in annoyance and threw him aside onto a pile of armor. Peter's vision swarmed with stars. He scrambled back to his feet, gasping painfully. Brine shouted something, but her voice was lost in the roaring in his ears.

Marfak West had tricked him. He'd pretended friendship, taught him things so that Peter would trust him, only so that he could stand and laugh at him now. Peter had known it all along, but he'd ignored the warnings. He'd wanted to believe that he was the only one who really knew Marfak West and, as usual, it turned out that he was wrong and the rest of the world was right.

He'd deal with the rest of the world later. For now, Marfak West was not going to get away with this. He wrested a sword out of a pile of treasure. "You can't go anywhere," he said, "you might as well surrender."

"That's what you think." The magician raised his arms and plunged them straight into the icy lake. He hissed in pain and then he stood up again and turned to face them all. A lazy smile lifted the corners of his mouth. It was a smile that said whatever anyone had been planning to do, it was far, far too late.

The sword fell from Peter's hand. Brine, struggling out of a quicksand made of coins, sneezed explosively and sat back down.

Marfak West held something roughly the shape of an egg,

but if it was an egg, it was the largest one Peter had ever seen. The bird who'd laid it would have had to be the size of a horse. It filled the magician's hands completely. And it glowed. Beneath a coating of frost, it shone softly, pure amber. It could have been made of rock or metal, or ice packed down into a hard ball, but of course it wasn't. Because something else survived the presence of magic, something besides gold and precious jewels, and Marfak West was holding it in his hands.

"Fools," said Marfak West. "All this way for a sight of Magical North and some common treasure."

Magic spilled out of the starshell and wound around Peter's legs like chains. Looking at the others, he saw that they were held fast, too. Magical North was not the end of the journey for Marfak West—it was the beginning. The beginning of a new reign of terror, only now he'd have the biggest piece of starshell in the whole world and not even Cassie O'Pia would be able to stop him.

The ground trembled. Marfak West calmly tucked a fold of his coat around the starshell and stepped backward into the lake. "Thank you for the use of your ship, Captain," he said. "Unfortunately, I've already sunk her and everybody is dead. I have my own transport from here." The lake began to churn around him.

Peter clenched his fists until they hurt. He'd been lied to, used, consistently pushed around. He'd had enough of it.

"Peter, do something," shouted Brine.

Why did everyone expect him to fix things when they went

wrong? His vision turned scarlet, and he did something that he knew was impossible—he caught up a thick blade of magic from the air and, without thinking, he used it like a sword to cut himself free. The spell gave way around his legs so suddenly he almost fell, but he kept his feet and plunged straight on into the lake. He crashed into Marfak West and grabbed hold of him as the water closed over them both.

They seemed to fall through water for a very long time. Peter's chest burned. He felt air leaking away from his nose and mouth. His arms became too heavy for him to hold on to Marfak West any longer, and he let go. His coat snagged on something, or maybe something grabbed his coat—he wasn't sure. A second before he opened his mouth, a great darkness rushed upon him and swallowed him whole.

CHAPTER 25

COLD FISH-BIRD SOUP

Ingredients:
1 fish-bird
Salt
Onions
Water (or you can use seawater and leave out the salt)
Cut the fish-bird meat into small pieces (can be done with a cutlass) and boil with the onions in plenty of salted water until falling apart. Allow to cool, and serve cold. If you are near any icebergs, you may chip off pieces and add them to the soup to chill it more quickly.

(From COOKING UP A STORME—
THE RECIPES OF A GOURMET PIRATE)

"Tim Burre!" shouted Ewan. He ran to the fallen mast and heaved. The deck creaked under him. Black spots danced across Ewan's vision, and he felt a muscle in his shoulder tear, but then the mast started to move. With a final gasp of effort, he hurled it aside, where it made another hole in the deck.

Tim Burre lay facedown just below in a pool of seawater.

He'd been lucky, Ewan thought: The mast had made a hole in the deck and he'd fallen straight through.

Not that lucky, though—he wasn't breathing.

Trudi came to join him. "I think we're supposed to kiss him or something," she said. She didn't look very eager to try it.

Ewan pushed her aside, clamped his lips over Tim's, and blew into his mouth. After a few seconds, Tim coughed, rolled over, and spat out water.

"I could have done that," said Trudi, clearly relieved that she hadn't had to. But she did hug Tim when he sat up.

Ewan looked at the crew gathered round him, silently counting up the damage. They'd lost eight people altogether. All but one of the rowing boats were smashed, as were three of the four masts, and the last one was leaning at an alarming angle. The deck had holes everywhere, and seawater came through as fast as they could bail.

A muffled squawk came from under a pile of timber. Ewan pulled it aside and found the cage with Tom's remaining messenger gull buried underneath. Miraculously, the gull was still alive. It huddled in the bottom of the cage, a bundle of damp feathers with accusing eyes. A moment later, Zen clambered out from under a neighboring heap of timber and shook himself.

"We should write a message," said Trudi, lifting the cat away from the birdcage. "At least people will know what happened to us."

They'd know, but they'd never believe it, Ewan thought.

For a moment, he considered it. It was the humane thing to do. One of the gulls had already died. Why keep the last one locked up here to die, too, when the *Onion* sank? He picked up the cage. The others seemed to know what he was thinking; they nodded. Trudi turned her face away.

Ewan stepped over the fallen mast and wedged the cage securely into a flap of sail. "We're not going to send any messages," he said, "because we're not going to die here. We'll make it back, and we'll tell stories so fabulous that all the islands will think we've gone mad. All right?" He turned, fixing a grin on his face.

No one met his gaze. Trudi tried to smile but didn't quite manage it. "Cassie will come back," she said, drawing a pattern in a puddle with her toe. "Cassie always comes back."

Ewan clapped her on the shoulder. "Of course Cassie will come back." He laughed aloud. The sound fell on silence. Ewan didn't care. He gazed around with narrowed eyes. Nothing had changed. If anything, they were sitting slightly lower in the water than before. They were alone and sinking in the frozen ocean. And yet . . .

He slapped his hands together. "Right, you lot, we've got work to do. Repair and salvage. Dry clothes, food, whatever might be useful, bring it all on deck. We can use some of these broken planks to build rafts. Whatever you do, keep out of the water. And don't let Zen eat the messenger gull—we might still want her later."

The pirates stirred into reluctant action. Ewan made his way to what used to be the prow. A broken square of wood bore part of the letter *O*. He held it in his hands for a long time before hurling it into the sea. Several fish-birds ducked out of the way and reconvened in a circle. Ewan wondered why they weren't attacking, but of course they didn't need to. All the birds had to do was wait, and the cold would soon do their job for them.

Ewan clamped his teeth together, determined not to shiver. Whatever else happened, he was not going to let everyone sit here, waiting to die. They'd escaped from worse catastrophes than this. Cassie would be back soon, and she'd know what to do. Cassie O'Pia always knew what to do.

━‥╫╫╍●

"Cassie, what do we do?" shouted Bill Lightning.

"I don't know!" Cassie yelled back.

Brine felt the magic give way around her, and she fell forward just as a stalactite crashed down. Another one landed as she ran to the lake.

"Peter!" She would have jumped into the water after him, but Rob Grosse grabbed her round the waist.

"It's too late," he shouted in her ear. His voice was almost lost in the roar of falling ice. "He's gone."

"Let me go!" Brine kicked him in the shins. He let go of her in surprise but grabbed her again straightaway.

Cassie seized a shield in one hand and Tom in the other. "Brine, he's right. There's nothing we can do. We have to get out of here, or we'll all die."

Brine didn't care if they all died. She shook with cold and fury. She'd let Peter go. She should have known what he was going to do and she should have stopped him. Instead she'd just stood there and watched, completely useless.

Cassie deflected another stalactite with her shield. It bounced away and smashed straight through a pile of treasure, leaving a gaping hole.

Tom gave a shout. "A tunnel! Boswell said there was a tunnel leading up. What if he came the other way?"

Then the tunnel would lead down. Brine stopped fighting Rob. Bill staggered across to join them, his face and clothes white with ice. Brine wiped her hair out of her eyes. Her hands came away damp with tears. Cassie was right: They had to get out of here.

A whole section of ceiling fell in with an angry roar and a snow-bear picked itself up, shook its head, and fixed its eyes on Cassie as if she were the source of all its problems. Cassie threw a goblet at it. "All those in favor of staying here and getting eaten by the snow-bear, say 'aye.'"

No one said a word.

"And all those in favor of seeing where this tunnel leads?"

They piled through the gap just as the snow-bear charged.

Brine's hand struck solid rock. She tried to back out, thinking the tunnel—if it was a tunnel—was blocked, but the others were pushing in behind her, and then, as she groped down, she found a gap she could squeeze through. Sounds of shouts and roaring and more ice falling followed her. After a while, every-thing became quiet. Only Cassie's voice drifted out of the dark-ness, saying the words that Brine had been bracing herself to hear.

"Well," said Cassie, "that could have been worse."

CHAPTER 26

I am writing this, not in any hope that someone will one day read my words, but because I wish to complete the record of my journey before I die. I set out to find Magical North, and I succeeded. Nothing else matters.

(From ALDEBRAN BOSWELL'S JOURNAL OF STRANGE
ADVENTURES IN THE YEAR OF DISCOVERY)

Something inside Brine snapped. "How?" she demanded. Her voice cracked. "How could this possibly be worse? Marfak West won. We practically handed him a giant piece of starshell. Peter's gone. We're trapped in a hole with snow-bears waiting to eat us. And even if we get back to the boats, there's no point, because Marfak West has sunk the *Onion*. With that much starshell, he can turn the ship to sawdust." Tears filled her throat.

"Also, my glasses are still broken," added Tom in a small voice.

"Let's not be so quick to give up," said Cassie. "We're all still here. Except for Peter, and we'll rescue him next. Marfak West may be a problem, but we'll think of something. The *Onion* has survived far worse than him. I bet they're all sitting about snacking on toasted fish-birds and wondering where we are. And"—she wriggled past Brine—"I do believe this tunnel keeps going down. Shall we take a look?"

Brine didn't have the energy to be angry anymore. *Why not?* she thought. Given that they were all going to die, why not see where one small tunnel led?

It led down, of course. They half slid, half crawled along it, bracing themselves against the sides with arms and legs. Gradually, the air became warmer—and lighter. A silver glow crept up to meet them. Brine could see her hands in front of her face again. She edged back. "What is it?"

"I don't know," said Cassie, "but as long as it's not more tunnel, I'm happy." She crawled on faster and then, without warning, she disappeared. A moment later, they heard her voice. "Everyone, you have *got* to come down and see this."

►╍┼┼┼●

It was a sight that was worth more than all the gold in the world: a river. It rushed away from them along the middle of a wide underground channel. Great ribbons of Stella Borealis lit up the rocky ceiling, and a gap in the roof let in a bright burst of sunlight. But even the relief of seeing the sun again was nothing compared to the wonder of seeing a ship.

She sat wreathed in silver mist, rising and falling with the movement of the water, changing as she moved. In one blink, Brine saw a vessel made of wood, so scorched and scarred it looked like it had been in a fight with a dragon. With the next

221

breath, she was looking at a ship out of a legend. A great, golden hull rose in a proud curve, four times the size of the *Onion*. Sails of pure copper stood stiffly on silver masts, the whole thing blazing like the setting sun. But whichever ship Brine saw, the same word curled around the hull. They all knew what it said—even Rob and Bill who couldn't read. The pirates had seen almost the same word every day for years. Only one letter was different.

ORION.

The back of Brine's throat ached, and she didn't think it had anything to do with her allergy to magic. This was Boswell's ship and Orion's, both at the same time. A century of magic had fused the real ship with the story until you couldn't tell them apart. She turned to see what Peter thought of it and remembered he wasn't there.

Cassie climbed the mooring rope and landed on the deck. "Come on up."

Bill and Rob followed, Bill limping from where he'd stabbed his foot back in the cavern. Brine stayed on the bank. All she could think about was how Peter was missing this, and it was all her fault. She'd yelled at Peter to do something, and he had.

"Peter will be all right," said Tom, seeming to guess what she was thinking. "Marfak West wouldn't have jumped into the lake without a plan. If Peter's with him, he'll be alive."

Brine shook her head. "Cassie told me to look out for him. If I'd been nicer—"

"Then things might be different, or they might not be,"

said Tom. "Does it change them now to stand here feeling guilty?"

Brine turned to look at him. He was so eager to explore the ship he couldn't keep his feet still. She sighed. "After you, then."

Everything on board had the same dual quality they'd seen from the shore, as if the ship were still trying to decide whether to be ancient or merely old. The ropes thrummed when Brine touched them. A small rowing boat tied up under a tarpaulin was called the *Celestial Shallot.*

Bill opened the hatch that led belowdecks, and they climbed down into darkness. Brine put her hands out and felt wooden panels on either side. A corridor, she guessed, then her eyes started to adjust and she guessed again. They were in the ship's hold, and she was standing between two rows of crates. Rob climbed up and pried the lid off one. "Empty," he announced.

"So's this one," said Bill. "These people must have sailed from the other side of the world to use up this many supplies."

"Or the crates were empty to start with," said Brine. "They were expecting to find treasure, remember."

Fire flared behind her and Cassie appeared holding a lantern. "I think I've found the captain's cabin."

A narrow door stood half-open. The room, like the rest of the ship, kept changing. In one view, it was cramped and dark, with cracked floorboards and a table and chairs made out of old crates. In the other, Brine saw an airy chamber with furs on the floor, tall windows, and delicate furniture made of white wood. But in both views, the table held a book with an old ink pot and quill next to it, and a pair of glasses.

Brine's heart thumped. She felt like she was tramping through somebody's grave. Cassie, who didn't care where she tramped, picked up the glasses and gave them to Tom. They all watched as he slid them onto his nose and blinked uncertainly. A broad grin spread across his face.

"I can see!" He adjusted the lenses with trembling fingers. "They're almost perfect—no, they *are* perfect." He turned full circle, then his newly perfect gaze fell on the book and he let out a shriek like a seagull.

Cassie yelled, too, and whipped out her sword. Bill attacked the nearest object, which happened to be the table.

"Stop!" bellowed Tom. The shout rattled the inkpot.

Bill gave a low chuckle. "Who'd have thought it? The librarian's got a voice inside him after all."

Tom glared at him over the top of his spectacles. It seemed to be a special, librarian sort of glare, because Bill shut up at once.

Brine picked up the book and blew the dust off the cover. *"Aldebran Boswell's Journal of Strange Adventures in the Year of Discovery,"* she read. "Tom, is this . . ."

Reverently, as if he was handling something infinitely more precious than mere paper, Tom took his copy of Boswell's journal out of his pocket and laid the two books side by side. He didn't even look at Brine as he began turning pages. He seemed to have forgotten anyone else was there.

He came to a place where his copy of the journal was blank. The original continued.

The twenty-seventh of Balistes. The first mate is dead, killed by a bear. Only ten members of the crew remain. They wish to leave, but the sun has not yet set.

The twenty-eighth of Balistes. Another man dead.

The thirtieth of Balistes. I am the only one left.

The thirty-first of Balistes. Orion's Day. Today, at last, the sun set. The stories are true. I stood at Magical North and I saw the world. Was it worth it? Who can say? All my supplies are gone, and I cannot sail this ship alone. Tomorrow I will leave this ship and walk into the snow. Maybe I will rise into the stars like Orion.

That was the last entry. Brine sat down shakily. Boswell had done it. He'd stood at Magical North. She wished he'd written down some of what he'd seen. "Why did he do it?" she asked.

Cassie picked up the lamp, sending shadows flapping up the wall. "Who knows why scientists do anything. Tom, did Boswell bother to mention where exactly Magical North is?"

Tom nodded. "That's the best bit. The ship is anchored right on it."

They gathered back on the foredeck. The Stella Borealis flickered around them, turning the sunlight that flooded the tunnel an eerie green.

"I can't see anything," said Cassie.

Of course she couldn't. Brine pushed a hand through her hair, gazing about. "It's no use. You can only see Magical North on Orion's Day when the sun sets."

"What's the date today?" asked Rob.

Tom rubbed his nose. "It's hard to tell because it's been light for so long. We crossed the Sea of Sighs on the twenty-eighth, and the sun hasn't set yet, so . . ." His voice trailed away.

Slowly, disbelievingly, Brine raised her face to the patch of visible sky. Sky that was turning orange. Her thoughts spun to a halt, and her chest tightened with a growing hope that felt painful. So much had gone wrong, but finally luck had turned in her direction.

Sunset.

The last shred of daylight faded from the tunnel. The only light came from the Stella Borealis. It coiled around the ship, flashing through every color in the rainbow. A silver circle appeared on the deck. It was just big enough for one person to stand in, and the air inside shimmered with the soft amber light of pure magic.

"It's Orion's Day," said Brine. "We did it." It didn't seem possible. She caught Cassie looking at her, and she smiled. "Luck's a funny thing."

Cassie nodded, but she frowned at the circle of magic as if

she was thinking of something else. "We don't know how long this will last. Brine, you'd better get on with it."

Brine's mouth fell open. "Me? But you're the captain."

"And I, as captain, order you to stand on Magical North," said Cassie. Her eyes were hard and bright. Brine wondered what it was that she was afraid of seeing. It didn't seem right to go first, though, when they'd all waited so long.

"Tom, you wanted to see the world," said Brine. "Why don't you do it?"

He shook his head. "I'd only want to see my mum, and I already know where she is."

"Bill? Rob?" asked Cassie. "Either of you want to try it?"

They both stepped back. "I've already seen more than most men alive," said Bill. "I don't want to push my luck."

"Off you go, then, Brine," said Cassie. "Quickly, before I decide to throw you in."

Brine shut her mouth hard. There were plenty of things she didn't want to see, either. Peter drowned, for one, and Marfak West gloating. Or Peter and Marfak West laughing together about how they'd tricked her. She ground her nails into her palms then let out a breath and forced her fingers to uncurl.

Cassie gave her a push from behind. Feeling as if she were walking a plank to her death, Brine stumbled forward and put both feet onto the exact point of Magical North.

CHAPTER 27

Stories deal in superlatives. No one wants to hear about the second greatest hero or the second most evil magician in the world.

(From ALDEBRAN BOSWELL'S SCIENTIFIC STUDY OF STORIES)

The ship vanished. Brine's eyes streamed, her ears filled with a high-pitched buzzing, and the pain in her nose grew until she was sure her face would explode. Then, as if her allergy had reached some sort of critical point where it couldn't possibly get any worse, the desire to sneeze vanished.

And she saw the world.

Marfak West had said it would appear as a map spread out before her. He was wrong. Brine saw everything in a stream of moving images: the whole story of the world, from the birth of the first ocean until the time far into the future when the last drop of water would dry up under the dying sun.

The knowledge was like a weight crushing her until she couldn't breathe. Now she knew who she was—she was nobody. An accidental scrap of life on a world that was already doomed.

She shut her eyes, not that it mattered, because she couldn't see for tears. No wonder nobody wanted to stand on Magical North. No wonder Boswell had doubted whether the journey had been worth it.

And yet, some other voice inside her wouldn't accept it. Boswell had been dead for a century, but he'd created a story that had stretched all the way back to the legend of Orion and forward to Brine's own time. Would Boswell say that didn't matter? Or what about the Book Sisters of Barnard's Reach, held captive by another story? Or Baron Kaitos and his fallen tower—a story to make you laugh every time you heard it?

The people who'd lived, the stories they'd created with their lives, the way they'd shaped the world, they all mattered.

Brine opened her eyes with a gasp. Straightaway, she saw her own story. A rowing boat, tossed this way and that on rough seas. Then the *Onion*, tiny against the oceans, old and tired but bright with dreams, and with the memory of something proud riding in the hull.

The images around her kept changing. Brine found that, if she thought about something, it would come into view. For a moment her thoughts flew to home and an island took shape before her, but she turned her back on it. Home could wait: They needed a way out of here. She concentrated on the present moment instead. The air shimmered and she found herself looking past the ship and along the tunnel, all the way to the frozen ocean. The ice there appeared impenetrable, but Brine saw where the river flowed and where the warmth of magic had weakened the ice so that it would crack if something as heavy as a ship should force its way through.

She almost called out to the others . . .

But then she saw Peter.

▶⁺⁺╫╫◖

There are many horrible ways to wake up. Regaining consciousness face-first in a pile of half-digested fish while an angry magician punches you between the shoulder blades was a new one for Peter.

He spluttered and spat out seawater. "Where am I?"

Marfak West stopped hitting him. "Take a guess."

Peter sat up unsteadily. His gaze took in piles of dead fish and pools of murky water that bobbed with unidentifiable lumps of stuff—stuff he was quite glad to leave unidentified. Domed walls made him think they were in a cave, except that they flexed slowly in and out and smelled even worse than the fish. The only light was a faint, silvery glow that came from the starshell tucked inside Marfak West's shirt.

"We're . . . ," began Peter. He couldn't say it. It was entirely too terrifying.

"In a whale of a belly," said Marfak West. "And the other way round as well." He sat back on what looked like the hump of an old rowing boat. He appeared perfectly at ease, as if being swallowed by a giant fish was all part of a normal day for him. He spread his hands out over the egg-shaped bump in his shirt. "Have you any idea how much magic this starshell contains?"

Peter shook his head, trying not to breathe in too hard because every time he did, it clogged his lungs with the stink of semidigested fish.

"Neither do I," said Marfak West, "but I'm guessing it's too much for even me to handle alone. Now that I have you, the task will be much easier."

"What task?" Every breath made Peter feel ill.

Marfak West stroked the starshell through his shirt. "I don't blame Cassie, you know. When she sank the *Antares* and left me for dead, I could respect that. She almost beat me. She should have tried a bit harder, but the Cassies of the world are like that—they never see a job through to the end. They know what needs to be done, but they don't quite have the courage to do it. Fortunately, I don't suffer from that problem." His face was a mask, hard and cold—or maybe everything up to this point had been a mask and Peter was finally seeing the magician for who he really was. His throat was so dry it hurt to swallow. Brine had known. She'd never been taken in by Marfak West, not for a second. Peter wished she were there. He didn't have the faintest idea what to do. A feeling like homesickness swept over him, and he had to blink away tears.

"You've beaten Cassie now," he said. "You've beaten them all. You've won. What do you want me for?"

Marfak West grinned at him. "You were the one who followed me, remember? You're wrong, though: I haven't won, not yet. Not until Cassie's story is erased and everything she did is undone. You're going to help me with that. To tell you the truth,

I've gotten used to having you around. I'm going to give you something I never had—proper teaching. I'm going to make you my apprentice, and you will repay me by obeying me, learning well, and carrying my work on into the future."

Peter turned colder than the inside of a fish. A lifetime with Marfak West. It would be a million times worse than Tallis Magus. "You can't do this," he said. His voice shook.

"Who's going to stop me? Cassie? She's dead. All your friends are—I persuaded this lovely whale to make a slight detour and sink the *Onion*. It's just you and me now."

The words fell like a hammer, and Peter believed them. Marfak West didn't lie—not when he knew the truth would hurt you. Peter already knew there was no hope. Even if the others had escaped from the cavern, there was still the long walk back to the boats, and without the *Onion*, they'd be trapped. Cassie, Tom, Brine—all dead. Peter wanted to curl up into a ball and cry, but he didn't want Marfak West to think he was weak. He stared straight ahead. "You might as well kill me, too, then, because I'll never be your apprentice. Never."

Marfak West's eyes narrowed. "That's what you think. We'll start your first lesson now. You're going to thank me for saving your life."

No—no way was he going to thank him, not for anything. He bit his lip and shook his head. That was when the itching began. It started at Peter's feet and crawled up his legs to his spine. By the time it had reached his head, he was scratching frantically.

"Lesson one," said Marfak West, watching him suffer. "Disobedience has consequences. If there's one thing I hate most, it's ingratitude. Is it so hard to say two small words to me?"

Peter ground his teeth. The itching continued—he wasn't sure how long, but it felt like an eternity. His skin burned. He dug his fingernails into his flesh until he bled, but that only made it worse. Itching piled upon itching, stretching out with no end in sight, until he knew he'd do anything, say anything, to make it stop.

"Thank you." The words were forced out on a gasp and felt like a betrayal of everything.

The itching stopped at once. "No, thank *you*," said Marfak West. He gave a little bow.

Peter collapsed back into a puddle. And then, not caring whether Marfak West was watching, or what he thought, he curled into a ball and cried.

CHAPTER 28

I wandered lonely as a ghost
That floats on oceans green and blue,
When all at once I saw a host
A crowd of onions in my view.
Beneath the trees, across the shore
Fluttering and dancing evermore.

And just as when I see the stars
That twinkle endless overhead,
My silly eyes filled up with tears
For my own *Onion* is dead.
Beneath the waves, beneath the sea
Forever gone and lost to me.

And now I will return to land,
Back to the home where first I came,
For nevermore will I command
A ship with any other name.
But when I die, please bury me
Beside my *Onion* at sea.

(LAMENT ON THE DEATH OF THE *ONION*, by Cassie O'Pia)

Brine saw Peter collapse, crying, and her own throat burned. She tried to call out to him that Marfak West was lying, that they were all alive, and they were going to escape and rescue him, but she couldn't make a sound. Then Peter's face faded and another image sprang into view. This time Brine did shout out loud, because she saw the *Onion*.

The ship—or what was left of her—listed low in the sea, with water slopping over the shattered edges of the deck. The sails were gone, and the masts. The crew scurried this way and that, tying together pieces of wood into a raft while, around them, fish-birds gathered in increasing numbers, waiting quietly while the sky slowly turned black. A few stars appeared overhead—the constellation of Orion, burning bright, and a last sliver of red sunlight sank slowly into the sea.

The sun vanished, and as night rushed in, the magical light around Brine went out. She stumbled backward, groping blindly in the sudden darkness.

A pair of strong hands caught her. "Steady," said Cassie in her ear.

A light flared. Tom held a lantern up. Brine pushed Cassie aside. "We've got to go. Marfak West's got Peter, and the *Onion* is sinking. *Now*," she added, afraid they were going to get into another pointless discussion.

Cassie's expression set hard. "Did you see a way out of here?"

Brine gulped and nodded.

Cassie swung away from her. "Then what are you all waiting for, you scurvy knaves? All hands on deck!"

The setting of the sun was worse than the never-ending daylight. Ewan Hughes had become used to the unnatural green sky. Night somehow felt wrong. He lit another lantern and watched the crew work. To his left, six pirates were lashing planks together to make rafts while, on the right, two human chains were jeering each other on as they raced to pass bundles of goods from belowdecks. Trudi, not one to let a little thing like the sinking of her galley stop her from cooking, had lit a barbecue mid-deck and was roasting skewers of meat.

"Fish-bird on a stick?" she offered Ewan. He took one. It tasted every bit as bad as he'd expected. Holding it, he surveyed the wreck of the *Onion*. Another section of wood broke away and splashed into the sea. Fish-birds darted after it and tugged it underwater.

"Cassie will come back," said Trudi. "There's plenty of time yet." She pushed her frizz of hair back off her face and smiled nervously. Tim Burre limped past backward, dragging a plank. Stepping out of his way, Ewan felt a frown forming. Everyone was staying far too busy, trying to fill up every second with activity so they didn't have to think about what was going to happen next. He walked to the side of the deck and stared out.

If Cassie wasn't back by sunset, she'd said, Ewan should leave without her. He shook the thought away angrily. Cassie was coming back. Cassie came back from everything. She was the greatest sea captain in the world, ever, and she wouldn't abandon her ship.

Ewan stood and watched—he wasn't sure how long—until faint fingers of light crawled back across the sky. The sun was coming up again. The sun that set only on the evening of Orion's day, he remembered. They'd missed seeing Magical North. He guessed it didn't really matter.

He glanced down at the half-eaten fish-bird kebab in his hand, shrugged, and tossed it overboard.

"I don't think you should have done that," said Trudi.

A faint rattle of sound swirled around them: the clattering of angry beaks. Fish-birds popped their heads out of the sea and more of them leaned forward from the ice floes, shuffling their feet and jigging their wings up and down in a vengeful dance. Ewan's legs trembled and he felt himself take a step forward. Too late, he remembered he was no longer tied to anything, and he didn't care. He wanted to give up and fall into the sea because there really wasn't any point carrying on.

But even as fish-birds closed in around what was left of the ship and Ewan's legs took him another step closer to the edge, he drew his sword. If there was such a thing as an afterlife, he promised himself, they'd all go into it fighting.

The fish-birds snapped their beaks: It sounded like applause.

And then, before another word could be thought or spoken, there came a rush of wind and a flapping of sails and the rising sun was momentarily blotted out as something dark and shaped like a ship shot around the side of the ice floes and headed straight for them. Suddenly released, Ewan collapsed to the deck. Hammers and swords and the untied ends of rope fell as every crewman, woman, and cat forgot everything else and stopped to stare in an utter eye-bogglement of disbelief.

The ship wasn't real. It couldn't possibly be. It was a figment of a desperate imagination, no more. Any moment now, it would vanish, and they'd be back with the icy sea and fish-birds trying to drown them. Yet, in the moment while he waited for reality to set in, Ewan saw a long hull of auburn wood that glowed as if a thousand lanterns were burning inside it. Above the white sails fluttered a flag marked with a gold ring, and on the prow, written in letters as tall as a man and edged in gold, one word: *ORION*. And, standing on the deck, waving frantically, was Cassie O'Pia.

"Ahoy, my hearties!" she shouted.

"Pieces of eight!" yelled Brine enthusiastically.

Fish-birds fled as the incoming ship cut through the ice floes. Ewan Hughes watched them go and wondered if this was part of the dream as well. He let go of his sword. The ship swung in a great arc and came to rest alongside the stricken *Onion*. A rope hit the deck by Ewan's feet.

Ewan shook himself out of his stupor. If he was having a dream, it was a remarkably stubborn one. And, by the look of the crew, they were all having it as well. A slow grin spread across his face. He stood and picked up the rope, leaned back on it to test it, and then—with a cry of "Happy day-after-Orion's-Day!"— he swung across the gap.

~~>++++||+&~~

The sight of the *Onion* had brought tears to Brine's eyes, but then she'd spotted people on the wreckage, and when Ewan swung across to Boswell's ship, she didn't think she'd been so glad to see anyone ever.

"I see you've had a spot of trouble," said Cassie.

Ewan Hughes was grinning like a madman. "Nothing we couldn't handle. Where's Marfak West?"

The urge to cheer died in Brine's throat. "He escaped," said Cassie, throwing a quick glance at her. "Peter went after him. While we all stood there, he ignored the danger and threw himself after the vilest man in the world. He's a hero."

Brine watched Tom's lips move silently, and she knew he'd be writing all this down later. Peter would like being the hero of the story—if he ever found out. And of course he would, because they were going to find him.

She kept that thought in her head while the crew brought across the supplies they'd managed to salvage from the wrecked *Onion*. The fish-birds watched, but they didn't seem to like the new ship, and they kept their distance.

Half an hour later, it was done. Brine looked overboard into the dark water, the last resting place of too many brave people.

The *Onion* didn't deserve to end up like this, none of them did—and this wasn't over yet, she reminded herself. They still had to find Marfak West.

Cassie clapped her hands, calling everyone to attention. "So here we are," she said. "We've lost friends, we've lost the *Onion*, but we're not defeated. We are going to find Marfak West, and we're going to send him to the bottom of the ocean where he belongs." She turned in Brine's direction. "But first," she added, "we have an initiation to perform."

Without warning, she swung round and seized Brine, lifting her off her feet so fast that they were halfway across the deck before Brine worked out what was happening.

"What are you doing, you mad pirate?" she shrieked. "Let me go!"

Ignoring her, Cassie carried her to the side of the ship and held her over the side. Brine immediately stopped yelling "let me go!" and started yelling "don't drop me!"

"You see how quickly someone can change her mind about what she wants?" Cassie joked. She adjusted her grip on Brine's arms and bobbed her up and down.

"Will you let me go?" shouted Brine.

"Certainly," said Cassie and dropped her.

A heartbeat of screaming, plummeting panic, then a hand caught Brine's wrist, nearly dislodging her arm from its shoulder as she jerked to a stop. She opened her eyes to see Cassie grinning down at her. Cassie helped her back over the deck rail, and Brine picked herself up, shaking and furious.

"What do you think you're doing?" Her heart hammered loud enough to deafen her. "Don't you know how cold that water is? You could have killed me."

Cassie stood back, a faint smile on her lips. "Did you really think I was going to drop you?"

Brine balled her fists. "I think you're all a pack of idiots, that's what I think. You don't know the first thing about pirating. You couldn't even sell me and Peter on Morning without making a mess of it. You listened to Marfak West and nearly got us all killed. And now Peter's been swallowed by a whale, and I bet you're not going to do anything about that, either." Her throat burned.

"But did you think I was going to let you go?" said Cassie.

Brine wiped the back of her hand across her eyes. "No, of course not. But—"

"Good." Cassie put a hand on her shoulder. "That means, deep down, you trust me. And that means next time I do something that looks incredibly stupid and dangerous, you'll back me up." Her gaze flicked round the rest of the people gathered. "I don't care if my crew thinks I'm stupid. I don't care if they make up silly songs behind my back." She gave Ewan Hughes a quick smile. "All I ask is for them to trust me when it matters. And that's especially important if you're going to be my chief planner."

Brine's mouth opened and shut. "I thought you never made plans."

"That was before we needed them," said Cassie. "Maybe if

we'd planned better, we wouldn't be here now." She glanced down. "Anyway, you seem to have a knack for it, and the rest of us haven't had a lot of practice, and . . ." She cleared her throat. "And anyway. What do you say?"

Brine gulped. She couldn't make plans. Or, rather, she did, and they always went wrong. Like on Minutes, and then Morning, and then when she'd rescued Tom from Barnard's Reach, which she hadn't really planned very much in advance . . . but it had worked. When she thought about it, most of the plans that had gone wrong had worked out all right in the end, because they had brought her here and, even if she didn't quite know how yet, she knew they were going to find Marfak West and rescue Peter.

She couldn't speak, since her throat felt too full of tears, but she nodded.

"Then you are officially a member of the *Onion* crew," said Cassie. "Welcome aboard."

The others crowded round. Ewan Hughes shook Brine's hand solemnly. "Anytime you feel like learning how to kill someone with your bare hands, I'll be happy to teach you."

"How about now?" Brine muttered, shooting a dark glance at Cassie. But she couldn't keep herself from smiling. She was part of the crew. She belonged.

Then she saw Tom. He was sitting against the deck rail. The cage with his messenger gull, brought across from the sinking *Onion*, stood beside him and the lone gull inside was squawking at him, but Tom paid no attention. He was looking down at a little bundle of sailcloth in his hands. Two feathers, one black, one white, were stuck carefully to the front. "My other gull," he said sadly, holding up the bundle for Brine to see. "She made it back after all. Ewan saved her for me."

Brine sat down next to him. "Of course Ewan did. You're one of the crew, too."

He shook his head. "I'm a librarian, not a pirate."

"You can be both. Look at Trudi. She's a cook and a pirate."

"Yes, but she's not a very good cook."

The thought made Brine giggle. She couldn't help herself. Tom looked like he was going to laugh, too, but his eyes filled with tears instead. He bowed his head. "I don't know why I'm feeling like this. She was only a bird. There are millions just like her. It's not as if one seagull really matters, not compared with everything else."

Brine pulled him to his feet. Holding his hand, she walked with him to the side of the ship. "She was a brave gull," she said. "She traveled where no gull had ever gone before, and she did her job. She came back, even though she had no message to carry."

Tom smiled through his tears. Gravely, he stood and released the gull's body into the water. They stayed there for a long time, looking down at the sea. It was the first day of Octopus, Brine thought. The first day of winter. She glanced up in time to catch the tail end of a twist of crimson as the Stella Borealis bled and sighed. All the pirates were gathered on the other side of the ship, and, as Brine walked to join them, she saw why: The *Onion* was sinking.

Waves washed the length of her deck. Every plank of wood rattled, as if the stricken hull was drawing one last, labored breath. Then she fell apart. The deck planks slid away one by one, the stump of the mainmast bowed to touch the foam-capped waves. A moment later, even the mast had vanished.

A lone rowing boat bobbed on the settling waves, and the pirates hauled it aboard. "It's the one we found you and Peter in," Cassie told Brine. Her eyes were red, her smile far too bright. Brine swallowed the lump in her throat. She nodded her thanks because she couldn't trust herself to speak. The salvage of one small boat was nothing compared with the loss of the *Onion*.

"Where to, Captain?" asked Ewan. His voice was rough and cracked.

Cassie looked at Brine expectantly. Brine looked down at her feet. She bit her lip. "Marfak West said he was going to undo everything you did. Where would he start?"

"The *Antares*, of course," said Cassie.

"The *Antares*, which you sank. Then you know where the wreck is."

"Yes . . . oh." Cassie brushed a hand across her eyes. "South," she said. "All hands on deck, and hurry. We have a whale to catch."

CHAPTER 29

Spellshapes are limited only by the magician's imagination. Most magicians never go beyond what they themselves have been taught, and this is a good thing, for magic is most dangerous when combined with an active imagination.

(From ALDEBRAN BOSWELL'S BIG BOOK OF MAGIC)

hift yourself, crybaby," Marfak West said. "We're leaving."

Peter glared at him sullenly. His head ached and his eyes were sore, but he didn't feel like crying anymore. He felt like punching Marfak West in the nose, although that was probably not the best idea. He stood up and almost fell straight back down as the meaty floor quivered.

Marfak West took hold of his collar. "Stay close."

He drew a circle in the air. For a second or two, Peter thought the magician was casting a finding spell, but then magic appeared all around them, enclosing them both in a shining bubble.

A deep groan ran through the whale's belly, then a noise like thunder. The whale's stomach shrank rapidly as a dark wall rushed toward them. By the time Peter realized he was seeing water and opened his mouth to scream, the flood had swallowed him. But instead of drowning him where he stood, it flowed up and over his head, beating at the edges of the magical light but not breaking through.

Peter drew in a cautious breath and found he was still breathing air.

"What—" he began.

Water surged, carrying him with it. His feet broke through the protective magic and plunged into freezing sea. Peter snatched them back. Marfak West laughed, apparently enjoying the whole thing.

With a final, agonized belch, the whale opened its mouth, and they tumbled out into the huge, black depths of the ocean.

Silence. Sudden, deep silence. All Peter could hear was his own breathing, slowing as fear gave way to a strange sort of wonder. The whale watched them with mournful eyes that could have been human apart from their size, then it swung slowly around and swam away.

Marfak West floated gently in the air bubble, smiling broadly.

"Are you going to turn us into fish now?" asked Peter, half hoping that the answer would be yes.

"You're wasting air." The magician gathered a handful of magic and cast a light down.

The wreck of the *Antares*—it had to be the *Antares*—spread out like a gigantic, half-finished puzzle directly below them. As the light glided over it, Peter saw the crushed timbers, shells, and seaweed heaped over the shattered masts. Remnants of sail tugged and drifted in the water. A fish flitted past Peter's face and landed inside the air bubble. Marfak West caught it and flicked it back into the sea with surprising gentleness and began drawing spellshapes, too fast for Peter to follow.

The *Antares* stirred. Shells flew off in flurries as if the hull were shaking itself awake. Broken pieces of wood crawled together and levered themselves upright to become masts.

Peter realized, too, as his legs suddenly became wet and cold, that the air bubble was shrinking. He was outside it from the knees down. He shot a glance at Marfak West, hoping the magician hadn't noticed. If he had, he might decide he needed the air more than he needed an unwilling apprentice.

Marfak West's head turned, and his eyes narrowed as if he'd guessed exactly what Peter was thinking. Peter gulped in a lungful of air. In the same moment, the air bubble shrank so it barely covered his head and shoulders, and Marfak West gave him a push that sent him spinning out of the bubble altogether and into the sea.

Oddly, Peter found he didn't care. He'd almost drowned once already, and it hadn't been too bad. There were fates worse than death, and at least he hadn't had to marry Penn Turbill's bladder-faced daughter. And he'd seen the world—not many people could boast about that. Not that he'd be able to boast about it, either, because you had to be alive to boast and he was just about to be disqualified. He wondered if his body would even float to the surface from this depth. He wondered . . .

His last thought faded away.

$\blacktriangleright\cdots\dagger\dagger\dagger\cdot\blacktriangleleft$

Brine stood at the prow of the new *Onion*—Ewan Hughes had repainted her name as they sailed. The ship was still changing, the deck planks shifting from pale ash to a dirty bronze and back, but the changes were happening more gradually now, and the color shifts were less extreme, as if the ship was settling on some halfway stage between legend and reality.

"Boswell said the universe is indecisive," said Tom, joining her. "It generally doesn't make up its mind about what it wants to be until somebody stares at it for a while."

At that moment, Brine couldn't have cared less what Boswell thought of the universe, but at least it stopped her from wondering how long someone could survive inside a giant fish, especially with Marfak West for company.

Tom frowned at her. "I read a story once about a man who was swallowed alive by a giant squid. He had to eat his way out. It took him a week, and forever after, the smell of fish sent him screaming inland."

Brine sighed. Tom blushed and took off his glasses to clean them. "I mean . . . you never know what might happen, that's all. I bet Marfak West could live inside a whale for a year if he wanted. What with him being the world's most powerful magician."

"Just as well he's so powerful, then, isn't it?" agreed Brine. She didn't want to be cheered up. She left Tom and wandered away to the back of the ship, where she leaned on the deck rail and watched the sea foam behind them. The sky was back to normal, and the wind was in their favor. Even the storms were staying away. Once or twice Brine heard a rumble of thunder in the distance, but that was all. She felt that she should be glad, but instead a weight the size of a whale settled on her shoulders. She couldn't get the image of Peter, crying, out of her head. Peter never cried. Even when Tallis Magus used to hit him, he'd pretend that it hadn't happened or that he didn't really care. To have witnessed him crying made Brine feel that the world was broken.

She didn't even smile when Zen pounced at her feet and missed, and when she spotted Cassie O'Pia making her way over, she groaned inwardly. Now Cassie was going to try to cheer her as well.

Brine stood up. "Don't try and tell me everything's going to be all right. You can't know that."

To her surprise, Cassie didn't argue. "True," she said. "Pirates have many abilities, but seeing the future is not one of them. I have no idea how this is going to turn out. But that's half the fun, isn't it? Would you really want to start a story knowing how everything will end?"

Brine shrugged. Cassie watched her for a while, twisting and untwisting the emerald around her neck.

"Don't you care?" Brine burst out. "We found Magical North, and Marfak West has stolen the world's biggest piece of starshell. Some of your crew are dead! Peter is kidnapped, and you lost the *Onion*, but you're all carrying on as if none of it matters."

Cassie dropped her gaze to the deck. Her fingers slipped from the emerald. "Things change," she said slowly. "That's the only thing you can rely on. The souls that have gone, let them rest in peace. As for the *Onion*, a ship is only a piece of floating wood. Anyone who goes seeking revenge because a large piece of floating wood gets sunk turns into . . . well, turns into Marfak West."

Brine bit her lip and said nothing. She hated that Cassie was right.

Cassie turned away from her to watch the flag that flew almost straight out from the mainmast. "We have to carry on. It's either that or give up, and the *Onion* never gives up. Otherwise everything and everyone we've lost will be for nothing." She laid a hand on Brine's shoulder. "We'll get Peter back. Don't worry."

"Who says I want him back?" grumbled Brine. Peter was a pain in the backside, and half the time she was with him, she felt like strangling him. And yet she'd grown so used to him being around that, without him, she almost felt she'd lost part of herself. In other words, Peter was the closest thing to a brother she was ever likely to have.

"Thanks," she said, and she found that she meant it.

Cassie flashed her a smile. "I was going to give you these," she said, taking out the box that held Marfak West's starshell. "But given your allergy, it's probably best if I hold on to them until we rescue Peter."

Brine nodded, although, strangely, her nose wasn't itching. At Magical North, she'd felt that her head was going to explode, but since then there'd been nothing, not a single sniffle. Something had changed inside her. She wasn't the child who'd once huddled in a rowing boat, terrified and sneezing. She straightened up and drew in a deep breath. "So what are we going to do?" she asked. "Charge in without a plan?"

"Certainly not," said Cassie. "We have a chief planner now, remember? This time we're going to charge in *with* a plan."

First came the feeling that he was flying, and then Peter felt a gentle warmth enfold him, as if the sun had somehow broken through a mile of sea to shine on him in his last second of life. And now a figure loomed over him, silhouetted in the light. The spirit of a long-departed ancestor, most probably. Whoever it was, Peter wished it would stop trying to talk to him. He was *tired*.

"If you're going to lie there all day," said Marfak West irritably, "you can at least move over a bit so you're not quite as in the way."

Peter opened his eyes with a start. He was lying on rough boards with the sky above him. Wind—real, fresh, nonfishy wind—ruffled his hair. Marfak West stood a few feet away, holding the giant starshell in both hands and grinning like a wide-mouthed shark.

It took Peter a full minute to sit up. After another minute, he managed to look around without feeling as if his head were about to fall off.

"Why didn't you let me drown?" he asked.

"You're my apprentice. Why should I let you drown? I knew I had enough air left to get you back to the surface—I just didn't want you wasting any of it. Say hello to your new home."

The thing Peter was sitting on was moving through the water, so it had to be a ship, but it was unlike any ship he'd ever seen before. The deck was a wide oval, roughly the color of old blood. Around it, eight legs spread out, crablike, into the sea. Little flecks of pure magic floated everywhere. Peter's eyes burned with staring. He staggered to his feet. "This is the *Antares*?"

"With one or two modifications." The tips of the magician's fingers were pure white from holding the starshell. "I'll have to rebuild her properly later, when there's time. For now, the magic is holding her together." He turned away from Peter and stamped on the deck. A hatch slid open, and a slender gold column rose out of it. Marfak West set the starshell on top. "I think you should start calling me Master West now."

Peter thought he should start calling him Stinkhead, but he didn't dare say so. He glared at the magician, tight-lipped. The world felt unreal, probably because they were plowing through the waves on a ship that looked like a giant spider. He watched as the glowing column sank back through the deck, taking the starshell with it.

"A ship like this needs a power source," Marfak West said, seeing Peter's curious gaze. He started peeling pieces of loose skin from his fingers.

"But you're not touching it. How are you still controlling it?"

"With magic," said Marfak West irritably. Peter noticed the way his chest puffed up. He liked to be asked things. He liked to show he was cleverer than everyone else.

"I thought I was supposed to be your apprentice," said Peter. "I need you to teach me."

"You need a good slap round the head," grumbled Marfak West, but Peter could see he was trying not to smile. "There are many ways of using magic. Most people know only one—hold on to some starshell, pull the magic out, make the right spellshape, and let the magic go. It's the way they were taught, and they never imagined there could be anything else. But you can, for example, learn to draw magic from a piece of starshell without needing to touch it. Or even straight from the air if there's enough magic around. Or you can write spellshapes straight onto a piece of starshell so that it will continue casting those spells, over and over, until the starshell runs out of magic. For example, my starshell is currently holding the *Antares* together and moving it through the water, and I'll be adding a lot more to that by the time I'm finished."

Peter only half listened. *Drawing magic from the air.* In the cavern at Magical North, he'd used magic, without thinking about it, without any starshell. Had he really done that?

"Can you become allergic to magic?" he asked, thinking of Brine. He had to swallow the lump that rose into his throat. Brine was as irritating as sunburn; she'd gotten him into trouble more times than he could remember, and yet he missed her.

Fortunately, Marfak West didn't seem to notice. "An allergy

is possible, I suppose. Overexposure might do it. Why do you want to know?"

"No reason," said Peter quickly. He made a show of looking around. The ship was traveling far faster than should be possible, its giant legs moving back and forth like oars. "Where exactly are we going?"

Marfak West's grin broadened. "You mean you haven't guessed?"

CHAPTER 30

Nine out of ten emergencies are caused by failing to follow procedures correctly. But a true emergency may arise, such as:

1. Fire
2. Flood
3. Attack by pirates

In the rare case of a true emergency, every Book Sister should follow the orders of the Mother Keeper.

(From THE RULES AND REGULATIONS OF BARNARD'S REACH, VOLUME 16: IN CASE OF EMERGENCY)

This is it?" asked Brine.

The *Onion* sat in a patch of ocean that was several shades darker than the waters around it. Cassie drew up a bucketful, and when Brine put her hand in, it felt warmer than it should. Warm with magic, maybe. Brine wished she would start sneezing to confirm it, but her allergy appeared to have deserted her just when it might have been useful.

Cassie emptied the bucket back over the side. "This is the exact spot. Right where we sank the *Antares*."

Beside her, Rob Grosse hung over the side of the ship, staring into the water as if he expected to see the *Antares* rising from the depths at any moment. "Maybe he hasn't gotten here yet."

Brine shook her head. Her insides were as empty as the ocean. They'd arrived too late; she knew it. Marfak West had already left.

"What now, Chief Planner?" Ewan asked her, breaking into her thoughts. Brine shot him an irritated glance. Ever since Cassie had made her the official planner, people seemed to think they weren't allowed to do anything without asking her first. The truth was, she'd been trying her hardest, but the place in her mind that should have been filling up with plans was still blank. Marfak West was the one with all the plans; the *Onion* had just been following behind, and far too slowly, it seemed. The magician could be anywhere by now.

No, that wasn't true. Marfak West could take all the starshell in the world, but he'd still be Marfak West. He could only be himself. What did he want most? Brine screwed her face into a frown, trying to remember every detail of the conversation she'd seen and heard from Magical North. First the *Antares*, then what? "He said he was going to erase Cassie's story," she said slowly. "He said he wouldn't have won until her story was gone and everything she'd done was undone." She fell silent. Her gaze shifted slowly to Tom, and a dreadful, empty feeling settled inside her. "Where do all stories live?"

One by one, everybody on board turned to look at Tom.

The color fell from his face, his eyes widening first in realization and then fear.

Ewan Hughes said it first, although everybody was thinking it. "Barnard's Reach," he said. "He's going to destroy Barnard's Reach."

▶┉┼┼┨❤

Barnard's Reach. Peter should have known. The island where all the stories in the world were written down. It was here, in the stories, that Cassie had become a hero and Marfak West a villain. The one place in eight oceans where Marfak West was not allowed to go—a group of librarians daring to tell the world's most powerful magician what he could and couldn't do.

Peter gazed out at the multiple images of the *Antares* reflected in the Mirrormist, and he shivered. Occasionally, in the reflections, he saw a close-up of his own face. The first time it happened, he gasped, wondering who the skeletal figure was. All he needed to do was grow tall and lose his hair, and he'd look like Marfak West.

"This is it," said Marfak West. "We are going to change the world together, Peter. With all their stories gone, people will have a blank page, a chance to start again, unhampered by any twisted notions of heroism or villainy. No longer tied to the past, we will truly be able to look to the future."

Peter shivered. "But even if you destroy Barnard's Reach, people will still know the stories. They'll still tell them."

"We'll deal with that later," said the magician. His face was set like stone. "Stories are an infection, and the only way to deal with an infection is to cut it off at the source. Barnard's Reach is the source."

The *Antares* slowed in the water, then stopped. Peter wondered why, then he saw that the Mirrormist had thickened right in front of it, acting like a shield to keep the ship out.

"We can't get through," he said, trying to keep the sudden surge of hope out of his voice.

Marfak West cuffed him around the head. "Don't tell me what I can't do. The Mirrormist won't let me through because it recognizes me as a threat. But you're so pathetic you couldn't threaten a sand snail. It's time you started earning your keep. Go and tell those boring book readers that they have one hour to surrender to me before I tear their island apart. Hold out your hand."

Peter obeyed and screamed as his flesh suddenly turned into a furnace. The black spot in the middle of his palm flared with bright amber magic. The pain quickly subsided, changing to a dull throb that pulsed all the way past his elbow.

"I've linked the *Antares*'s magic to the starshell in your hand," said Marfak West. "I'll be able to work magic through you, and I'll be keeping an eye on you, so watch what you say. Now, stand still."

A glowing circle appeared on the deck around Peter's feet. "What are you doing?" he asked, or rather he started to, because the ship abruptly vanished and he was standing on top of a cliff, surrounded by seagulls, with the same circle of magic turning the grass brown. He yelled in fright and fell over.

When he made it back to his feet, people were watching him. Six women stood in a line. They were all dressed in brown robes identical to Tom's, and five of the women carried swords.

"I can see you, remember," Marfak West's voice said in Peter's ear.

The women watched Peter curiously. His heart thrummed. He wanted to run away, but he could barely stand up, his legs were shaking so much.

The unarmed woman pushed back the hood of her robe. She was the Mother Keeper, Peter guessed. She fit Brine's description of her—pale face, yellow hair, and a mouth that was set in an angry straight line. "A boy?" she said. "Is that the best he can do? You're breaking the rules, boy. Men are not permitted here—not even undergrown ones."

Peter's legs stopped shaking, and he backed up a step. Couldn't she see he didn't want to be there? He was only a messenger, and a most unwilling one at that.

His palm tingled warningly, reminding him that Marfak West could see and hear everything. "Marfak West is back," he said. "He's alive, and he's right on the other side of the Mirrormist. If you don't surrender, he'll destroy Barnard's Reach."

"This is exactly why men should not be allowed to read," said the Mother Keeper icily. "It gives them ideas, and men with ideas are always trouble." She clasped her hands in front of her. Her fingers were stained blue with ink. "Go back to your master and tell him Barnard's Reach will not surrender so much as a single book to him."

Marfak West was not his master, but there was no point trying to tell the Mother Keeper that. "I don't need to tell him," said Peter. "He can hear you."

The Mother Keeper's eyebrows rose. A thin, bright pain cut through Peter's head, making him gasp. "Never doubt my power," he heard himself say, but his voice was the voice of Marfak West. "I am giving you one chance to live. Surrender."

The Mother Keeper laughed. It was the worst thing she could have done.

Peter's palm flared with heat. He knew with a sick certainty what was about to happen. He closed his fingers over his palm and tried to keep the magic in, but Marfak West was controlling it and Marfak West was a lot stronger than he was. Peter could only watch as a thin snake of magic crawled out of his hand and twisted itself into a shape that seemed to writhe and crawl in the air. Peter tried to drag it into a harmless arrow or circle, but he might as well have been trying to pull down a mountain with his bare hands.

The librarians raised their swords threateningly, but the spell blazed to life quicker than any of them could attack. A ball of magic struck the Mother Keeper between the eyes. For a second, she stood, swaying, her mouth open in shock, and then she began to shrink. Her features disappeared, her arms shriveled away. Her robe tumbled onto the grass and lay still, a discarded puddle of cloth. A fat, pink worm crawled out of one sleeve.

Peter's stomach heaved. He would have collapsed if Marfak West hadn't held him upright. "You have one hour," he said in Marfak West's voice. "Surrender or you'll all die." Then the island blurred and Peter felt a wrenching sensation, as if his insides were being pulled out. He looked down and saw a circle forming around him; he shut his eyes. When he opened them again, he was back on the *Antares*.

Marfak West grinned at him. "Well done, apprentice."

"I'm not your apprentice!" Peter yelled, shoving him away. He stumbled to the edge of the deck and threw up over the side. "They won't surrender," he said. He wiped his mouth on his sleeve. "It doesn't matter how much time you give them."

"I know. I need the hour to get through the Mirrormist, but let them think I'm being generous. Now, would you like to see what I've been doing while you were away?"

Peter shook his head. Whatever Marfak West had been doing, it couldn't be good. His ears filled with a dull pounding. He thought he was imagining it, but then he started to feel the vibration through the floor: a rhythmic thumping like the tramp of hundreds of feet.

A door opened across the deck and Cassie O'Pia came out and waved at him.

Peter's legs nearly gave way. *Cassie, here?*

Then the rest of the crew came marching out. Ewan Hughes took up his usual position at Cassie's shoulder. Rob Grosse and Bill Lightning stood together, Trudi and Tim Burre fell in behind them. Everyone was there except Brine and Tom. This wasn't happening. Cassie was Marfak West's sworn enemy. She wouldn't have joined forces with him, not willingly. The magician must be controlling them.

"Let them go," said Peter.

Marfak West laughed.

Another door opened. Cassie O'Pia came out of it and waved at him. Peter blinked. A pair of Ewan Hugheses took up position on either side of her, then three identical Trudis, another Tim Burre, and, last of all, Brine, who for some reason was completely bald.

"Peter, meet the crew," said Marfak West. "I call them my pirate copies. Attention!"

The last word was snapped to the pirate copies, who stamped to attention and saluted. Some of them hit their neighbors in the face. Some of them hit themselves in the face.

"They're not particularly bright," said Marfak West, "but they make up for it in numbers. Now, I'd like you out of the way for the next hour. Pirates, take the boy to the brig."

Twenty Cassies advanced across the deck. Peter screamed. The circumstances seemed to require it.

CHAPTER 31

Rules are a statement of how the world usually works, and this is their problem—they deal with the usual. When faced with the extraordinary, rules fail us.

(From ALDEBRAN BOSWELL'S BOOK OF SCIENTIFIC KNOWLEDGE)

Ready?" asked Brine.

Tom nodded, cradling his trembling messenger gull against his chest. With his long hair blowing in the wind and his library robe tucked up into his belt, he looked like a warrior from a story, about to go into battle.

Imagine the stories if we succeed, Cassie had said once. Brine bet that even Cassie had never anticipated this happening. And now, if they didn't succeed, all the stories of Barnard's Reach would be lost.

Tom released the gull. The pirates all watched her fly to the top of the mainmast, perch there for twenty seconds or so, and then, as if finally realizing she was free, spread her wings and take off into the sky.

"You think she'll really be able to find her way to Barnard's Reach?" asked Brine. Every direction looked the same to her.

Tom nodded. "Messenger gulls always find the way home. Mum will know we're coming."

He kept staring up into the sky, his face creased with worry. Cassie nudged him. "I can't wait to see the look on your mother's face when we turn up at the last minute to rescue her."

Tom smiled, but the worry didn't leave his eyes. "If you don't mind, I'd like us to turn up before the last minute. Just so we have a bit more time to do the actual rescuing."

The crew went back to work, and as the *Onion* sped on, Brine stood beside Tom, both of them watching the horizon. The gull had already vanished into the clouds, and there was no sign of anything ahead, just a big, blue, empty sea.

The *Onion* picked up speed. Brine listened to the familiar sound of the wind in the sails and the slap of water on the hull. The creaks and thuds settled in a rhythm and she seemed to hear another sound beneath them—a quiet and steady *thud-thud, thud-thud*, as if someone was beating a drum very gently just below her feet. She tapped her fingers on her leg in time with it, counting the seconds go by. The new *Onion* traveled fast, but Barnard's Reach was still over an hour away and Marfak West might be at the island already.

"We'll get there in time," said Brine, but it sounded very much like she was trying to convince herself.

Ursula had been on hourglass duty when she heard the cries. She abandoned the glass without a thought and ran.

Outside, one Book Sister was clutching an empty robe. Another was holding a pink worm in her cupped hands. Others were in tears. Ursula couldn't think properly. A gaping hole had opened up where all her thoughts should have been, and a single word echoed in the emptiness: *Tom.* Something terrible had happened to Tom. She didn't know how she knew it; she just did. She seized the nearest Sister. "What's happening?"

"Marfak West," the Sister said.

Of all the answers Ursula was expecting, that didn't even come close.

The Sister pointed across the grass toward the sea. "Marfak West is alive." Her voice was flat with shock. "He turned the Mother Keeper into a worm, and if we don't surrender within an hour, he'll destroy the island."

Ursula's hand slid from the Sister's robe. She couldn't feel her fingers. Marfak West was dead; she'd helped send out the news herself. This had to be a trick, someone using his name to frighten them.

Or, a quiet voice said in her mind, *maybe evil like Marfak West doesn't die that easily.* And now he'd done what everyone had expected: He'd come back.

She waited for someone to tell her what to do next, but nobody did. Nobody was going to, she realized. The Mother Keeper was the only person who gave orders; everyone else just followed them. There were no extra rules to tell you what to do if the library was attacked by an evil magician.

No rules, maybe, she thought, but they had something better—they had stories. Rules were the opposite of stories. Rules only allowed you to do one thing, but stories opened up a thousand possibilities.

Ursula stepped forward.

"Everyone, go back inside and start packing up the books. Seal them in boxes and make sure they're watertight. We'll throw them into the sea if we must, but we're not going to let Marfak West have them."

The Sisters stared at her. For a moment, Ursula thought they weren't going to do it, but then one of them nodded and started back inside. Another followed her, and another, until they were all hurrying back through the door.

They worked furiously, carrying heavy boxes up the stairs. On her fourth trip back out, Ursula noticed a bright patch in the Mirrormist. She stopped. One by one, the Book Sisters joined her and they all stood and watched in terrified silence. The patch in the mist was growing. The dense white fog that protected the island from intruders was slowly giving way to the pale blue of defenseless sky.

One of the Book Sisters began to moan softly. Ursula's heart thumped in her throat. Mirrormist was gathered from all the magic that flowed north. The sea fogs caught it and the movement of the tides through the caves that riddled the island drew the fog around it like a shield. Over the centuries, the Book

Sisters had carefully chipped away at the stone passages to direct the sea and keep the Mirrormist constant around the shores of Barnard's Reach. Ursula couldn't begin to imagine the power it would take to cut through it like this.

"Get back inside," she ordered. "We'll keep working as long as we can, and after that . . ." After that, she didn't know, but she'd think of something.

The Book Sisters obeyed. Ursula stayed outside, watching the sky and the ever-expanding patch of amber light. She almost didn't see the gull that swooped out of the fading Mirrormist straight at her. It fell into her hands with a shudder of exhaustion, and Ursula saw the canister on its leg.

Two minutes later, she was running into the library and down the stairs, waving a slip of paper and not caring how much noise she was making. Book Sisters stopped as she burst into the science library.

"We're saved," Ursula gasped. "The *Onion* is coming. They're coming back." Tom was coming back: that was what she meant. He was alive, and nothing else mattered compared with that.

The room shook as she spoke. Bookcases trembled, spilling their contents. The Book Sisters stood frozen for a moment, then raced to gather them up.

Ursula's euphoria faded. She left the Sisters to their task and headed on down the stairs. *The* Onion *had better come soon*, she thought, *or there won't be a library to come back to.*

CHAPTER 32

Even magic cannot create something out of nothing. It is possible to change matter from one form into another, but you can't hold things in the wrong shape for long. Physics doesn't like it.

(From ALDEBRAN BOSWELL'S BIG BOOK OF MAGIC)

Brine stood with Cassie's telescope to her eye and turned slowly. She ought to be able to see something by now, but save for a bright patch in the sky up ahead, every direction looked the same.

Tom was reading Boswell's journal again. Brine wondered at his ability to shut out all the noise on the ship and lose himself between the pages. She put the telescope down but kept watching the sea. You can't plan ahead when you're floating about on the ocean, she remembered Cassie saying—and Cassie, as usual, was three-quarters right. You could make plans, but you had to be ready to change them all. You got to choose your starting point and a general direction, but a lot of the time, you just had to go with the waves and see where they took you. Like a child in a rowing boat.

She looked back at Tom. He was lucky, she thought—his upbringing was beyond weird, but he knew exactly where he came from. Still, at least Brine knew where she was going now. That made a difference. She didn't feel so adrift anymore.

She kept watching until, after what seemed like hours, Tim Burre shouted from the top of the mast. "Ship ahoy!"

If it was a ship, it was the least ship-shaped one Brine had ever seen. It didn't float; it loomed. It squatted on the sea with wooden legs, and everywhere Brine looked, she saw spikes and sharp angles.

And even that was nothing compared with the light that came off it. It blazed in pulses from between the ship's front legs, and each new burst looked like a miniature shooting star. Pulse after pulse smashed through the tattered remains of the Mirrormist and into the cliffs of Barnard's Reach with a fury that made the sea tremble.

Cassie took the telescope from Brine, whistled softly, and then fell silent, watching intently. Ewan Hughes took a look and nodded, his face grim. "I guess we're going to fight that thing, then."

Cassie shrugged. "I suppose we might as well. It'd be a shame to come all this way for nothing."

>-++}}}●

Peter sat in a cage in the dark and scratched at the bump in the palm of his hand. One tiny fleck of starshell against all of Marfak West's magic. He might as well give up now, he thought miserably.

But he didn't. Cassie would never decide she was beaten, no matter how bad things became. He looked again at his hand. One tiny speck of starshell, but it was warmed by his flesh, fed by his blood—and, all of a sudden, his blood felt ready to boil over.

He reached through the bars of the cage and felt the lock. As far as he could tell, it was an ordinary, nonmagical one, much like the one Marfak West had taught him to open on the *Onion*. Of course, when he'd done it last time, he'd had Marfak West's starshell to work with, not this useless splinter in his hand.

You can draw magic straight from the air if there's enough around. Marfak West had said so, and Peter had already done it once before. The *Antares* was held together with magic—it could spare a little. Peter held out his hand and concentrated. He had no imagination, Tallis Magus used to say, but Peter knew what it felt like to hold pure, raw magic in his hands. He imagined that, imagined magic leaking slowly out of the ship and filling the starshell splinter in his palm.

"'A great magician is like a skilled artist,'" he said aloud, quoting Boswell. "'With the tiniest amount of magic, he can perform wonders.'"

He wasn't sure if what followed counted as a wonder. There was a lot of prodding and pushing, trying to feel the hidden pieces of the lock and move them into the right position so they would turn and open. His palm burned with the effort. But just when he thought he couldn't do it, something gave way inside the lock and it dropped softly off the cage into his hand. The door swung wide.

Peter suppressed a shout of triumph. He contented himself with a quick and silent grin and stepped out into the room. All right, so he was still on a ship powered by magic, crewed by an army of pirate copies, and captained by a madman who wanted to destroy the whole history of the world, but at least he wasn't in a cage anymore. As Cassie would say, it could be worse.

It soon was. The door opened. Peter scarpered back into the shadows just in time as two Cassies came marching in.

They saw the empty cage and stopped. And Peter did the first thing that came into his head. He sang.

Oh, she's strong and she's swift, and if you get my drift,
She is all that your heart could desire.
For one chance to see her, fair Cassie O'Pia,
A man would walk naked through fire.

The song made him think of the *Onion*, and that thought gave him courage. He stepped out into the room, gathering a slender thread of magic from the starshell in his hand as he moved. He didn't bother forming it into a shape. As he sang "fire," he squeezed it into a ball and threw it. An amber streak hit the first Cassie between the eyes. The second one managed to draw its cutlass before another burst of flame set it on fire from head to foot. It staggered, arms waving, then collapsed in on itself. A few last flames flickered. The air stank like charred fish.

Peter's new courage evaporated. His knees shook and almost gave way. He'd just killed two . . . two somethings. What if they'd been real people? He couldn't afford to think about it. He clenched his teeth and sidled past the mess on the floor, then crept out the door.

Small patches of amber light lit the corridor at intervals. The walls looked like they were made of copper and buzzed softly. Peter ran his hand over one. The surface might have looked like metal, but it felt like wood, and each piece trembled as if it was on the point of bursting apart. The various parts of the *Antares* were being held together against their will.

He reached a place where the corridor forked in two, and he paused. One of the corridors felt much colder than the other, and when Peter turned in that direction, he could see his breath on the air. He could also see a group of Ewan Hugheses waiting for him. He threw a handful of magic, driving them back, and with that, the starshell in his hand ran dry.

For a moment, he just stood there, hand still raised, trying to think of an appropriate swearword. The Ewans stared back with unblinking eyes. Peter looked around for a weapon and counted several swords and cutlasses—unfortunately all in the hands of the Ewans.

The first Ewan ran at him. Peter sidestepped, and the pirate copy smacked into the corridor wall, a cutlass sliding from its hand. Peter grabbed the weapon and backed away. The cutlass felt far too light for its size, and the hilt was slippery.

Ewan Number Two swung at him. Peter ducked under the blade in a reflex action that was pure luck. He slid and almost fell as he turned, but managed to head-butt the Ewan in the back. His hands felt clammy. No, worse than that—cold, wet, slimy. He looked down. Instead of a cutlass, he was holding a large and very dead haddock.

Even magic cannot create something out of nothing. Boswell had said that somewhere. The pirate copies must have started their lives as something else. Now that Peter knew what he was looking for, he could see the magic coiled around them in a shape that reminded him of the spell Marfak West had used to turn the Mother Keeper of Barnard's Reach into a worm.

"You're fish," he said in surprise. "You're all fish." He slapped the nearest Ewan with the haddock. "This is what you ought to look like, remember?"

The spell that had held the Ewan together began to unravel. The pirate slid to the floor, legs—no, *tail*—flapping. Seconds later, an oversized flounder was gasping its last breath at Peter's feet. He snatched it up and, with a fish in each hand, advanced on the remaining Ewans. One of them managed to skewer Peter through the arm before turning into a crab and scuttling away. Peter gasped but kept moving. He was hurting and covered in fish, yet strangely elated. Marfak West must surely have heard the commotion by now, but Peter didn't care. Let him come. The last Ewan fell. Tucking a spare fish into his belt, Peter ran until he saw a doorway filled with amber light, and he knew he'd found the starshell.

Five minutes. Brine's stomach churned. She wished she hadn't eaten Trudi's seafood pancakes for breakfast. Or any breakfast at all, for that matter. Five minutes, and they'd be within range. She forgot for a moment that she was Brine, planning officer on board the *Onion*, and she went back to being Brine the servant, hiding in the kitchen while Tallis Magus shouted outside.

She put a hand on her cutlass hilt to steady it. Tallis Magus was half an ocean away, she told herself firmly. She didn't even need to be thinking about him. And while the *Antares* looked like something she might dream about on a bad night, it was only a ship. Cassie had defeated it once before, and they'd do it again now.

Brine heard the clink of metal behind her and turned. Tom was walking across the deck, clutching a sword and shield. His face was the color of damp clay. "Don't try and stop me," he said. His glare was fierce but his voice trembled. "This is my home, and I'm coming with you." He brandished his sword awkwardly.

Brine smothered a smile. She and Tom together had to be the least fearsome warriors ever.

"You can't come," she said. "You have to stay on board—it's part of the plan."

"What plan?" Tom's mouth grew tight. "You're making this up, aren't you?"

Then Cassie was behind him, plucking the sword from his hand. "You said that the pen is mightier than the sword. It's true. A sword can only destroy. A pen creates. Anybody can wave a sword around and hit someone. But to put words on paper in just the right order, to take the dull truth and gild it with the first layer of legend, that takes real talent." Her gaze traveled from Tom's sword to his face. "There are three kinds of people in the world—those who listen to stories, those who tell them, and those who make them. Think what would be lost if we fought the greatest battle in the world and no one could put it into words."

Slowly, Tom began to smile and Brine could almost sense the words of a new story forming behind his eyes.

Cassie slid Tom's sword through her belt and Brine slowly released her grip on her own cutlass. Cassie beamed at them both. "That's settled, then. You'll stay on board the *Onion*. Both of you."

Brine gave a squawk of protest, echoed by the circling gulls.

"You're my planning officer," said Cassie. "You don't plan a battle from the middle of it." She turned to Tom. "And while Brine is planning, somebody has to captain the *Onion*, and I'd be a whole lot happier knowing it was someone with a shred of common sense."

She paused, waiting for Tom to understand what she'd just

said. It took him a couple of seconds. His mouth fell open. "Me? *Captain?*"

"I can't think of anyone better. I hereby appoint you Acting Captain in Case of Emergency, and in my book, this is the exact definition of an emergency. What do you say?"

She held out her hand. Tom studied it as if he'd forgotten what hands were for. Eventually, he reached out and took it. A grin spread across his face, so wide it made his glasses wobble.

"I say get to it, you scurvy knaves!"

>++++++⦿

Peter skidded to a halt. He was in a room lit by burning torches. The starshell sat on its pedestal in the center, streaming magic. A million colors appeared and disappeared across the amber shell, pulsing as if something inside it were breathing. Peter stood transfixed, watching. This was starshell—true, real starshell as it ought to be. All these years, he'd called himself a magician when he'd just been messing about with tiny, broken scraps. Now Peter understood what had driven Marfak West to the top of the world. If Peter had known this existed, he'd have gone anywhere, done anything to lay his hands on it.

Then the starshell flared with light, and a bolt of magic shot out, fast as a spear. The floor shook, and a few seconds later, Peter heard a rumble as if rocks were being torn apart. Marfak West was attacking Barnard's Reach already, Peter thought. He started forward. However beautiful the starshell was, he had to destroy it. It was the only way to save the island.

"Sorry," he said. He didn't know who he was apologizing to—the starshell couldn't hear him. A couple of Ewan Hughes copies came running through the door. Peter turned them back into herrings and slapped his hands flat onto the starshell.

It was like being hit over the head with a storm. Peter let go with a yell. His hands felt as if they were on fire. He didn't know how Marfak West could stand it, not even for a second.

A passable imitation of Marfak West came through the door. Peter hit it in the face with a fish.

Nothing happened.

"Nice try," said Marfak West. His voice was like acid.

Peter tried to run, but his muscles locked rigid. It was all he could do to twist his face into a scowl. The euphoria that had filled him turned cold. It was a lot easier to believe he could beat Marfak West when he wasn't actually standing nose to nose with him. He watched the starshell flicker. It was absorbing magic, drawing it in from the air as fast as it could—so fast that it was taking the heat out of the air along with it. That was why it was so cold in here.

Peter suddenly found that he could move again. He sagged. "Why don't you just stop? You don't need Barnard's Reach. You can have any island you like."

Marfak West stared at him. "Stop the attack? Why would I do that? Their stories turned me into a villain: They've got only themselves to blame when I act like one. Soon we will build new stories together, on the ruins of the old ones. But first we're going to put our hands on the starshell, draw out every last bit of magic, and drown Barnard's Reach in a tidal wave so great they'll feel it on Morning."

Peter swayed. He bit his lip and concentrated on staying upright. The sharp taste of blood in his mouth told him he'd bitten a little too hard. Marfak West was mad. Peter had known it before, but now he saw it with horrible certainty. Maybe magic had corroded away his sanity or maybe he'd been born that way, but the result was the same.

A bell clanged overhead. Marfak West glanced up. "Enough of this. I can control you through the starshell in your hand, remember. Either you will do as I say or I'll make you." He jerked his head at the remaining pirate clones that were lurking by the door. "Bring him," he ordered them.

The bell stopped ringing as they emerged onto deck. Barnard's Reach was on fire—everywhere. Instead of Mirrormist, all Peter could see was thick, black smoke. But then he saw what else was out there.

It was the *Onion*, but not the *Onion*. It cut through the waves toward them, like a ship through butter. Gulls circled its masts, and Peter was sure he could see people on the deck waving. His heart leaped.

"Cassie's dead, is she?" he said.

Marfak West slapped him across the back of the head, but the magician was smiling. He'd hoped this would happen, Peter thought, and a thrill of surprise ran through him. Now he understood why the magician had saved him from drowning at Magical North, why he'd kept him alive, and why he was so determined to turn him into his apprentice. For all his talk of revenge and rewriting the past, there was something he wanted more than anything else: an audience. In the absence of Cassie O'Pia, he'd made do with Peter, but now Cassie had arrived, and she'd done it just in time to see Marfak West tear Barnard's Reach apart.

CHAPTER 33

All you villains dismay, for she's coming your way,
And soon you will villain no more.
You'll die with a cheer, because Cassie O'Pia
Is a sight that is worth dying for.

(From THE BALLAD OF CASSIE O'PIA,
Verse 210, Author Unknown)

Deep underground in the book cellars, Ursula could barely see for the dust that filled the air. Most of the Sisters were coughing as they emptied the bookcases and packed manuscripts into boxes. The floor trembled almost constantly, each new quake more violent than the one before. Pieces of bookcases littered the floor, several Book Sisters were nursing injuries, and one unlucky Sister hadn't been quick enough to move when a set of shelves fell; she lay frighteningly still.

The case Ursula was emptying shuddered and toppled forward. Ursula jumped aside as books and manuscripts crashed down around her. She felt cold water soaking through her shoes, and she looked down to see water bubbling through a crack in the floor.

"Everyone, get out," she ordered. She snatched a pair of manuscripts out of the water. Their edges were wet, but the writing was still readable. "Take what you can carry. We've lost this room."

"But the books," protested a Sister, pale with shock.

"We can't save them." Ursula choked on the words. Some of these books were older than the library. Centuries' worth of stories about to be lost forever.

There was no time. She hurried the Sisters to the stairs. The crack in the floor suddenly opened wide, and the sea flooded in behind her.

She locked the door and ran up the stairs. While the Sisters ran to the next set of books, Ursula headed for the gull room.

The birds were all huddled fearfully in their cages. The moment Ursula entered the room, they sent up a shrieking that made her ears ring. She unlatched the windows and pushed them wide, then she started opening cages. It took the first gulls a few moments to decide they were free. The others caught on quickly. They surged through the open windows, calling out as they beat their way up into the sky.

Very soon, Ursula was standing in an empty room, surrounded by feathers. She wiped a splodge of white droppings off her shoulder. The Mother Keeper would be furious, she thought, before she remembered the Mother Keeper was a worm and probably beyond caring about anything.

From a distance, Brine had thought the *Antares* looked like a floating nightmare. Close up, it was worse than a nightmare: a mass of splintered wood and sharp bits of metal that bent in the wrong places. It looked like a spider that had been trodden on and put back together by someone who'd never seen one. But then she saw Peter standing next to Marfak West, and her heart leaped. He was alive.

"Surrender!" shouted Cassie. "Hello, Peter."

Peter waved. Marfak West slapped his arm down. "The *Antares* refuses to surrender."

"Does it refuse to sink?" asked Cassie. The *Onion* swung around so it was sideways to the monstrosity. Cassie caught hold of a rope, preparing to swing across.

"Do that, and I'll make you regret it," warned Marfak West.

"Oh, yes? You and whose army?"

A spiteful grin split the magician's face. "Funny you should say that."

Doors snapped open all around the deck of the *Antares*, and Ewan Hugheses marched out. They came in formation, ten at a time, each row pausing to salute Marfak West before marching on to take up position around him. Within a minute, they filled the entire deck, and still they kept coming, until every doorway was crammed full of sword-waving Ewan Hugheses.

"Meet my Ewan Hughes army," said Marfak West.

Brine rubbed her eyes. She had to be dreaming.

For half a second, Cassie stood, immobilized by astonishment—but only for half a second. Her sword rang free.

"Charge!" she cried.

"Repel boarders!" shouted Marfak West. He took hold of Peter, and the two of them sank through the deck of the *Antares*, vanishing from sight. And with a yell that made the ocean tremble, every pirate attacked.

---

wan Hughes—the real Ewan Hughes—paused next to Tom with his foot on the deck rail. "If this goes wrong," he said, "I don't want you to waste time trying to rescue us. Your job is to keep the *Onion* safe. If it looks like we're losing, don't wait. Turn around and get out of here. It doesn't matter where you go, just go. Sail like you've never sailed before."

"I never *have* sailed before," said Tom with a worried frown.

Ewan clapped him on the shoulder. "Great—then you'll be good at it." He winked at Brine.

"How are they going to know you're the real Ewan Hughes over there?" she asked too late. Ewan had already gone. They all had—only Bill Lightning and a few of the crew remained behind. Brine's hand ached with the effort of keeping it away from her cutlass. She should be over there with the others, not standing here uselessly with Tom. Besides, if she didn't get to rescue Peter, how was she going to gloat about it forever afterward?

"I guess there's nothing to do for a while," she sighed.

Tom nodded and sat down with Boswell's book. Brine paced the deck restlessly. New fires sprang up on Barnard's Reach. The sky above the island was black with smoke, and the sea was littered with pieces of the shattered cliff. Wooden boxes bobbed past. Brine watched one of them sink. Another one had split open, and she saw books inside. She didn't know what was happening inside the library, but she guessed it wasn't good.

"Brine," said Tom, "you should read this."

Brine wanted to be fighting, not reading. She snatched the book out of his hand impatiently. The faded writing made no sense for a couple of seconds, then, slowly, the trailing curls of ink resolved themselves into letters, and the letters sorted themselves out into words. And the words . . .

The story of these creatures is interesting. When the time comes for one to die, they say, it flies far away to the top of the world. There, it builds its own funeral pyre from wood and gold, and with one last, fiery breath, it lights the pyre, and thus it dies. And so, say the stories, the life cycle is renewed, for out of the ashes comes a new egg. As the parent died in fire, the egg will one day hatch in fire. It is only a story, but if it were true, it would explain a great deal.

Beneath was a drawing of an egg, complete with measurements that seemed impossibly large. Brine handed the book back to Tom. "What has this got to do with us?"

"Didn't you think," he asked, "that the starshell Marfak West found looked a bit like a giant egg?"

Had it? Brine really couldn't remember. There'd been so much happening at the time—Marfak West trapping them all with magic and leaving them to die, for example—that she hadn't taken proper notice of anything else. "But if the starshell is an egg, what is it supposed to hatch into?"

Tom turned back a page. Brine's eyes opened wide. "Oh," she said. "But that's just a story. Like Orion."

"And like Boswell and Marfak West and Magical North?"

Another ball of amber magic burst from the front of the *Antares* and flew into Barnard's Reach. Brine felt the shockwave as it hit. Marfak West was doing this, she thought. He was going to drain the starshell completely of magic, and he wouldn't stop until it was dead and Barnard's Reach was in pieces.

Without a word, Tom caught one of the hanging ropes and held it out. Brine gave it back. "Cassie's right this time. I should stay here."

"No. You should go," said Tom. He straightened his glasses. "I'm the captain, and I am giving you an order."

Brine hesitated one moment more and then, with a quick nod, she launched herself off the *Onion* and into battle.

CHAPTER 34

Why does magic exist at all? I somehow feel it is not solely for the benefit of magicians, although many magicians seem to believe it is.

(From ALDEBRAN BOSWELL'S BIG BOOK OF MAGIC)

Brine landed in the middle of a group of Ewan Hugheses. Rob Grosse appeared out of nowhere and decapitated two of them. There was surprisingly little blood, just a thin oily ooze. Rob's face was slashed from his ear to his chin, but he didn't seem to have noticed.

"Does Cassie know you're here?" he asked.

"Not yet." Brine drew her sword and pushed her way after him. A whole crowd of Ewans knocked her down. She yelled and rolled backward, head over heels. A sword hit the deck right beside her, and she got her sword in front of her just in time to parry another blow. No time to think—too many people were trying to hit her.

Then Cassie was there, a cutlass in each hand. Her hair swung around her, and she moved so fast she appeared to be dancing, or flying. Pirates rushed at her and fell beneath her blades, but as each one died, another took its place.

"Behind you!" shouted Brine.

Cassie twisted mid-leap, away from a Ewan that was stabbing at her shoulder blades. She kicked the Ewan back, skewered it through the heart, and came down facing Brine. "I thought I told you to stay on the *Onion*."

Another Ewan ran at them. Without thinking, Brine threw her cutlass at it, finishing it off. Brine grinned. She was Brine the pirate warrior, and she was armed and dangerous. Well, not armed anymore, but still dangerous. "We have to find the starshell," she said. "Marfak West is killing it."

Cassie booted a Trudi backward. "You can't kill starshell. It's not alive."

"Yes, it is," Brine said, searching around the deck. There had to be a way down somewhere. She caught a flash of silver on the edge of her vision and spun toward it. "Over there. A hatch." Pirate copies blocked their path. Cassie fought them all grimly. Brine kept close behind her, her breath tight in her chest. A sharp pain went through her leg, and she looked down to see a little Ewan Hughes, only knee-high, brandishing a sword. Brine gritted her teeth and trod on him without looking. Something squished unpleasantly beneath her feet.

Cassie pulled her aside to avoid another batch of Ewans, and then Brine saw it again—between the staggering feet, the outline of a hatch. Silver flashes popped around the edges. Brine ran to it and dropped to her knees. There was no handle. She tried tugging at the corners, then pushing on them, then she grabbed a dagger from the deck and tried jamming it in the crack. The square of wood fit so tightly into the deck that nothing would go in.

"Open, will you?" said Brine. She punched the deck in frustration.

"I don't think it's working," said Cassie helpfully.

Brine glared at her. "You do something, then. You're the hero."

"Me?" Cassie shrugged. "I just hit things with swords." She hit the hatch with her sword. It didn't move.

A Ewan Hughes loomed over them, bigger and uglier than all the other ones. Brine screamed and then realized that this Ewan was bleeding in several places, missing half a front tooth, and grinning as if he were in the middle of a party.

"Having trouble?" he asked. He handed Brine his sword, drew a pair of daggers, paused a moment, then raised his arms and drove them with a yell straight down into the deck.

They connected with a thud that must have bent the blades. Brine caught her breath as Ewan Hughes ground his teeth and pulled. The hatch, caught on the very tip of one blade, lifted a fraction, then a fraction more.

Brine thrust her fingers under one side. Cassie caught the other. It was like trying to move a mountain, but they all heaved together, and little by little, the hatch creaked open.

It flew back suddenly as a battalion of Ewan Hugheses

leaped out at them. Cassie somersaulted into them with a shout. A flurry of sword-waving later, she reappeared.

"Coming?" she asked.

▶︎⊶┼┼┼╞

Tom saw Brine land on board the *Antares* and quickly lost sight of her. From this distance, it was impossible to tell who was winning, or even who was who. It didn't help that the sea was becoming choppy and the *Onion* lurched from side to side. Tom clung to the mast and somehow stayed on his feet. Around him, the few crew members who weren't fighting on the *Antares* struggled to keep the ship steady. Tom might as well have been invisible for all the notice they took of him. He'd never felt so useless. Cassie had trusted him to do the right thing, and he didn't even trust his own knees to hold him up.

The *Onion* tilted, almost throwing him into the sea. Bill Lightning ran to the helm, shouting orders.

"What's happening?" asked Tom, and then he saw and his heart turned to ice.

The sea was rising up. It looked like the Dreaded Great Sea Beast of the South emerging from the deep. Wave piled upon wave; waters gathered together and rolled up higher and higher until they formed a wall that was at least twenty times taller than the ship. And, looking down, all Tom could see was a gaping, empty hole, edged with black waves, reaching down and down, all the way to the bottom of the ocean.

Brine tore through the corridors belowdecks with Cassie and Ewan on her heels and a lot more Cassies and Ewans just behind. Something was wrong with them. They staggered and tripped, bouncing off icicles and trampling over one another, but they kept coming.

Cassie and Ewan stopped and turned to face them. "Go," shouted Cassie to Brine. "Find Peter."

Brine ran. She heard the sound of fighting from behind and Cassie's voice shouting at her to hurry, then she turned a corner and the sounds became muddled. The corridor turned cold as she ran, and the floor grew slippery with ice. Spotting a doorway full of light, she plunged through it and skidded to a halt.

The floor was littered with fish. In the middle, the starshell egg sat on top of a column of shining ice. Peter and Marfak West stood on either side of it, neither of them moving. Icicles hung from Peter's ears and from Marfak West's nose. Peter's face was twisted up, and he was leaning back from the starshell as if he'd been trying to get away when his hands had frozen to it. He looked dazed and bruised, so pale that Brine wondered if he'd died and she was seeing his ghost.

She threw a fish at him. "Peter, you squid-brained idiot," she said.

Peter jumped and turned his head. "Oh, n—" he began. That was as far as he got.

Marfak West swung round, one hand raised. Brine reacted without thinking, diving flat as the magician released a blast of magic that shattered the wall where she'd been standing. She scrambled up, terror turning her mind blank. All her planning hadn't prepared her for this.

Then she heard Cassie shouting her name and Marfak West turned toward the door. Brine found she could think again. "Peter," she gasped, "the starshell is an egg. It's trying to hatch."

"Of course it's an egg, you silly girl," said Marfak West over his shoulder. He waved his hands across the doorway, filling it with thick ice just as Cassie and Ewan appeared outside. As they beat on it, he turned back to face Brine. "I know what it is," he said softly. "I know more than you can possibly imagine. You want to know who you are? I can tell you that. The Western Island, the floating castle. You don't remember any of it, but I've seen it all."

Brine's mouth turned dry. "You're lying," she said, but she knew he wasn't. Marfak West didn't lie, not about the things that mattered. She tried to look like she didn't care. "If you're going to tell me you're really my father—"

"Do I look like your father?" The magician's voice dripped scorn. He paused and smiled. "I did meet him once—a long time ago, when you were just a baby."

Marfak West knew her father? Marfak West had seen her when she was a baby? Brine took a step back. The magician spread his hands wide. The room they were in filled with amber light, and the *Antares* groaned and shuddered. All the torches in the room went out, then flared back to life brighter than ever.

"I'm tired of Peter as an apprentice," said Marfak West. "I'm thinking I might just take on a non-magical assistant instead. Join me and we'll sail the *Antares* across the Western Ocean to Orion's Keep, where you began your life. We'll find your family together."

"Brine, don't do it," said Peter.

Brine had no intention of doing anything Marfak West suggested. She didn't care what the magician knew about her; she saw the emptiness at his heart, and it terrified her. People feared him, and everyone hated him. He needed somebody like her or Peter, someone he could turn into a copy of himself, just so he wouldn't be quite so alone.

Brine pulled herself up straight and released a shuddering breath. "I already know who I am," she said, and it was true. Whoever she might have been, she was Brine Seaborne: once the magician's servant, now the friend of pirates. Brine Seaborne, pulled out of the waves to start life over again. She was Brine, and right now there was only one thing she wanted to do.

"This isn't about me," she said. Outside, Ewan was stabbing the ice with his daggers while Cassie fought pirate copies. "That egg contains a . . . a legend. You can't kill it."

"Legends are stories, and stories are lies," mocked Marfak West. "We're better off without them. Magic exists to be used. Used by people like me. Now, how would you like to die?"

"Of old age?" suggested Peter.

The ice in the doorway splintered. Ewan Hughes's arm broke through. "Peter!" he shouted. He tossed something that glittered gold and amber as it fell.

Peter snatched it up: a gold chain hung with three slender pieces of starshell.

CHAPTER 35

How long does it take for something real to become a legend?
In my reckoning, the last member of the species *Draconus basilicus* become extinct over eight hundred years ago. Now they exist only in stories.

(From ALDEBRAN BOSWELL'S JOURNAL OF STRANGE
ADVENTURES IN THE YEAR OF DISCOVERY)

Tom tore his gaze away from the sea. The great wave hung motionless, but very soon, he thought, it would come crashing down, and when it did, it would crush the *Onion* to nothing. He needed a plan.

"We're too close," he said. "We need to pull back." He strode over to Bill Lightning. "Are you listening to me? Turn the *Onion* around."

"The *Onion* doesn't retreat," said Bill.

Tom's cheeks stung. "I am Acting Captain of the *Onion*, and when I am speaking to you, you will do me the courtesy of paying attention."

"Do you the what?" Bill was paying attention now, but he looked as if he might be about to start laughing.

Tom's blood pounded. He saw the rest of the crew smiling at him with a mixture of kindness and pity, as if everyone knew that Cassie hadn't really meant it when she made him Acting Captain, and he was just a boy who ought to stay out of the way while the grown-ups sorted everything out.

A month ago, Tom would have agreed. A month ago, even a week ago, he'd never have dared talk back to anyone, let alone a pirate. Stay out of the way, be quiet, don't touch anything: that was life on Barnard's Reach. The *Onion* was the opposite. You jumped in, did something, anything, and if it went wrong, it didn't matter, because you could always do better next time.

Tom took off his glasses and gave Bill the full force of his librarian's glare. "I am a keeper of books," he said. "A writer of stories. When I write down the story of this battle, what would you like me to write about you?"

Bill thought about it. The others all looked at the deck.

"We're not going to retreat," said Tom. "Get ready with ropes. Keep the *Onion* behind that wave and be ready to start rescuing people. I think they're going to need it."

Bill paused for a few seconds more, then saluted. "Aye, aye, Captain."

And then the sky filled with birds.

It was as if every single bird that had ever nested on Barnard's Reach had chosen the same moment to take flight.

They swept overhead: black gulls, white gulls, gulls of every color, screeching and cawing, their beaks open and their feet outstretched. Tom's heart leaped to see them. All the gulls of Barnard's Reach, and some of them still had canisters on their legs. Someone on the island must have let them free. He hoped it was his mother.

"What's happening?" Bill asked.

Tom laughed. "The seagulls are coming." He shouted it: "The seagulls! The seagulls are coming!"

The flock parted as it reached the *Onion* and rose up high above the masts, and then, as if the birds somehow sensed an enemy that must be destroyed, they plunged down upon the *Antares*.

Trudi Storme was fighting six Ewan Hugheses when a seagull landed on the head of one of them.

The gull was momentarily surprised to find that the thing that had smelled so much like a fish was in the shape of a man. But on the other hand, nothing reminds you that you're really a fish like being attacked by a hungry predator. The Ewan reacted as any fish would. It thrashed wildly and tried to dive underwater, but there was no water, only the deck.

Trudi lowered her sword. The Ewans that had surrounded her a moment ago were gone. In their place, seagulls were pecking at . . . "Fish!" she shouted. "They're all *fish*." Her eyes gleamed as she snatched up an extra sword. "Right! You lot are casserole."

Brine barely dared breathe. Peter stood between her and Marfak West, and Brine could see Peter's hand shaking as he clutched the three pieces of starshell. Outside, Cassie and Ewan were still fighting for their lives against pirate copies.

Marfak West's eyes narrowed to slits. "That starshell is mine. Give it to me."

Peter shook his head. "You're not the only magician in this room, you know."

"Are you challenging me?"

His attention was wholly on Peter. *Move*, Brine told herself. She scraped her feet backward over the icy floor. Outside, Cassie dropped to one knee and barely fended off a blow that came straight at her head.

Marfak West spread his fingers, and Peter suddenly left the ground and slammed into the ceiling. Peter's face twisted in pain.

One more step. Brine felt the wall behind her. She reached up, unhooked a torch from above her head, and threw it.

As the parent died in fire, Boswell had written, *the egg will one day hatch in fire.*

The torch cartwheeled across the room in slow motion, end over end, trailing fire. Marfak West let out an angry cry, but he was too late to stop it. The torch struck the starshell egg and burst into flame so bright that Brine had to close her eyes, and even then, she could still see it.

Fire and smoke boiled up together, engulfing the egg in a storm of red and black. It rocked back and forth, cracking the ice that held it steady. The ice everywhere started to melt; the room filled with rain and then steam.

Ewan and Cassie burst through the ice in the doorway. They were both bleeding, and Cassie had a fish in her hair. Peter dropped from the ceiling and landed on them. They all picked themselves up quickly.

"You've lost, Marfak West," said Cassie. "Surrender."

The fire went out.

They all stared at the egg, which lay still, a few coils of steam rising, but the heat was already fading out of it. Brine's eyes stung with tears. She'd failed. The knowledge emptied her of feeling. She hadn't thrown the torch hard enough, or the fire hadn't been hot enough, or maybe the egg was already dead and no amount of fire would make it hatch.

Marfak West laughed. "What exactly did you think would happen?"

Every single torch flared toward the center of the room and then died. Brine blinked in the darkness. What was Marfak West doing now?

A light appeared in the middle of the room, egg-shaped and scarlet. Brine thought the magician was taking the last of the power out of the egg, but then the egg began to move again. A shrill humming made Brine's ears ache. The ice began to fall, and it didn't even have time to melt: It just broke away in chunks and turned to steam before it hit the floor.

Brine felt like singing. The egg rocked from side to side.

Alive. A single egg, sitting alone at Magical North for centuries, patiently waiting—until now.

"It's taking the magic back." Peter's voice was raw as he staggered to his feet. "All the magic."

"The magic is mine!" snapped Marfak West. He seized the egg in both hands and shook it.

"Is that a good idea?" asked Cassie.

Apparently, it was not.

The egg burst back into flame. Marfak West's shouts turned to screams. He tried to hurl the egg away, but his hands stuck to it once more, and he couldn't let go. Black smoke poured out of his clothes. The walls trembled. The ceiling creaked, and bits of it started to fall in.

Peter drew a shape in the air. "Everyone get close to me."

Brine squeezed in between Cassie and Ewan. A magical shield sprang up around them. She had half a second to wonder where Peter had learned that spell before the starshell exploded.

It happened with a crack like thunder, echoed by a deeper tearing right down in the heart of the *Antares*. White light burst through the room and blew the ceiling apart. Brine ducked as a lump of wood bounced off the shield by her head. Her hands and face stung.

Slowly, the room settled around them. The magical shield wavered and collapsed, and Peter slumped to the floor, gasping. Brine sat up, blinking in the sudden rush of sunlight from the hole above her. Her hands were speckled with a rash of tiny burn marks.

Marfak West was gone. Pieces of starshell smoked gently around a wide, charred hole in the floor. Brine crawled over and looked into it. In the deck below was another hole. In the deck below that, another one, and so on all the way down to the sea.

Peter stirred. "Uh, Brine."

Something rustled right next to her. Cassie and Ewan limped across to join them, and all four of them stared openmouthed at the tiny dragon that rustled its silver wings, raised its head, and stared back with a look that suggested it didn't know what was going on but it didn't approve of any of it. Who could blame it? It had, after all, been asleep for more than eight hundred years.

CHAPTER 36

Running away is sometimes the best thing you can do. Walk into trouble but run out of it.

(From BRINE SEABORNE'S BOOK OF PLANS)

Tom saw the whole wall of water tremble. Foam started to slide down from the top. "Get back," he shouted. "Retreat!"

This time Bill didn't argue. The giant wave came tumbling down, and the *Onion* fled. They bounced over the waves as if they were flying, shooting up into the air, then slamming back down with jolt after jolt that jarred every bone in Tom's body. He wrapped his arms around the mast and clung on, half-drowned and blinded by seawater. Seagulls still shrieked around him, and fish fell across the deck, dropped by the fleeing birds. Tom felt every meal he'd eaten for the last day clamoring to get out. He wasn't sure how much longer he could hold on, or even if he wanted to, because a swift death in the sea might be preferable to this agony of crashing and flying.

Then it was all over. Tom peeled himself from the mast

cautiously and wiped his hair out of his eyes. Looking out to Barnard's Reach, he saw that it was still in one piece. The giant wave, rather than engulfing the land, had collapsed back in on itself, filling the hole in the sea. All they'd felt on board the *Onion* was the aftershock.

Tom stumbled across to join Bill and the others.

Bill seemed as surprised as Tom to find they were still in one piece. "Well, that was interesting," he said. He walked unsteadily past Tom to the side of the ship. "With your permission, Captain," he said, "I think we should start picking up survivors."

The *Onion* might have survived intact, but the *Antares* hadn't been so lucky. Dragged unnaturally from the seabed, shaken, prodded, pulled this way and that, the ancient timbers had reached the point where they couldn't take any more. As Tom watched, they started to come apart. The *Antares* bobbed helplessly. Water spurted through its deck and showered down on the surviving pirates. Two of the ship's legs snapped off and slid away into the sea.

"I can't see Brine," said Tom worriedly.

Bill turned the *Onion* back toward the sinking wreck. "Don't worry. She's with Cassie. They'll be fine."

Cassie stood up, one hand pressed to a sword wound in her side. "Well," she said, "that could have been—" She caught Brine's gaze and stopped.

Brine felt a grin break out over her face. "It could have been worse," she agreed. She bent to pick up the baby dragon. It hopped sideways out of reach and shot a stream of yellow flame at her.

"I hate to mention it," said Cassie, "but the ship is on fire."

"But that's all right," said Ewan, "because we're sinking."

The rest of the ceiling caved in as he spoke. The dragon retreated, hissing steam. Brine squatted down. "It's all right," she said softly. "My parents left me, too. We're both on our own."

Any hope she harbored that she might prove to be the world's first natural dragon tamer died as the dragon snarled and scrabbled back from her.

Peter dropped to his knees and began gathering up the pieces of broken dragon shell. "Leave it," ordered Cassie. "There's no time."

A crash and a roar from outside made them all jump. The dragon wailed in fright and flung itself into Brine's arms. Its scales felt warmer than she'd imagined and perfectly dry. When it burrowed its head into her shoulder, it left little trails of warmth that seemed to sink inward until they filled her completely. She knew at that moment that she wouldn't let anything happen to this small creature. She'd protect it with her life, if necessary.

Cassie tried to pick Peter up. He struggled and kicked her. "Peter," she shouted, "we found a magic ship, we crossed the Gemini Seas in three days, and we fought an army of pirate fish to get you back. We're not leaving you here now."

Some of her words seemed to penetrate. Peter went limp, then stood up and nodded, his face set.

"Let's get out of here," said Ewan.

They ran. Peter's hands were full of dragon shell, and Brine's hands were full of dragon. The little creature clawed its way up Brine's front and clung around her neck as they raced along the corridors: a savage, silver necklace with eyes of flame. She scratched it behind the ears with one hand. She was on a sinking, burning ship with a dragon around her neck—she wondered why she wasn't afraid. The ship was falling apart around them, and yet the whole world felt completely right, as if a final missing piece had been put into place.

The ladder to the deck was smoking but still intact. Brine pounded up it behind Cassie and Ewan and stopped when they did, gasping in the sunlight. The deck was covered in fish, and seagulls wheeled above in screeching circles. Here and there, people were still fighting, but the last of the pirate copies were turning back to their proper forms and slithering into the sea.

Rob Grosse hit a Bill Lightning copy in the face with a fish. The copy sprouted tentacles and grew to the size of a house. Grosse groaned, then grinned and attacked. Cassie grabbed him as they ran past.

The *Onion* drew alongside them. "Ahoy!" shouted Tom.

Ropes slapped down on what remained of the deck of the *Antares*. Peter grabbed one and offered it to Brine. Pausing only to tuck her scaly passenger firmly into her shirt, she launched herself out over empty space.

CHAPTER 37

Magic corrodes everything. Wool, leather, iron, and steel all waste away and turn to dust. Only gold and a few precious stones survive. Maybe this explains why dragons are known to collect vast hoards of treasure. They are, in fact, building nests.

(From THOMAS GIRLING'S NEW BOOK
OF SCIENTIFIC KNOWLEDGE)

A nd that's it," finished Brine. "The end of the extraordinary story of the voyage of the *Onion*."

She sat with Tom and Ursula in the science library of Barnard's Reach. Racks of books lay drying around them and Book Sisters crept about, carefully turning and smoothing the pages so they wouldn't dry wrinkled. Though Brine guessed that most of the Sisters were using the books as an excuse and really were staying around to hear the end of the story.

Two days had passed since the battle of the *Antares*. Two days with no storms, no birds or bears trying to eat them, no evil magicians trying to kill them. It had almost been too quiet. Of course there'd been the usual arguments with Peter and the excitement of learning how much food a baby dragon needs (lots) and how often it needs the toilet (oftener than you'd imagine). Much of those two days had been spent on Barnard's Reach.

The libraries had escaped, but not without damage. The lower book cellars were still full of water, and everything down there was beyond saving. Whole rooms might never be usable again.

The Mother Keeper remained a worm. Brine had taken her across to the *Onion* so Peter could try to turn her back, but nothing he did had had any effect. The Mother Keeper was living in a jar now while the Book Sisters researched ways of bringing her back. In the meantime, Ursula was serving in her place.

The library rules were changing, Ursula said. There wouldn't *be* so many rules, for a start, and anybody would be allowed to come in and read, men and women, boys and girls. Maybe if they started treating knowledge as something to be shared and not hoarded, she said, there'd be fewer people like Marfak West around. Ursula had, however, introduced one new rule: No dragons allowed. She'd been very polite but very firm about the presence of a fire-breathing lizard in a room full of books.

Peter had stayed behind on the *Onion* with the dragon. Someone had to look after him, he'd said, although Brine had seen from his face that that wasn't the only reason. He still hadn't told her what had happened during the time he was with Marfak West, and Cassie had warned her not to ask. He'd talk about it when he was ready.

Brine sighed. She ought to feel happier than this. She'd stood at Magical North, helped defeat Marfak West, and saved Barnard's Reach. She ought to be celebrating, but all she felt was the sadness of a story ending.

Ursula blotted a page. "Actually, Brine, I think you're wrong. This is not the end. This voyage of the *Onion* may be over, but your own story is only just beginning. Tom told me you want to find your parents. I was Assistant Keeper of Geography once, remember. I found a few books for you."

She pulled out a box from under one of the racks and carried it to the table. "They're a little out of order," she apologized, "but they might be helpful. You can borrow them if you like."

Brine didn't dare look. Tom reached past her and took the first book out. Stories about the Western Ocean. A book of maps. And, right at the bottom, a book that looked even older than Boswell's journal. The cover was made of dark brown paper, stained unevenly.

The Western Island and the Floating Castle.

Brine gazed at it, speechless, not daring to open it. She heard Marfak West's voice in her mind all over again. Here it was at last—home. Suddenly she was afraid. What if she found her way home and nobody remembered or wanted her? Wouldn't it be better just to stay on the *Onion*, not ask too many questions, not try to know too much?

"Go on," said Tom.

Cautiously, her heart thumping in her throat, Brine opened the book to the first page.

The words on the cover were the only words in the whole book. The rest was a series of pictures—forests and mountains, strange-looking plants and even stranger animals. Then she turned a page and saw a picture of what had to be a dragon. She almost dropped the book. "There are dragons on the Western Island? Is this real?"

Ursula raised her hands in a shrug. "No one thinks so. But nobody thought Magical North was real, either." She slipped the book back into the box. "Take it all with you. You'll be needing it."

▶┈┼┼┼●➤

Peter was waiting for them when they got back to the *Onion*. The baby dragon was curled up with Zen in a patch of setting sun. Peter had been sorting through the pieces of starshell he'd saved. Some of them were already beginning to glow. Brine wondered what he was going to do with them all, but she decided it would be better to let him work that out for himself.

She sat down on the deck and let the dragon crawl into her lap. "He needs a name," she said. "We can't keep calling him 'the dragon.' We don't even know for certain that he *is* a dragon."

"He's got wings and scales, and he breathes fire," said Peter. "How much more dragony does he have to be?" His eyes looked bruised and tired. He swept all the starshell aside. "We should throw this lot overboard. Magic brings nothing but trouble."

Brine put her hands over his. "Magic is part of the world,

Peter. You can't go throwing away parts of the world because you don't like them. Anyway, magic is only trouble if the wrong people get hold of it. You're one of the right people."

He nodded, but he looked away from her. "That's the problem," he said. "I don't know what sort of person I am. I've only ever been a magician, and the only other magicians I know are Tallis Magus and Marfak West."

"Magic didn't turn them bad," said Tom. "I bet you they were both horrible people before they became magicians. Magic just meant they could be horrible in different ways."

"Maybe," said Peter. "Or maybe Boswell is right and magic corrupts people." Slowly, he gathered up the starshell pieces and put them in the box Ewan Hughes had given him. When he was finished, he held it out to Brine. "I want you to take care of this," he said. "Until I've worked things out."

Brine's heart hammered. He couldn't mean it—not this much starshell. "You really trust me with this?" she asked.

"Right now I trust you more than I trust myself," said Peter. For a second, he met her gaze. "I need to know who I am without magic, and that means no spellcasting."

Brine couldn't think of what to say. Or rather, she could think of lots of things, and all of them seemed wrong. She nodded solemnly and took the box.

The dragon flapped inexpertly at her. Peter scooped the little creature up. "We should give him a name. Is he a he? What does Boswell's book say?"

"Not much," said Tom. "Males are supposed to be smaller than females and breathe fire earlier, so it could be a boy, but it's hard to tell with no other dragon for comparison."

"Let's say that he is for now," said Peter. "If he lays an egg, we can rethink. How about calling him Boswell?"

Boswell purred like a cat, and for the first time in days, Peter smiled. Brine smiled back. Peter would be fine. He just needed a new adventure—a good adventure this time. One without freezing cold or evil magicians. She put the starshell box to one side and set her box of books down in their place. "Here, take a look at these."

Peter opened the first book and gave a low whistle. "There really is a floating castle. And are those flying creatures dragons?" He scratched Boswell under the chin. "He's going to be lonely. How would you like to be the only dragon in the world? We're going to have to find some friends for him."

Brine knew he was thinking about the lonely years growing up on Minutes. Tom, also, had a faraway look in his eyes as he turned his head back toward Barnard's Reach. Once again Brine found herself wishing she could remember her own childhood, but then she saw Cassie sitting cross-legged on the deck with Aldebran Boswell's map spread out in front of her, her fingers already trailing the western edge. Some people always looked to the future, Brine thought, and the promise of a new adventure surged inside her.

"We'll find more dragons," she said confidently. "If Boswell's egg survived, there must be others. Will you come west with us, Tom? You could go back home now that the rules have changed."

"And miss the next voyage? You've got to be kidding." He got up and held his hands out to them. "We're friends," he said. "That means we stay together, wherever the seas take us."

"Wherever the seas take us," they both agreed.

The setting sun laid a trail of amber light across the waves before them, disappearing into the west. West, where home was. And, if they were lucky, dragons.

ACKNOWLEDGMENTS

Just as one person cannot sail a ship alone, this book would never have set sail without the hard work of many, many people.

My gallant captains, Noa Wheeler and Rachel Kellehar, who steered me through these exciting new waters with skill and great care. Also Oriol Vidal for the amazing artwork. And special thanks to Julia Sooy and everyone at Henry Holt for their time, effort, and expertise. You are all brilliant.

My most wonderful agent, Gemma Cooper, who fell in love with the *Onion* and stormed on board to become my navigator, my chief adviser, and much, much more. This book would not be the same without you.

My motley crew of fellow writers and friends who shared the ups and downs of the journey, suffered through my early drafts, and supplied me with more tea, cake, and friendship than anyone could wish for. A big thank-you to Peter and Anna Bell, Sarah Burrow, Helen Clifford, David and Alison Williamson, Caleb and Beverley Woodbridge. Thanks also to Rob Harper and Sarah Callaghan for silly rhymes, Vee and Keith Griffiths for revels in the sky, and everyone at Team Cooper for all your advice and encouragement.

This magical voyage began when my opening chapters won a place in the final of Undiscovered Voices, run by the Society of Children's Writers and Illustrators. I am tremendously grateful to the Undiscovered Voices team for their work in discovering and developing new writers.

Finally, and most of all, I would like to thank my husband, Phillip. Ewan Hughes to my Cassie, my fellow adventurer and tireless helper. I can't imagine doing this, or anything else, without you.

GO FISH

CLAIRE FAYERS

What did you want to be when you grew up?
A dinosaur! And then a pirate or an explorer. For a while, I thought I'd be a music teacher because that's what everyone told me, but it turned out I had other dreams.

When did you realize you wanted to be a writer?
I always loved books and used to make up stories all the time, but I never thought that I could write for a living. Then, when I was sixteen years old, my two English teachers gave me a lot of encouragement and even read some of my attempts at creative writing (which I'm sure were awful). Thanks to them, I went to university to study English and I have never stopped writing.

What's your most embarrassing childhood memory?
I was short-sighted, clumsy, and had a weird sense of humor. My whole childhood is one embarrassing memory.

What's your favorite childhood memory?
Going to see *Star Wars*. I was eleven, and my mother had given us the choice of either going to the circus or to see this new film that everyone was talking about. My sisters wanted to go to the circus; my brother and I chose *Star Wars*. He

wouldn't take me, so he went to see it first, then my mother took me to the cinema, bought me a ticket, and pushed me into the right screening. I sat there alone, completely immersed. I'm still a *Star Wars* fan.

What was your favorite thing about school?

Leaving! I loathed school—I was bullied very badly and it was a really miserable time. There were some good points, though. I read a lot and I became very self-sufficient, and then, when I was sixteen I got a place in college to do A levels (this was in the UK). There, I met people who inspired and encouraged me to write, and I made some good friends. If anyone reading this is going through rough times at school, hang in there. Things can, and do, get better.

What were your hobbies as a kid? What are your hobbies now?

I was a musical child. I played the piano and cello, and I was fascinated with how instruments worked. I used to try out new instruments for just long enough to find out how to play them, then I'd get bored with them and move on to the next one.

I still love music now. The front room of my house is a music room with a piano, a cello, and a saxophone belonging to my husband (which I have never been able to play despite a lot of trying. The neighbors are very glad I've given up!).

I took up skiing a few years ago, and I love it. I also enjoy gardening: growing my own fruits and vegetables to turn into things. I have an entire wardrobe full of pickled things in my spare bedroom.

Did you play sports as a kid?

I was the least sporty child you can imagine. I was the one who was always at the back and picked last for every team.

What was your first job, and what was your "worst" job?

My first job was also my worst job—as a student I worked in a factory making plastic goods. My job was to pour plastic into the top of the machine and then pick up each plastic disc as it came out, check it, and put it in a box. I worked ten to twelve hours a day for less than minimum wage and barely saw sunlight for the whole summer. But at least it was quiet.

What book is on your nightstand now?

I have just finished reading *A Snicker of Magic* by Natalie Lloyd, and I adored it. I'm also looking forward to reading the second book in the hilarious Ministry of SUITs series by Paul Gamble.

How did you celebrate publishing your first book?

I was very fortunate because the UK edition of *The Voyage to Magical North* was chosen as the July book of the month by the bookstore chain Waterstones. I spent much of my launch month visiting bookshops and becoming wildly excited as I told *Onion* stories to groups of bemused children whilst wearing my giant pirate hat. And I had two book launches— one on a Saturday afternoon for friends who were coming from farther away, and then an evening one for all my old work colleagues. It was great fun.

Where do you write your books?

Mainly at home. I have an office with doors opening onto the garden so my two cats can wander in and out. I've also started meeting a fellow author in a coffee shop twice a week for writing sessions. As a full-time author, you end up spending a lot of time alone, so it's great to write with some- one else for a change.

What sparked your imagination for *The Voyage to Magical North*?

I wanted to write something fun, and I've always loved quest and adventure stories. The story really took off, though, when I started thinking about Brine. Why did she join the *Onion*, and what was she going to get out of their voyage north? Once I'd worked all that out, the story fell into place around her.

What challenges do you face in the writing process, and how do you overcome them?

So far, I've found the middle of the book the hardest thing to write. Starting a story is quite easy, and I'll usually have an idea of what will happen at the end, but getting from start to finish is hard work and I'll often become stuck. Sometimes it's because I don't have any ideas at all, and sometimes I have too many and can't decide which one to use. When this happens, I take a break and go for a walk, do some work in the garden, or make lots of cake. Cake-eating is an essential ability for an author.

What is your favorite word?

A Welsh word—*llongyfarchiadau*. It means "congratulations."

If you could live in any fictional world, what would it be?

I'm a huge fan of Studio Ghibli films. They are always beautifully animated and have the most wonderful characters. I'd most like to live in the world of *My Neighbor Totoro*, which is full of magical creatures, including a marvelous cat bus.

Who is your favorite fictional character?

I have so many! Heroes and villains (I love a good villain). But the warmest place in my heart is reserved for a character so minor I have trouble remembering his name—Monsieur

Mabeuf from Victor Hugo's *Les Misérables*. He's an old scholar who runs out of money and has to sell all his possessions to buy food. In the end he only has his books left. He takes them to the market, one by one, coming home with a handful of coins and a loaf of bread, but sometimes he spends the money on a new book and is hungry but joyful for a while. He's just sold his last book when the revolution happens and he joins up to fight without a thought. His story occupies about five pages of the twelve-hundred-page novel, but he's the one I remember.

What was your favorite book when you were a kid? Do you have a favorite book now?
I didn't have a favorite book, but I loved adventure stories, especially if they involved deadly peril and lots of sword-waving. Then, when I was fourteen I discovered *The Lord of the Rings* and fell in love with fantasy.

I have many favorite books now. The one I reread most often is *The Count of Monte Cristo*. I love all the twisty, revenge-laden plotting.

If you could travel in time, where would you go and what would you do?
Ooh, everywhere and everything! But first, I'd go back to nineteenth-century Europe. There was so much happening then—wars and revolutions, great books being written, great discoveries being made. And I'd get to wear a really big dress and hat. After that, I'd have to visit the dinosaurs, of course, but I'd probably have to get in line behind all the other time travelers because everyone wants to see the dinosaurs.

What's the best advice you have ever received about writing?
Never give up.

What advice do you wish someone had given you when you were younger?

It's normal to be nervous if you're trying something for the first time. Go ahead and try, and you don't have to do everything perfectly on your first try, either.

What do you want readers to remember about your books?

Stories are powerful—they can change the world. Be careful about the stories you tell. And never try to copy any of Trudi's recipes.

If you were a superhero, what would your superpower be?

It'd have to be something where I could shout and wave my arms around dramatically. Maybe shooting lightning out of my hands. Or I'd transform into a giant, tentacled monster to fight crime.

Do you have any strange or funny habits? Did you when you were a kid?

I sing to my cats. Because, obviously, talking to cats would be silly.

You have conversations with your characters—what is that like? Do you really hear their voices?

I create their voices in my head, pretending that I am the character. So I'll say, "Hello, Cassie." And Cassie will say, "Hello, Claire, isn't it a fine day for swashbuckling?" And I'll say, "So, what do you think about having Brine and Peter onboard the *Onion*?" And Cassie will frown and say, "Can I give you some advice? Next time you want me to rescue someone, don't stick them in the sea right in front of my ship. I nearly ran them down." And the conversation will continue. It gives me a better idea of how the character sounds, and how well I know them. When they start answering me back and insulting me, I know they're coming to life in my imagination.

Tell us more about Tallis—the magician and the feline friend?

Tallis Magus started his life with a different name, but my agent didn't like it. I was struggling to look for a new name for him when I looked around and saw a very large cat thoughtfully shredding wallpaper—and I thought, *I know, I'll name him after the cat. No one will ever know.* So now you know.

Tallis the cat is a British Cream. He weighs around sixteen pounds and has a big, round teddy bear face. He doesn't move very fast except when there's food about, and then he develops supersonic speed. Zen, the ship's cat, is a little like him.

You live in Wales, which seems like a land steeped in mythology. How do you think it influences your imagination and writing?

Wales certainly is steeped in mythology. We even have a dragon on our flag. Many of the myths and legends are tied to certain places—the Lady of Llyn y Fan Fach, the mountain of Cadair Idris, King Arthur's Cave. So it felt right to me that the *Onion*'s crew was trying to find the most magical place in their world.

How did your time as a librarian influence your imagination of Barnard's Reach?

I'd actually written most of that before I started work at the library at Cardiff University. (My colleagues at the library were most disappointed that I hadn't based any of it on them!)

During the editing stage, I slipped in some extra bits. Because I was working in the science library, I added a science library to Barnard's Reach. And my work gave me a much bigger appreciation of the role of librarians. Libraries are there to make sure knowledge is shared with anyone who comes looking for it, and that's a very important thing.

SQUARE FISH

It's westward ho in search of dragons,
no matter the obstacles. All manner of strange and
dangerous threats await the crew when they land
on the Western Island. Will Brine and Peter be
able to protect everyone and take care of that angry
volcano before they all go up in flames?

Keep reading for an excerpt.

CHAPTER 1

Dragon eggs absorb magic. We know this—for centuries, magicians have collected the discarded shards, not knowing what they are. They call them starshell and use them for spellcasting. This uses up some of the magic in the world, but stories suggest that dragons themselves use much, much more. Yet dragons, with one exception, are extinct.

So, what happens to all the spare magic?

(from THOMAS GIRLING'S BOOK OF PIRATING ADVENTURES)

B rine Seaborne was bored. She shouldn't be—she was sunbathing on the deck of a pirate ship with a dragon in her lap. But after two months of sailing with a good wind, calm seas, and nobody attacking them, she was beginning to wish something would happen.

"Are you still keeping notes about our journey?" she asked Tom.

Tom looked up from his notebook. "Of course I am. Mum said it was important to keep accurate records so we can separate out the truth from the stories."

He'd grown taller in the past months, and the constant sunshine had tanned his skin an even brown. He still kept his dark brown hair long, and he wore his knee-length librarian's robe belted over his trousers. He said he needed it because of all the pockets, but Brine suspected he wore it because it reminded him of home in the underground libraries of Barnard's Reach.

"How much longer do you think it'll take us to find Dragon Island?" asked Brine. They'd passed the island of Auriga last week, which was the farthest west anyone had ever sailed before, so they must be getting close. Unless the people of Auriga were right, and if you carried on west, you'd sail off the edge of the world—which was nonsense, of course. Nowadays, everyone knew the world wasn't a bowl full of the sea, but a ball that had no edge or end.

"It'll take about an hour less than the last time you asked," said Peter, his shadow falling across her. The young magician sat down between Brine and Tom.

While Tom's skin had tanned in the sun, Peter's had developed pink patches, and his hair, which used to be dust-beige, had become the dirty yellow of dried sea-cabbage. He reached out to stroke Boswell's warm scales. The dragon let out a contented puff of flame and rolled over to let Peter scratch his belly where his scales were still pure silver. Over the past month, he'd been shedding, and the scales that grew back were the green of a stormy sea.

"Do you think we'll really find dragons on the Western Island?" asked Peter.

The rest of the crew didn't think so. Maybe there were dragons in the west once, but they were probably all extinct now—that was what pirate captain Cassie O'Pia and first mate Ewan Hughes said. And Tim Burre, who came from Auriga, was sure they'd fall off the edge of the world long before they found anything.

As far as most of the crew was concerned, they were sailing west in search of adventure and Brine's home—a home she still couldn't remember. Just because some of the books from Barnard's Reach talked about dragons, it didn't mean they'd find any. Brine knew that stories were usually made up out of a pinch of fact and several buckets of exaggeration, but even so, she couldn't help hoping.

"We *better* find dragons," said Tom. "My calculations show—"

"Yes, we know about your calculations." Peter grinned. "I'm telling you, the absence of dragons is not making the world fill up with magic. Excess magic burns off into the sky—it's how we get storms and the Stella Borealis. *Everyone* knows that."

"Then *everyone* is wrong," said Tom. "Some magic burns off, but not all of it. Dragons were supposedly the biggest consumer of magic in all of the eight oceans, but dragons have been extinct for so long that most people think they're just stories. Also, we've just lost Marfak West, and he used a lot of magic. So we've got a whole load of magical energy just hanging about the world, and increased magic means increased strangeness."

Brine started as Boswell gave a fiery snort, singeing her trousers. "I haven't noticed anything strange," she said, rubbing at the burnt fabric.

"Anyway, magic corrodes," said Peter. "That's why dragons build their nests out of gold and jewels, because they're the only things that don't disintegrate. Too much magic would make things fall apart. I'm a magician—I should know."

"You're a magician with a splinter of starshell in your hand," said Tom, raising his eyebrows. "But your hand hasn't fallen off yet."

"That's because the splinter is too small to make any difference." Peter sighed.

"What about this ship, then?" said Tom, patting the scuffed wooden deck of the *Onion*. "It's full of magic, and it hasn't fallen apart. And these"—he took his glasses off—"they belonged to Boswell the explorer, so how come they're exactly right for me?"

"Coincidence?" suggested Brine.

"Or maybe, the huge levels of magical energy concentrated at Magical North reshaped them to be what I needed," Tom argued. "Magic *changes* the world."

"Well, magic or not, right now I'd like the world to change to be a little more exciting," said Brine, shading her eyes as she peered at the featureless ocean. "In a good way, please—not with evil magicians trying to kill us."

Neither Tom nor Peter answered. Good—she'd finally gotten them off the subject of magic. Then she noticed how still they'd become.

"Umm . . . ," said Peter.

Something skittered on the deck behind them.

And then Cassie O'Pia shouted, "Giant spiders! Why is my ship full of giant spiders?"

Boswell fell off Brine's lap. Brine sat up in a hurry and put her hand back, straight through something that was warm and squished horribly. She shrieked.

"Don't just sit there screaming!" shouted Cassie. "All hands on spiders!"

Brine jumped up, shaking congealed spider off her hand. The rest of the gray-green spider lay behind her, a handprint through its crumpled body.

"That's gross," said Peter, his face matching the green of Boswell's scales.

"I know it's gross." Brine scrubbed her hand on her trousers. "Do something!"

Everywhere, pirates scrambled for weapons. More spiders came crawling over the deck rail. Brine counted at least twenty in a single glance. They were exactly the worst size imaginable. Big enough that you could count their eyes and see the slime hanging from their jaws. But small enough that they could scuttle straight up your body and cling to your face. Brine jumped back as a spider dropped from the rigging in front of Boswell. The little dragon toasted it with an enthusiastic belch of flame.

"They look like sea-spiders," said Tom with fascination, "though I've never seen a sea-spider that big before. Peter, did you magic them?"

"Of course I didn't!" Peter put a hand over his mouth. His eyes bulged as if he was going to be sick. "Why would I make giant spiders? I haven't done any magic since . . ."

Since Marfak West had captured him and made him do all sorts of terrible things, Brine thought. She shuddered.

Cassie rushed past, her long hair flying and her emerald pendant flashing against her bronze skin. Ewan Hughes was right behind her, as usual. Meanwhile, Trudi, the ship's cook, was trying to squash spiders with a frying pan.

"Remind me to scrub that before she uses it for cooking again," muttered Peter.

Never mind scrubbing it, Brine thought: She was going to throw it overboard.

An arrow hit the deck at her feet and she looked up to see Tim Burre in the crow's nest, waving a bow.

"Sorry!" he called cheerfully.

"They're only sea-spiders," Tom called back. "They're not dangerous!" He lifted his feet out of the way of one of them. "Just a million times bigger than they should be," he added uncertainly.

Cassie hacked down a sheet of green web from the mast.

"Tom, you're supposed to be killing them, not studying them. Squash them with a book or something."

Brine winced at the thought of Tom using a book as a weapon. She drew her sword and thrust it through a spider. The creature made a noise like wet leaves squishing underfoot, waved six of its eight legs at her, and died.

"Yuck," said Tom.

Boswell bounded across the deck on the heels of another spider. Did spiders have heels? Brine wondered. The dragon let off a burst of flame that missed the spider and set fire to a bucket.

"Nice job, Boswell," said Peter, running to grab him.

There were hardly any spiders left now, anyway. And then, after a few more minutes, there was only one, running in terrified circles. Cassie cut it in half and then threw the pieces into the sea.

"Well," she said, wiping slime off her cutlass, "that could have been worse."